PRAISE FOR

"Manuel Vilas writes both novels and poetry, and this book falls somewhere in between. It's a meditation on yearning, solitude, and self; a soul storm, a mirage of phantom figures—resurrected images of dead ancestors, childhood memories, the changing face of Spain itself. And all of these visions come in waves to Manuel after his parents' deaths, as he struggles to make sense of his own midlife sorrow and emptiness. It's a book of deep reckoning—of the meaningful and mundane—but written with an airy, even whimsical touch. . . . Despite the melancholy at its heart, this is ultimately a book of light." —*The New York Times Book Review*

"It's beyond impressive that Vilas can pack so much emotional resonance into [these] pages without resorting to anything manipulative. And when it comes to limning the everyday sadnesses of the world, Vilas is a master."

—NPR

"[A] sober yet elegant autobiographical novel . . . Painfully observant and poetically inclined." —*The New Yorker*

"Sometimes there arises a snapshot so striking and definitive it resembles the universal. Manuel Vilas's *Ordesa* is one such novel. . . . With the cadence of poetry, *Ordesa* unearths a fraught but tender reality in which each moment we've inhabited with those we love is synonymous with the present moment—inextricable from everything that comes after." —*ZYZZYVA*

"[A] poignant and sensitive portrait of a wounded man . . . A journey both nostalgic and melancholic." —*Library Journal* (starred review)

"Vilas is a Spanish poet, novelist, and essayist born in 1962 who has enjoyed critical and commercial success in his homeland with this book. . . . [He] conveys—and Rosenberg smoothly translates—many moments of pain and happiness any reader might recognize as the narrator plunges into the maelstrom of closely examined memory. A dark and challenging but emotionally rich work." —*Kirkus Reviews*

"[A] vibrant English-language debut . . . Despite lacking a central arc, the novel hums with magnetic and lively scenes. This is an indelible portrait of a man facing the costs of a life dedicated to remembrance." —*Publishers Weekly*

"*Ordesa* is a poet's novel, or maybe a novelist's prose poem. It's both things at once, and also the saddest and most candid autobiography I've read in recent times. I've been through this book twice and I still don't know how Vilas does it. I know, however, that this book is a gift, and maybe that's enough." —Juan Gabriel Vásquez, author of *The Shape of the Ruins*

"[*Ordesa*] is the album, the archive, the memory without lies or consolation. . . . What's left in the end is the clean emotion of truth and the distress of everything lost."

—Antonio Muñoz Molina, author of *Like a Fading Shadow*

"A book full of compassion toward the underdogs of history, the everyday men. An extraordinary book." —*El País* (Spain)

ORDESA

ORDESA

MANUEL VILAS

Translated by Andrea Rosenberg

RIVERHEAD BOOKS | NEW YORK

RIVERHEAD BOOKS
An imprint of Penguin Random House LLC
penguinrandomhouse.com

The Library of Congress has catalogued the Riverhead hardcover edition as follows:

Names: Vilas, Manuel, 1962– author. | Rosenberg, Andrea, translator.
Title: Ordesa / Manuel Vilas ; translated by Andrea Rosenberg.
Other titles: Ordesa. English
Description: First American edition. | New York : Riverhead Books, 2020. |
"Originally published in Spain by Alfaguara, an imprint of
Penguin Random House Grupo Editorial, Barcelona, in 2018"—Title page verso.
Identifiers: LCCN 2020014200 (print) | LCCN 2020014201 (ebook) |
ISBN 9780593084045 (hardcover) | ISBN 9780593084069 (ebook)
Subjects: LCSH: Vilas, Manuel, 1962– —Fiction.
Classification: LCC PQ6672.I473 O74413 2020 (print) |
LCC PQ6672.I473 (ebook) | DDC 861/.7—dc23
LC record available at https://lccn.loc.gov/2020014200
LC ebook record available at https://lccn.loc.gov/2020014201

First Riverhead hardcover edition: December 2020
First Riverhead trade paperback edition: November 2021
Riverhead trade paperback ISBN: 9780593084052

Printed in the United States of America
1st Printing

BOOK DESIGN BY LUCIA BERNARD

Gracias a la vida, que me ha dado tanto . . .

—VIOLETA PARRA

ORDESA

1

If only human pain could be measured with precise numbers, not vague words. If only there were some way to assess how much we've suffered, to confirm that pain has mass and measure. Sooner or later, every man must confront the insubstantiality of his own passage through this world. Some human beings can stomach that.

Not me—not ever.

I used to look at the city of Madrid, and the unreality of its streets and houses and humans felt like nails through my flesh.

I've been a man of sorrows.

I've failed to understand life.

Conversations with other humans seemed dull, slow, destructive.

It pained me to talk to others; I could see the pointlessness of every human conversation that has been and will be. Even as they were happening, I knew they'd be forgotten.

The fall before the fall.

The futility of conversations—the futility of the speaker, the futility of the spoken-to. Futilities we've agreed to so the world can exist.

At that point I'd start thinking about my father again. The conversations I used to have with him seemed like the only thing that was worth a damn. I'd go back to those conversations, hoping for respite from the universal deterioration of things.

It felt like my brain was fossilized; I couldn't perform simple mental operations. I would add up cars' license plate numbers, and the activity plunged me into a deep sadness. I stumbled over my words. It took me a long time to get a sentence out; when I went silent, the person I was talking to would look at me with pity or scorn and end up finishing it for me.

I used to stammer, repeating the same thing over and over. Maybe there was beauty in my stuttering emotions. I called my father to account. I was constantly thinking about my father's life. Seeking an explanation for my own life in his. I became racked by fear and delusions.

When I looked in the mirror, I saw not my own self growing old but someone else who'd already been here in this world. I saw my father growing old. It made it easy to remember him in meticulous detail; all I had to do was look in the mirror and he'd appear, like in some unfamiliar liturgy, a shamanic ceremony, an inverted theological order.

There was no joy or happiness in this reunion with my father in the mirror—only another turn of the screw of grief, a further descent, the hypothermic pall of two corpses in conversation.

I see what was not intended to be visible; I see death in the breadth and basis of matter; I see the universal weightlessness of all things. I was reading Saint Teresa of Ávila, and she had similar sorts of thoughts. She called them one thing, and I call them something else.

I started writing—only writing offered an outlet for all those dark messages flooding in from human bodies, from the streets, the cities, from politics, the media, from what we are.

The great ghost of what we are—a construction bearing little resemblance to nature. And the great ghost is effective: humanity is convinced it actually exists. That's where my problems start.

In 2015 there was a sadness that stalked the planet, invading human societies like a virus.

I got a brain scan. I went to see a neurologist. He was a bald, burly man with neatly trimmed fingernails and a necktie under his white coat. He ran some tests. He said there wasn't anything funny in my head. That everything was fine.

And I started writing this book.

It seemed to me the state of my soul was a blurry memory of something that had occurred in a place in northern Spain called Ordesa, a place full of mountains. And that memory was yellow, the color yellow spreading through the name Ordesa, and behind Ordesa was the figure of my father in the summer of 1969.

A state of mind that is a place: Ordesa. And also a color: yellow.

Everything turned yellow. When things and people turn yellow, it means they've become insubstantial—or bitter.

Grief is yellow, is what I'm saying.

I'm writing these words on May 9, 2015. Seventy years ago, Germany had just signed its unconditional surrender. Within a couple of days, photos of Hitler would be swapped out for photos of Stalin.

History, too, is a body with regrets. I am fifty-two years old and I am the history of myself.

My two boys are coming in the front door, back from a game of paddle tennis. It's scorching out already. Insistent heat, its unrelenting assault on people, on the planet.

And the way that heat on humanity is increasing. It isn't just climate change—it's a sort of reminder of history, a vengeance taken by the old myths on the new. Climate change is simply an updated version of the apocalypse. We like apocalypse. We carry it in our DNA.

The apartment where I live is dirty, full of dust. I've tried a few times to clean it, but it's no use. I've never been good at cleaning, and not because I don't put in the effort. Maybe there is some aristocratic residue in my blood. Though it hardly seems likely.

I live on Avenida de Ranillas, in a northern Spanish city whose name currently escapes me. There's nothing here but dust, heat, and ants. A while back there was an ant invasion, and I killed them with the vacuum cleaner. Hundreds of ants sucked into the canister—I felt like an honest-to-God mass murderer. I look at the frying pan in the kitchen. The grease stuck to the pan. I need to give it a scrub. I have no idea what I'm going to feed my kids. The banality of food. Through the window I can see a Catholic church impassively receiving the light of the sun, its atheistic fire. The fire of the sun that God hurls at the earth as if it were a black ball, filthy and wretched, as if it were rot, garbage. Can't you people see the garbage of the sun?

There's nobody on the street. Where I live, there are no streets, just empty sidewalks covered with dirt and dead grasshoppers. Everybody's gone on vacation. They're at the beach enjoying the sea. The dead grasshoppers, too, once started families and celebrated holidays, Christmases and birthdays. We're all poor souls thrust into the tunnel of existence. Existence is a moral category. Existing obliges us to *do*, to do something, anything at all.

If I've realized one thing in life, it's that men and women share one single existence. One day, that existence will gain political representation, and that will mean we've taken a major step forward. I won't be around to see it. There are so many things I won't be around to see, so many I am seeing right now.

I've always seen things.

The dead have always talked to me.

I've seen so many things, the future ended up talking to me as if we were neighbors or even friends.

I'm talking about those beings, about ghosts, about the dead, my dead parents, the love I had for them, how that love doesn't leave.

Nobody knows what love is.

2

After my divorce (a year ago now, though time's a tricky thing in this case, since a divorce isn't really a date but a process, even if officially speaking it's a date, even if in legal terms it may be a specific day; at any rate, there are a lot of significant dates to keep in mind: the first time you consider it, then the second time, the accumulation of times, the piling up of moments full of disagreements and arguments and sadnesses that eventually end up pointing toward that thing you've been considering, and finally the moment you leave your home, and the leaving is what sets off the cascade of events that culminate in a particular judicial proceeding, which is the end of the road from a legal point of view, since the legal point of view is essentially a compass on the precipice, a kind of science, because we need a science that provides rationality, the illusion of certainty), I became the man I used to be many years earlier; by which I mean that I had to buy a mop and a scrub brush, and cleaning products, lots of cleaning products.

The superintendent of the apartment building was in the lobby. We'd chatted a bit. Something about a soccer game. About people's lives too, I think. The super is Asian of some sort, though he's from Ecuador. He's been in Spain a long time, so long now he can't remember Ecuador. I know deep down he's envious of my apartment. However bad you've got it in life, there's always somebody who envies you. The cosmos has a twisted sense of humor.

My son helped me clean the house. There were piles of mail covered in a layer of dust. You could pick up an envelope and feel the grimy sensation that the dust, so thick it was almost dirt, left on your fingertips.

There were faded letters of old love, innocent and tender letters of youth from my son's mother, the woman who was once my wife. I told my son to put those in the memory drawer. We also put photos of my father in there, and one of my mother's purses. A cemetery of memory. I didn't want to, or couldn't, let my eyes linger on those objects. I touched them with love—and with pain.

You have no idea what to do with all these things, do you? my son said.

And there's more, I told him. Receipts and papers that seem important, like insurance documents and letters from the bank.

Banks flood your mailbox with depressing messages. Loads of

statements. Letters from the bank make me nervous. They aim to tell you exactly what you are. They force you to reflect on your lack of significance in the world. I started leafing through bank statements.

Why do you like having the AC cranked up? he asked.

I can't stand the heat—my father couldn't either. Do you remember your grandfather?

It's an uncomfortable question, since my son thinks that in asking it, I'm seeking some sort of advantage, some kindness on his part.

My son has a knack for diligence and hard work. He was very thorough in helping me clean my apartment.

Of late, it's started to seem like the place isn't worth the money I'm paying for it. That realization, I imagine, is the most obvious evidence of a human mind's maturity under the tyranny of capitalism. But thanks to capitalism, I have a home.

I thought, as always, about financial ruin. A man's life is, at bottom, an extended effort not to fall into financial ruin. No matter what your profession, that's the great failure. If you can't feed your kids, you don't have any reason to exist in society.

Nobody knows if life outside society is even possible. Other people's esteem ends up being the only record of your existence. Esteem is a moral system; it entails values and other people's assessment of you, and your position in the world is derived from that assessment. It's a battle between the body, your body, where life resides, and your body's value to others. If people seek you, if they seek your presence, you'll do well.

But death—that sociopathic madwoman—equalizes all social and moral assessments through the active corruption of the flesh.

There's a lot of talk about political corruption and moral corruption, and very little about the corruption of the body once death gets her hands on it: the swelling, the explosion of foul gases, the corpse turning to stench.

My father never talked much about his mother. He only recalled what a wonderful cook she'd been. My grandmother left Barbastro in the late sixties and never went back. It must have been around 1969. She took her daughter with her.

Barbastro is the town where I was born and raised. When I was born, it had ten thousand residents. Now it has seventeen thousand. With the passage of time, the town has acquired the power of a destiny that is at once cosmic and intimate in scope.

The ancients use the term *allegory* to denominate that desire to take formlessness and turn it into a character with form. For nearly every human being, the past is as precisely drawn as a character from a novel.

I recall a photo of my father taken in the 1950s, in his SEAT 600. You can barely make him out, but it's him. It's an odd photo, very much of its time, on a street that looks newly built. In the background is a Renault Ondine and a huddle of women—women with their backs turned, holding their purses, women who must be dead now, or very old. I can make out my father's head inside the SEAT 600 with Barcelona plates. He never mentioned that, the fact that his first SEAT 600 had Barcelona plates. It doesn't appear to be summer or winter. It may be late September or late May, to judge from the women's clothing.

There isn't much to say about the decay of all the things that have ever been. I can only note my personal fascination with that car, the SEAT 600, which was a source of joy for millions of Spaniards: a source of concrete, atheistic hope, a reason for faith in the

future of personal machines, a reason for travel, a reason to see other places and other cities, a reason to ponder the labyrinths of geography and highways, a reason to visit rivers and beaches, a reason to shut yourself off inside a cubicle, away from the world.

It's a Barcelona plate, and the number is long gone: 186025. Something of that plate must still exist somewhere, and believing that is a bit like having faith.

Class consciousness is the thing we must never lose. My father did what he could with what Spain provided: he found a job, worked, started a family, and died.

And there aren't many alternatives to those options.

Family is a demonstrated form of happiness. People who decide to stay single and alone—statistics back me up on this—die sooner. And nobody wants to die before his time. There's nothing fun about dying, plus it's old-fashioned. The desire for death is an anachronism. We've only recently discovered this. Western civilization's latest discovery: It's better not to die.

Whatever you do, don't die, especially since there's no need. There's no need to die. We used to think there was—we used to think it was necessary.

Life didn't have as much value back then. It's worth more now. The production of wealth and material abundance has meant that the outcasts of the past (those who in previous decades were indifferent to being dead or alive) now love being alive.

The Spanish middle class of the 1950s and 1960s passed down to their heirs more sophisticated aspirations.

My grandmother died in I don't know what year. It might have been 1992 or 1993, or 1999 or 2001, or 1996 or 2000, somewhere in there. My aunt called us up to let us know my father's mother had died. My father wasn't on speaking terms with his sister. She left a message on the machine. I heard the message. It said that even if the two of them didn't get along, they had the same mother. That was the thing: they had the same mother, which was reason enough for them to have a relationship. I pondered awhile when I heard that message. Bright light always poured into my parents' house, making things lose their solidity, since light is more powerful than any human action.

My father sat down in his armchair. A yellow armchair. He wasn't going to the funeral—that's what he'd decided. She'd died in a far-off city, some three hundred miles from Barbastro, some three hundred miles from the place where my father had just received the news of his mother's death. He took a pass, is what happened. He didn't feel like it. All that driving. Or being on a bus for hours. And having to find the bus.

That decision led to a flood of further consequences. I'm not interested in judging the past, only in narrating it or describing it or celebrating it. The morality of any fact is always a cultural construction. In and of themselves, facts are certain. Facts are nature; interpreting them is politics.

My father didn't attend my grandmother's funeral. What kind of relationship did he have with his mother? None at all. Yes, sure, they had one at first, back in I don't know, 1935 or 1940, but that relationship gradually disintegrated, disappeared. I think my father should have attended that funeral. Not for his dead mother, but for himself, and also for me. In washing his hands of it, he was deciding to wash his hands of life in general.

The biggest mystery is that my father loved his mother. He refused to attend her funeral because his unconscious rejected his mother's dead body. And his conscious self was bolstered by laziness.

A thousand stories are jumbled up in my head, stories about poverty and how poverty ends up poisoning you with the dream of affluence. Or how poverty leads to immobility, a lack of will to climb into a car and drive three hundred miles.

Capitalism went under in Spain in 2008—we were lost, no longer knowing what to aspire to. The arrival of economic recession set off a political firestorm.

The dead seemed almost enviable.

My father was burned in a gas furnace. He never gave any indication of what he wanted us to do with his corpse. We simply got rid of the deceased (the recumbent body, the thing that used to be someone and that now was unrecognizable to us), the way everyone does. The same way that will happen to me. When someone dies, we're obsessed with erasing the corpse from the map. Extinguishing the body. But why the rush? Because of the decay of the flesh? No, now we've got these state-of-the-art fridges where we can store bodies. We're afraid of corpses. We're afraid of the future, of what we will become. We're terrified to ponder the ties that bind us to the corpse. We're frightened of the days we spent at the corpse's side, the many things we did with it: going to the beach, eating lunch, traveling, having dinner, even sleeping next to it.

At the end of people's lives, the only real problem that presents itself is what to do with the corpses. In Spain there are two possibilities: interment or cremation. Two beautiful words whose roots stretch down into Latin: to become earth or to become fire.

The Latin tongue ennobles our death.

My father was cremated on December 19, 2005. I regret it now—it may have been a hasty decision. On the other hand, the fact that my father didn't attend his mother's—my grandmother's—funeral influenced our decision to burn him. Which is more relevant, referring to my relationship and saying "my grandmother," or referring to my father's by saying "his mother"? I'm not sure which point of view to choose. My grandmother or his mother—everything is encapsulated within that choice. My father didn't attend my grandmother's funeral, and that influenced what we did with my father's body; it influenced our decision to burn him, cremate him. It had nothing to do with love, but with the cascade of events. Events that produced other events: the cascade of life, water endlessly flowing while we go mad.

I am also aware, at this precise moment, that my life has not been marked by momentous things, and yet I carry a deep suffering within me. Grief is in no way an impediment to joy, as I understand grief, since for me it's connected to the intensification of consciousness. Grief is an expanded consciousness that encompasses all the things that have ever been and ever will be. It's a sort of secret benevolence toward all things. Courtesy toward everything that ever was. And benevolence and courtesy always produce grace.

It's a sort of overarching conscience. Suffering is an outstretched hand. It is kindness to others. We smile while crumbling on the inside. If we choose to smile rather than falling down dead in the middle of the street, it's out of grace, affection, courtesy, love for others, and respect for them.

I don't know how to structure time, how to define it. I return to this afternoon in May 2015 that I'm experiencing right this moment and I see a bunch of medications strewn chaotically across my bed. There are all kinds: antibiotics, antihistamines, anxiolytics, antidepressants.

Still, I celebrate being alive and I always will. Time continues to pile up atop my father's death, and I often have trouble remembering him. But this doesn't make me sad. I find it extraordinarily beautiful that my father is heading toward complete dissolution now that I, along with my brother, am the only one who remembers him.

My mother died a year ago. When she was alive, I sometimes tried to talk about my father, but she always dodged the conversation. I can't talk about my father with my brother much either. This isn't a criticism, not at all. I understand the discomfort, the discretion. Because talking about the dead, in some cultural traditions, or at least in the one that happens to be mine, entails a powerful, pungent degree of indiscretion.

And so I'm alone with my father. I'm the only person in the

world—I don't know about my brother—who remembers him daily. Who daily contemplates how he's fading, becoming purity. It's not that I recall him daily, it's that he's permanently within me, it's that I've pulled away from myself to make room for him.

It's as if my father didn't want to be alive to me, meaning he didn't want to reveal his life, the sense of it, to me—no father wants to be a man to his son. My whole past caved in when my mother did what my father had done: she died.

3

My mother died in her sleep. She was tired of dragging herself around, since she could no longer walk. I never found out what specific illnesses she had. My mother was a chaotic narrator. As am I. I inherited narrative chaos from my mother. I didn't inherit a literary tradition, either classical or avant-garde. A mental degeneracy provoked by political degeneracy.

In my family we were never precise in our narrations. This is where I get my difficulty putting into words the things that happen to me. My mother had a multitude of maladies that overlapped and crashed into one another in her stories. There was no way to organize what was happening to her. She was trying, or so I've inferred, to incorporate her own disquiet into her narratives and also seeking to find meaning in the events she narrated; she was interpreting, and in the end it all led to silence; she started leaving out certain details she'd already relayed, details she felt didn't put her in a good light.

She manipulated the facts. She was afraid of facts. She was

afraid that the reality of what had happened might go against her interests. But she was never quite clear on what her interests were either, beyond what instinct told her.

My mother always left out anything she thought worked against her. This is something I have inherited in my storytelling. It's not lying. It's just the fear of making a mistake, fear of putting your foot in it, dread of other people's atavistic judgment of your failure to live up to society's incomprehensible code of conduct. We didn't understand, my mother and I, what a person is supposed to do. But the doctors and geriatricians who treated her were never able to impose their medical narratives over her chaotic, wandering descriptions. My mother cornered medicine's logic and drove it off the cliff. She asked her doctors remarkable questions. She once managed to get a doctor to admit that in fact he didn't know the difference between a bacterial infection and a viral one. In her moral chaos and her desire to be healthy, my mother's intuitive, visionary observations were more compelling than the doctors' explanations. She saw the human body as a hostile, cruel serpent. She believed in the cruelty of blood running through veins.

She was a one-woman show. Her melodramatic tendencies bested doctors' patience. They didn't know what to do with her. The bones in one of her legs were in really bad shape. She had a hip replacement that got infected. It was installed around the same time the then king of Spain, Juan Carlos I, got his. People talked about it on TV. We used to make jokes about it. When the prosthesis got infected, it couldn't be removed because that would have required an operation and my mother had cardiovascular conditions too.

She suffered from a long list of illnesses. She used to list her aches and pains, some of them amazingly original.

In the end she was alone. She would sit there in her apartment, totally alone, listing maladies.

She also suffered from asthma. And anxiety. She was a compendium of all named illnesses. Ultimately, her own awareness of life became a minor ailment in and of itself. Her illnesses weren't fatal—they were little everyday torments. They were suffering, that's all.

She lived in a rented apartment: fifty-four years old and living in a rented apartment. She smoked a lot when she was young. She must have smoked till she turned sixty. I'm not sure exactly when she quit.

I can try to calculate when she quit smoking in an approximate sort of way. It would have been 1995 or thereabouts. So she would have been about sixty-two.

There was a fashionableness about the way she smoked, and her smoking also made her different from the other women of her generation. I remember my childhood as being full of tobacco brands that I found fantastic and mysterious.

For example, Kent cigarettes, which I always loved because of their pretty white packaging. My mother smoked Winstons and L&Ms. My father didn't smoke much, but when he did, he smoked Larks.

All the packs of cigarettes lying on the tables and nightstands in my house are connected to my parents' youth. There was joy in my house back then, because my parents were young and they smoked. Young parents smoked. And it's amazing how precisely I remember that joy, a joy from the early 1970s: 1970, 1971, 1972, maybe even 1973.

They would puff away and I'd watch the smoke, and so the years passed.

Neither my father nor my mother ever smoked dark tobacco.

They never smoked Ducados, no dark tobacco at all. That's how I took a dislike to that brand, to Ducados, which I thought was sordid, nasty stuff. My parents didn't smoke it. I associated dark tobacco with grime and poverty. I did notice that some rich people smoked Ducados, but I continued to view dark tobacco with disdain or fear. With fear, really. Fear, at least in personalities like mine, is linked to the spirit of survival. The more fears you have, the longer you survive. I've always had fears. But fear hasn't really kept me out of trouble.

I now sense an enormous gap between us. By evoking the brands of tobacco my parents smoked, it seems, I'm discovering an unexpected joy in my parents' lives.

By that I mean that I think they were happier than I. Even though at the end they were let down by life. Or maybe they were let down by the deterioration of their bodies.

They weren't normal parents. They were historically unique. In every way. They were original—they did bizarre things, they weren't like everybody else. The reason for their eccentricity, or whatever of that eccentricity ended up affecting me as their son, seems to me a fond enigma. My father was born in 1930. My mother—it's a guess, since she was always changing her birth date—in 1932. I think he was two years older than her, maybe three. Sometimes six, because occasionally my mother insisted she'd been born in 1936; it struck her as a famous date because she'd heard it mentioned so many times for whatever reason.

In reality, she was born in 1932.

4

My mother was born into a peasant family and grew up in a tiny village near Barbastro. My paternal grandfather was a storekeeper, but after the Civil War he was accused of being a red, a republican, and was sentenced to ten years in prison, which he didn't end up finishing because of his health. He spent six years in a Salamanca prison. I don't really know the details; my father sometimes used to mention a history of friendship between my grandfather and the militants. It seems he had friends in the Popular Front. Somebody turned him in when the nationalists occupied Barbastro. My father knew who had turned him in. But the man is dead now. My father didn't inherit any hate. What he inherited was silence. I'm not sure what sort of silence it was—I think it wasn't a political silence but a kind of renunciation of words. As if my grandfather didn't want to talk, and my father was fine with wordlessness.

I'm going to die not knowing whether my father and grandfather ever talked. Maybe they never did. They were enveloped in an Adamic idleness. I'm going to die not knowing whether my father ever kissed my grandfather. I don't think so, I don't think they were affectionate. My ancestors' idleness is beautiful. I never met either of my grandfathers, not on my mother's side or my father's. No photos of them exist. They left this world before I arrived, and they left without leaving a photo. Not a single portrait. So I don't know why I'm here in the world. My mother didn't talk about her father, and my father didn't talk about his. It was silence as a form of sedition. Nobody deserves to be named, and this way we will keep talking about that nobody even after that nobody has died.

5

My parents never went to mass like my schoolmates' parents did; this always seemed weird to me and made me uncomfortable around my friends. My parents didn't know who God was. It's not that they were agnostic or atheist. They weren't anything. They didn't think about those things. They never talked about religion at home. And now that I'm writing this memory, I'm fascinated. Maybe my parents were aliens. They didn't even curse. They never mentioned God at all. They lived as if there were no such thing as Catholicism, and that is remarkable, admirable, in the Spain they were born into. For my parents, religion was something invisible. It didn't exist. Their moral universe proceeded without a fetishization of good and evil.

In the Spain of the 1960s and '70s, they would have done well to go to mass. In Spain, people have always done well to go to mass.

6

My mother smoked, so I started smoking too. In the end, smoking together was what we did. My mother baptized me into addiction, unaware of what she was doing. She always misjudged the importance of things: she attributed relevance to trivial things and neglected what was actually vital. Her entire life was spent smoking, until they told us we were rotting our insides. She used to send me down to the shop to buy cigarettes. I ended up getting to know all the tobacco shops in Barbastro.

The dead don't smoke.

I once found a thirty-year-old Kent cigarette in a drawer. It had been hidden. I should have stuck it in an urn.

I'm looking for meaning in the fact that there's nothing left. Everyone loses their father and mother—that's just biology. But I'm also obsessing over the dissolution of the past, and thus its ultimate inexpressiveness. I see a laceration in space and time. The past is the part of life that's been handed over to darkness's holy office. The past never leaves; it can always return. It returns, eternally returns. The past contains joy. It is a hurricane. It is everything in people's lives. The past is love too. To live obsessed with the past prevents you from enjoying the present, but enjoying the present without the weight of the past pressing desolately upon it is not a pleasure but a form of alienation. There is no alienation in the past.

7

They seem alive. But they're dead.

The day they met comes to me. A Saturday afternoon in April 1958. The afternoon is alive. The presence of that afternoon conceals another, more distant presence.

Death is real, and it is legal. It is legal to die. Has any government declared death illegal? It comforts me that our laws make room for death; dying is not a subversive act—even suicide is no longer subversive.

But what are they doing, the two of them, my parents, evading lawful death? It's clear they're not entirely dead. I see them often. My father tends to come before I go to bed, as I'm brushing my teeth. He stands in front of me and looks at the kind of toothpaste I'm using, studies it with curiosity. I know he wants to ask about the brand, but he's not allowed.

And this isn't about me remembering them, about the fact that they live on in my memory. This is about the place they're in now, where their spirits are still suffering. It's about ugly deaths and beautiful lives.

There they are. And in some way they're ghastly spirits.

When my parents died, my memory became a cantankerous, frightened, and wrathful ghost. When your past is wiped off the face of the earth, the universe is erased and everything is sunk in indignity. There is nothing more undignified than the gray dullness of nonexistence. Extinguishing the past is heinous. Your parents' death is heinous. It's a declaration of war that shapes your reality.

When as a child (because of my as-yet-unformed personality or my timidity) I was tormented by my inability to fit in with people, with my schoolmates, I always used to think of my father and mother, and I trusted that they must have an explanation for my social invisibility. They were my protectors, the people who guarded the secret of the reason for my existence, even if it eluded me.

With my father's death, the chaos began; the person who knew who I was, and who could, what's more, take responsibility for my presence and my existence, was no longer in this world. This may be one of the most remarkable things in my life. The only true, accurate reason you're in this world is contained in the will of your father and mother. You are that act of will. Will made flesh.

The biological principle of will is not political in nature. That's why I'm so interested in it, so moved by it. If it's not political, that means it is something approximating truth. Nature is a vicious form of truth. Politics is the agreed-on order, sure, but it's not truth. Truth is your father and your mother.

They created you.

You come from semen and ovule.

Without semen and ovule, nothing exists.

The fact that your identity and existence take place within a political order does not undermine the principle of will, which precedes the political order—and is, furthermore, a necessary principle, whereas although the political order may be perfectly fine and exactly what you want, it is not necessary.

8

I regretted having opted for cremation. My mother, my brother, and I wanted to forget everything. To get rid of the corpse. We were shaking with fear, but we pretended to be on top of the situation, tried to laugh at a few comical details to shield ourselves from terror. Humans invented tombs so that the memory of the living could seek refuge in them, and because bones are important, even if we never see them: knowing they're there is enough. But in Spain our tombs are niches. Tombs are noble; niches are depressing, expensive, and ugly. Because everything is ugly and expensive for the Spanish lower middle class, more lower than middle. That combo term is a dastardly invention—and a lie.

We were lower class, but my father always dressed well. He knew how to dress the part. But he was poor. He just didn't look it. He didn't look it, and in that sense he was a fugitive from Spain's socioeconomic system in the 1970s and '80s. They couldn't throw you in prison for that, for having style even though you were poor. They couldn't throw you in prison for dodging the visible stamp of poverty.

My father was an artist. He had style.

Before he was cremated, my father's body lay on display at the funeral home for several hours. People came to see him. When funeral directors stage the little theater piece of putting death on display, they hide everything except a face caked with makeup. You can't see the corpse's hands or feet or shoulders. The lips are glued shut. I stared at my father, wondering whether it was an industrial-strength glue they used to seal lip against lip. Just imagine the glue fails and suddenly the corpse's mouth falls open. A man came whom I recognized. He wasn't a friend of my father, at most an acquaintance. The guy realized he had no business being there. He came up to me and said, "It's just that we were the same age. I came to see what I'll look like as a corpse." The guy was serious. He took another look and then left.

I later learned the guy died two months after my father did. I remember the expression on his face, even the tone of his voice. I remember how he stared at my father's dead face through the glass of the case where the casket lay, trying, with an act of imagination, to replace my father's face with his own, to see what he'd look like as a dead man.

I stared at my dead father too. The watchman, the caretaker, the commander on duty of my childhood, was taking his leave of the world. I contemplated the disintegration of humanity. The arrival of the corpse. The birth of insubstantiality. Madness. Magnificence. The corpse in all of its mystery.

9

I awoke with a start, coming out of an intense dream. I'd taken an antianxiety pill to sleep. Once upon a time I used to take them in alarming quantities, and I'd combine them with alcohol. The first time I mixed the two aggressively was in 2006. My marriage was in crisis because I had a lover. She wasn't just any lover, she was special, or that's what I felt at the time; maybe the infatuation was completely one-sided, since a partial confession isn't enough to confirm love—you'd have to get a second opinion from the other person. The will to live is always confounding: it starts with an explosion of joy and ends in a spectacle of vulgarity. We are vulgar creatures, and most vulgar of all is anyone who fails to recognize his own vulgarity. Recognizing it is the first gesture of emancipation toward the extraordinary. All of the crises in my marriage since then have combined alcohol and anxiolytics. As the effects of the alcohol dissipate, you go into a state of panic, and that's when you take a stiff dose of anxiolytics.

At bottom, drugs are capitalism's greatest enemy.

It had been an intense dream, and I came out of it with a sensation of drained or exhausted terror. I'd dreamed about a bedroom, the bedroom of a house that had been mine not so long ago.

I had a lot to do that day. I drank some coffee, took a shower. I'm never sure which to do first: have coffee and then shower, or shower first and then have coffee. I was nervous, excited. I was supposed to put on a suit and go to an official banquet with the king and queen of Spain. The idea of meeting the king of Spain while I was on drugs was an appealing one, but you've got to have a revolutionary courage for that sort of thing. It had been many years since I'd worn a suit, maybe not since my wedding. You don't need a suit for a divorce.

Since I don't know how to tie a necktie, my brother had pre-knotted mine. I put on a navy blue suit. It didn't look bad on me. I maybe even looked handsome with my white shirt. I'd slimmed down a bit—I've been locked in combat with food all my life. Food gladdens the heart, but so does being slim. It had gotten late, or that's what I thought, but when I checked the clock I saw that it wasn't too late.

Then I sat down in a chair and thought about the suffering of the necktie's fabric—the knot had been there for several days. I remembered my father. He definitely knew how to tie a necktie. He could do it in a flash with his eyes closed.

A man in a tie is automatically older.

I headed to the royal banquet in my car. A few days earlier, I'd given the palace authorities the license plate number.

I had trouble finding the entrance to the Plaza de Armas.

My nervousness increased.

Then, when my brain was about to burst, I heard a voice: "Relax, buddy, it's all good, you're just going to a banquet. Your suit looks nice. Your parents are dead. You seem to be alive. You've got a decent car, and you still look young. What difference is one meal going to make in your life?"

It always does me good to hear that voice. It's a voice that comes from inside me, but it seems like it's someone else. My internal someone else.

I drive through Madrid. The wheels of my car touch the city of Madrid. I touch the knot of my tie. I consult the GPS. There's a lot of traffic. The GPS isn't working well because it's old; I didn't want to get a new one because it cost fifty euros. People have money in Madrid, you can tell.

10

Madrid is beautiful.

Madrid has been everything in this country; it's got everything. My father came to Madrid a number of times. All Spaniards from the provinces traveled to Madrid at some point. In that sense, Madrid was cruel. People from the provinces were frightened by how big Madrid was.

But it wasn't so big, really. Not as big as London or Paris, for example. Maybe it's catching up. It was a disparaging term, "the provinces." And it was absurd. Madrid's aristocratic elevation over the provinces was the invention, initially, of the monarchy, and later of Franco, but it doesn't matter.

In fact, nothing matters: history is dead and people have realized that the things history describes don't exist in the present, and people no longer wish to inherit the phantasmagoric burdens of times past, of times fictitious.

A guard points out where I should park. Then another guard gives me further instructions. They're elegant, the guards of the royal palace in Madrid.

A wide staircase stretches up before me, flanked by soldiers in their dress uniforms, with gleaming but harmless spears. Their tips probably haven't been sharpened in more than a century. Castrated spears, spears with historic value at best, but useless when it comes to piercing a body.

I climb the stairs. I observe the guards, look them in the eyes.

I feel as if the guards know my past, as if they recognize me as an impostor, as if they realize that, in fact, I should properly be there with them, wearing a showy outfit and holding a spear. How much do they earn? I figure about 1,450 euros a month, maybe, 1,629 euros if they're lucky. I doubt they make as much as 1,700. We hide our salaries, but it's the only thing about ourselves we can actually confess. Finding out someone's salary means seeing them naked.

The large windows of the royal palace are still there, seeing things, filtering the light of days that have accrued in the form of centuries.

The guests are smiling.

Madrid is like the heart of a wild animal.

11

The monarchy inspires fascination, a fascination that doesn't preclude condemnation. There they were, Felipe VI and his wife, Doña Letizia, king and queen of Spain without anyone asking them, though of course they both know such a request is unnecessary because history is a succession of horrifying political maneuvers, and it's best not to delve into that abyss since they, Felipe and Letizia, are a solid, dependable solution given that everything that could replace them is uncertain, unstable, and very likely to end in devastation, death, and destitution. They know that the service they're providing to Spain is objective and measurable—it can be tallied and weighed, it is money. They facilitate international agreements, persuade foreign governments and companies to invest in Spain. Thanks to them, yes. It's true. They inspire confidence in international investors. Confidence is money; it is people coming off the unemployment rolls.

Still, people end up organizing, so you've got to be on the alert—that's why there's a glint of shadow on Felipe VI's face, and a whisper of whips in his wife. They have to be careful. She is creating a moral space, a sort of political temple where "irreproachable" majesty takes place.

They are husband and wife, and so I feel some compassion for them. It's normal to feel compassion for married couples, especially as their years of conjugal bondage pile up. We all know that marriage is the most terrible of all human institutions, since it requires sacrifice, renunciation, going against one's instincts, and lies upon lies—all in exchange for social stability and economic prosperity.

Doña Letizia takes a step away from her husband and situates herself in a more comfortable historical realm, closer to absolution. She is thinking about that illuminating idea, thinking this: "Nobody will ever be able to reproach me for anything." They are silent. I stand motionless, observing their silence, which is occasionally broken by affirmative-sounding monosyllables.

Somebody has told them, "Always say yes."

The monarchs are presiding over the official lunch to celebrate the awarding of the Cervantes Prize to an elderly writer named Juan Goytisolo, a genius who has written brilliant books, the best books of his generation, books written in Spanish. He is, therefore, a Spanish writer. It's not actually self-evident to note his nationality. Spain is a country perpetually on the verge of saying no—that's why Doña Letizia has been instructed to always, if she can, say yes.

It is April 23, 2015, a spring morning in Madrid, with an outside temperature of sixty degrees. The guests gather in circles to chat with some measure of enjoyment; the conversations are polite, relaxed. They are also reserved. All of the guests know they are part of a common framework, a family photo, a sociological reality that could be labeled "Spanish culture, literary sphere, in the year 2015."

A photo at which time can now hurl the merciless cavalry of the dead. I think of myself, right this moment, as the man with the necktie whose knot was tied by another man. It's like a courtly sobriquet from a chivalric novel: he whose necktie was knotted by another man.

Relatively easily, I join several circles; I even move from one circle to another and greet illustrious writers with courteous affability. I feel sophisticated in my suit. Even though fear prevails deep down in my psyche.

I am afraid. I'm afraid of power and the state, I'm afraid of the king—I can't help it.

There is fear everywhere. Even in those who seemingly have nothing to fear, such as Their Majesties the king and queen of Spain, there may also be fear. In other guests, in frequent guests, fear may have been displaced by habit and routine.

Those veteran guests seem to be in their element. There is an obvious recent development: Juan Carlos I is no longer king; his son is. Still, the protocols remain identical.

On the inside, I become someone else, and I give myself a nickname: the man with the fake necktie.

I see myself, ultimately, as someone else.

The specter emerges. I am now the specter.

The man with the fake necktie is a rookie—it's his first time eating with the king and queen.

He's afraid he won't be up to the demands of protocol. Nor is he part of the elite hierarchy of Spanish literature. He toils in a middlingly obscure middle class. He thinks now about that middle class, about the kind of writer who reeks as swiftly of failure as he once did of "This kid is good," except this kid is now over fifty. But it doesn't matter, because everybody, across the entire globe, is headed toward places where hierarchies are fickle and wretched and disintegrating, and stink of old age, where in the end nothing means anything anymore, and that's new.

Hierarchies are breaking down. The ancien régime is breaking down. History, like water, flows on where you least expect it.

Things and people are ceasing to have a clear meaning, and that is subversive, liberating.

Many of those present are over fifty, even over sixty and seventy. The average age at this banquet may be about sixty-five. Indeed, the youngest people here are the king and queen of Spain.

Once upon a time, royal protocols sagely laid out the method by which two people can greet more than a hundred people, or two hundred, in an orderly and coherent manner. It was a revolutionary, democratic notion: nobody should go without being acknowledged.

All guests should be greeted by the hosts.

It seems like a masterly idea.

An idea that is itself a masterpiece.

So the king and queen of Spain settle in an adjoining room, at an unexpected angle. They look like they're coming out of the dark or descending from heaven. All the guests are going to have their photos taken with the king and queen; they will each have exactly six seconds of visibility in their audience with royalty.

There dawns on the man with the tie knotted to his vulgar

neck a method for creating historical unease. He occasionally gets ideas that are above his social station. It's an uneven distribution of genius, a phenomenon that history indulges in from time to time—when people with irrelevant ancestors conceive some relevant thought.

It occurs to the sad necktie man (it's the tie that's sad, not the man—the tie's sad because it's wrapped around a neck that is inadequate to its aesthetic standing, since neckties have destinies too, like Asian elephants) to wield a new weapon that's only recently appeared in the world. It's a political weapon. He pulls a cell phone, a Samsung Galaxy, out of his pocket and goes to the stopwatch function. A revolutionary bit of technology.

He measures how long his encounter with the king and queen of Spain lasts. He measures it with his stopwatch. It's six seconds and ninety-two hundredths of a second. That is the amount of time granted to each guest.

12

Nor can he say good afternoon or good evening or good morning or hello how are you nice to meet you to the king or queen. His muteness is to be expected—it is the product of the Iberian peasantry's stingy night of bread and meat, night of madmen and the cognitively impaired, and his genetic code contains only terror and anguish and error.

Terror and anguish, next to light and wealth, next to the security and love emanating from the king and queen.

Their smile, from three feet away, is one of the greatest sights a Spanish citizen can behold, since it contains the life of millions of now-dead Spaniards whose historical dignity is nestled within that smile. All that Spain has been able to build politically is encoded in that smile, at whose edges millions of fiery serpents nest.

The serpents are ablaze.

The celebrated writer, a doddering geezer, a faded man, a creature from another era, walks with the queen on his arm. Thanks to her punishing high heels, she stands two hands taller than Juan Goytisolo's nearly bald pate. The man with the sad-knotted tie ponders the public display of torture to which the queen is subjecting her feet by placing them in those shoes (stretching and deformation of the bones, joint pain, arthritis), and he ponders what the celebrated writer might be thinking. The man is exhibiting a certain discomfort, a gruffness. It may be that few of those in attendance have read him. And even if he were widely read, it wouldn't actually do him much good, since nobody loves him, and in that sense it's as if he hadn't been read at all. There is no love here, no love anywhere. And maybe he knows it and accepts it. We all know it and accept it, because literature is something that's become irrelevant, since there's no love in it. There's no love in it, thinks the man in the yellow tie, and there should be, since only love has meaning, and where is his love, and what is he doing in this place when he's not going to find love here, and he then recalls his father, whose entire life was determined by the power structure that the woman in severe heels symbolizes.

His father would have loved to see him there, next to the king and queen. He would have loved for him to tell them some anecdote; maybe that's why the son's come in the first place, out of love for his father.

The writer and the queen walk the length of the table with the guests standing at attention. They walk slowly, arm in arm. The queen slows her steps to match the writer's weary gait.

The voice returns and tells the man with the flaming tie, "See, this is it, this is the end of the great Spanish writers, a palace stroll on a queen's arm, a protocol—but people would kill their own mothers for the sake of that final protocol, because life is empty, quite empty in and of itself."

The man with the frightened tie has never seen such a large table, a table for more than a hundred people. He dreams of celebrating Christmas Eve at that table, and he dreams that the people he's sitting with at the table are the lowborn ghosts of his ancestors: his parents, his grandparents, his great-grandparents, his great-great-grandparents.

He'd like to talk to his great-great-grandfather, if he ever existed. There was a man who in biological terms could be considered an ancestor, and thus a great-great-grandfather according to the generational math, but it never occurred to that man that he'd be another man's great-great-grandfather.

There is no bond.

There is nothing.

But the monarchy is a bond. The king's ancestors' portraits hang in the Prado Museum. The king can go whenever he wants to see his great-great-grandfather and talk to him.

Everything is yellowing, and the color of the monarchy is yellow. The royal family is the family chosen to have the yellow pomp of memory imposed on it, the memory that thousands upon thousands of Spanish families lack, that was lost in the spent days of history, that was lost to famine, war, and poverty.

The man with the sad-knotted tie will never be able to go to a museum to be reunited with his great-great-grandparents as painted by Francisco de Goya. But if just one family can, that is enough. This is the moral mystery of monarchies. It is the symbol, the great discovery.

The man with the humiliated necktie would like to know if he has anything in common with his great-great-grandfather: some gesture, some physical resemblance, anything that implies a need, a meaning, an explanation for this historical, biological, genetic present.

While all the guests are watching the old man and the queen, the man with the doomed tie takes the opportunity to observe the table, now that nobody else is. The enormous table, too, serves a function, a being there as a piece of furniture; it fulfills the little-desired role in Spanish history of "being there, enduring, performing one's role."

The award-winning elder has a look on his face that suggests something more than what it actually says, a nose sloping toward the very saddest cliff imaginable. It's a savage sight, his hand clasped in the hand of the queen of Spain. A beautiful woman, inscrutable, with silent, blameless arrogance. The two ghosts walk, pacing within the so-called superstructure of Spanish democracy, which doesn't help a person die in peace.

A democracy doesn't help a person die in peace.

Nothing that is human helps a person die in peace; only drugs do that, and they're a state-run monopoly.

And what is the state? It's a yellowing superimposition of exhausted intentions that no longer think, which had their last thought many decades ago, and which laziness, the mother of intelligence, perpetuates.

13

On October 1, 1991, after passing a public exam, the man who would, twenty-four years later, sit wearing a false necktie near the king of Spain was given a position as a high school teacher specializing in language and literature in a northern city, whose name the man who would, twenty-four years later, sit near the king of Spain does not wish to recall.

It was the best thing that ever happened, financially speaking, to that man.

I even thought God might exist after all and that he'd decided to watch over my passage through the world: I was going to be earning a guaranteed income.

There was gladness in the heart of the man who, twenty-four years later, would sit near, but not very near, not too near, the king of Spain, wearing a depressed tie around his flushed and flustered neck.

The man was twenty-nine back then, that man who became what I am today—which is to say, another man. A man built atop another man, or several. Being twenty-nine is the best killing machine in the world. Nobody realizes it at twenty-nine. It was the moment for enjoying life. Everybody that age longed to have a steady job back then—coming out of the democratic transition period, Spain was obsessed with steady jobs.

The school I was assigned to was named after Pablo Serrano, a famous sculptor. I bought a car, a Ford Fiesta. And I drove that car to teach at the school, which is still standing. Luckily, it had a parking lot with trees that was reserved for the teachers. The trees shaded the cars. I would park my car in the shade. All my life I've been obsessed with parking in the shade. I inherited that obsession from my father. My father always tried to park in the shade. He'd get irritated if he couldn't. We didn't understand that obsession, not my mother, nor my brother and I, when we were younger. We used to go places according to whether there was shade to park in. When my father had a little money and used to take us to the seaside for summer vacation—this was in the late sixties and early seventies—we would get up early to go to the beach, because if we got there too late, he wouldn't be able to find a spot to park the car under the eucalyptus trees. I was very young and didn't understand why we had to get up at six in the morning when we were on vacation and didn't have school. I tried to figure out the reason. And the reason was the shade of the eucalyptus trees. I used to stand staring at those trees, and I ended up internalizing that shade as something amazing, divine in essence. If my father didn't park the car in the shade, he'd be unhappy, distressed. Years later they cut down those eucalyptuses and widened the esplanade. Those trees no longer exist.

Today I understand the desire to park in the shade because that obsession is inside me, with me, in my heart. I nurture that obsession because it's something passed down from my father. It tormented him when the car was in the sun. He was a singular man in every way.

And so I became part of Spain's army of educators. At the time the country still offered a vocational training program. And the shade of the trees in that parking lot in 1991 brought back memories of the eucalyptuses of 1971.

Since I was new, I was assigned the worst groups in the school. It was my job to teach the students in the electrical trade program.

They were fourteen-year-old kids whom nobody loved, kids who'd been referred for so-called vocational training by the state. I was also assigned a group of hairdressers. And a group of administrative assistants. I spent my days explaining the diacritical accent. All Spaniards who have gone to school end up learning about the difference between the pronoun *tú* (you) and the adjective *tu* (your). The *tu* in *tú piensas* (you think) is different from the *tu* in *tu pensamiento* (your thinking). In the first instance, it's a pronoun and has an accent, while in the second it's a determiner and doesn't have an accent. And that was what I did. I spent twenty-three years contemplating the blasted *tu* versus *tú* distinction. That's what they paid me to do. I spent the whole day teaching it, how *tú vienes* (you come) is not the same as *tu venida* (your coming)—it was ridiculous, especially when absolutely goddamn nobody ever came. But I did it because I'd never been paid so well in my entire life as they were paying me. I was assigned to a group of first-year students in the electrical program. Teachers in Spain's public education system are responsible for keeping abreast of the disciplinary and pedagogical details of their students. I soon realized that was a farce. When I walked into the classroom in mid-October, the weather was still hot. A third-year management student asked about something that had just happened in the United States. I thought it was a serious question.

On October 16, 1991, George Hennard killed twenty-three people in the city of Killeen, Texas.

I offered a long reflection on violence, but they weren't listening. My students weren't listening to me. So I let them talk.

"On TV they showed the shattered skull of one of the people he shot. The guy was carrying a semiautomatic pistol—he fired a hundred bullets, it's freaking awesome," said Castro, the most talkative student. "He took out twenty-three people, and he made sure each one was dead before moving on to the next."

The group burst out laughing. And I heard the voice, maybe one of the first times or even the very first time I did: "These kids don't know the victims, they don't know what it means to die, they don't know what it is to murder, to shoot at another body, they don't know anything, and you don't know anything either. In fact, you don't even know whether you care about those twenty-three bullet-riddled bodies. You have to repudiate violence because you're broke and you're doing this job because you get paid at the end of the month. And you're a teacher. And you have to teach them responsible values, you have to make them see you can't just go around killing people. But when you start moralizing about things, they tune you out. Come up with something, dumbass. You're just thinking about your salary, but I get it. You think if you talk like them, you'll get fired and lose your monthly paycheck. And that'll end up killing you. People tend to be invested in their work. And that isn't delusional in the least; it's useful to be invested in something—it makes people's lives better. But from the start you've been infected with a historical and genetic virus passed down from your mother: a dissatisfaction that spreads like an oil slick, relentlessly, over the oceans of the world."

The newbie teacher that I was (again the specter emerges) stood staring at Castro and then pointed his finger like a gun.

He aimed at Castro and said, "Bang, bang, bang."

"I just blew your head off, Castro," I said. And everyone went quiet.

The class ended and I left with a sense of triumph.

"Wow, look at you," the voice said.

A few weeks later, a first-year electrical student who skipped class a lot—in fact, hardly anybody remembered his face—showed up at my classroom door. The newbie teacher that I was looked at him in surprise.

"No, I'm not here for class," he said. "I'm here to beat the crap out of that asshole"—and he pointed at one of his classmates.

He was pointing at Maráez, who was universally known as "Cauliflower."

"That jerk Cauliflower got caught shoplifting at El Corte Inglés, and the bastard told the security guard he didn't have his ID on him but gave them an address. And he gave mine, my address and my name, and yesterday the cops came by my house looking for me, and my old man split my head open with a saucepan." He pointed to a seeping wound on his head.

Cauliflower laughed. Everybody laughed. The newbie teacher that I was stood staring at the wound.

Today I still remember that wound, and it provokes in me a mixture of numb rage and somber tenderness. Today a luminous word comes to mind: *mercy*. We should all be more merciful. I even thought I needed to write a book called *Merciful*. I would have liked to plunge my fingers into that wound and open it further until the boy bled out, and then tenderly drink that blood, in a ceremony of despair.

I've often felt these sensations of profound hopelessness throughout my life. I don't know where they come from. They're miscegenated emotions, violence and melancholy blended together. And euphoria too. I think these feelings come from my most remote ancestors. There must be something in me that has made me resistant despite my emotional warping and decline; otherwise, I wouldn't be in this world.

Resistant to biological bacteria and social bacteria alike.

"Well, since you're here, come on in," I said.

Horcas—that was the kid's name—came into the classroom, saying, "I'll eat your liver during the break, Cauliflower."

"You hear that?" the voice said. "He wants to eat Cauliflower's liver. What does a fourteen-year-old kid's liver taste like? Behold the Spanish lower class—it's a historic show to which few people have tickets, so enjoy. These kids are like rivers of young, cheap blood, they live in crappy apartments and sleep in smelly beds, and their parents aren't worth anything. Their mothers don't have fortunate bodies and their fathers lack professional abilities. Not many people are lucky enough to get a ticket to see this. But you are. Look at them killing each other. You've got a box seat. You're a writer, or you'll end up one eventually. Spain is irredeemable. You get paid to explain bullshit like the diacritical accent mark and how to make sure they don't mix up Quevedo and Góngora, even though who gives a crap who Quevedo was or who Góngora was. Definitely not the two of them, since they're extremely dead. The only ones who care that you're pumping out this bullshit and forcing kids to memorize it are the members of the Spanish cultural elite, who have nothing to do with you or these sad sorts that society has abandoned. But these kids should actually know who Góngora and Quevedo were, because if anybody ever offers them a leg up, it'll be the dead. As if Góngora and Quevedo were some kind of charitable organization, because a charity will end up serving as history for those who need it most—that is, for those who have nothing except history. You should write a history for those who have nothing but history."

Years later I read about Cauliflower's death in the paper. He'd crashed his car into a wall. An old car, but stolen. He could have stolen a new car and not an old one, but Cauliflower had style, and most of all he had a sense of humor. I'm sure the bastard stole the car from Horcas.

Cauliflower left this world at twenty-seven.

Poor Cauliflower, whose life spooled out so swiftly, whom nobody knew, not even him. There's a startling purity in that too. Purity and poverty were wed in the bosom of that dumbass Cauliflower's meager life.

I like to remember him that way, as "that dumbass Cauliflower," where the word *dumbass* signifies peace, honor, and virtue. I knew it was Cauliflower because they printed his full name in the paper: Iván Maráez.

It was him, Cauliflower.

He'd gained a lot of weight, poor Cauliflower. All of my students ended up gaining weight. They all got fat.

The all-time great Spanish bastard: Cauliflower.

And that's even though your parents, Cauliflower, when you were born, gave you a nice name, seem to have put some effort into it. I mean, they thought about your name, and that counts for something.

They called you Iván.

It must have been the best day of your life, the day your parents decided you would have a name. But there's no way you remember that day. Nobody remembers the day they receive the name their parents have chosen. It must have been the best day of your life and you didn't know it—you didn't savor that day, you didn't enjoy it.

Well, Cauliflower, I think that on the day of your baptism, you were loved. I don't know, it seems like there's a kind of beauty in the fact that they named you Iván, a bit of intention, a desire for you to be okay in this world.

Or maybe that day your parents flipped their lids.

Or maybe it was one of your grandparents who took care of your baptism, dear Cauliflower. And decided to name you Iván for some ludicrous and insignificant reason.

Cauliflower took the reason for his name to the grave.

Hey, Cauliflower, here's something funny for you: the guy who taught you Spanish in 1991 later ended up sitting near—though not too near—the king of Spain. What do you think of that, Cauliflower? Not that it's important, since nothing's important when you are dead and were unlucky when you were alive.

It isn't important, but it is funny.

It's funny, and I figured it would make you laugh.

Because to a certain extent you were a victim of an entire historical ordering of society, the construction of hierarchies, the confirmation that in fact biological determinism does exist, and I was the official bearer of Spanish state news, I was the delivery man, the notary. That's why somebody placed me near the king many years later. It's as if everything ended up making a sort of sense, if a terrible one.

Hey, Cauliflower, your bones will have been buried in the common grave by now. I think it's been five years, and I don't think your parents, if they're still alive, would pay for five more.

Hey, Cauliflower, that Christmas of '91 I told my father about you. My father took a liking to you. I described what you were like. He was curious about you. My father was a magnet for the unfortunates of this world. I remember how my father laughed about that time you got nabbed at El Corte Inglés and gave your friend's name. It was my first serious job, and my father liked for me to tell him things. Cauliflower, you were in my father's thoughts. You know something, Cauliflower? My father in Barbastro was beloved of the ill, the developmentally delayed, the poor, the mad, the wretched. He was a magnet for misery. Where did that rare gift of his come from? It was a gift that arose from the depths of the earth that saw him be born; it was from there, from that land, from the Somontano. My father was a rare bird—why were people always going up and talking to him? I think it was because my father was profoundly good.

His goodness was legendary.

"Tell me more about Cauliflower. What a kid," my father said on Christmas Eve 1991, sitting before a chicken my mother had stewed.

My father loved you, Cauliflower.

I didn't.

I didn't back then, Cauliflower, but now I do. Because your eyes, which I can picture right this moment, were good, and bad luck should never keep us from gazing up at the sky, giving thanks for having contemplated the sighs of all the men chained in the air.

14

I remember the year 1983, in August. Two friends and I traveled to the city of Zaragoza to look for a student apartment. I remember the apartments we were shown.

I think the apartments were between twenty and twenty-five thousand pesetas a month. We were looking for one with three bedrooms, a living room, and a kitchen. There were also some that cost eighteen thousand, even fifteen, but farther out from the city center.

An orgy of cheap apartments sprawled before me.

We were three broke students with our scholarship funding in hand. We were good guys. Maybe the three of us were ugly. Maybe me not so much. All three of us were full of exuberant expectation about the future.

We rented one that cost twenty-eight thousand pesetas. It was outside our budget, but we liked it, it was right downtown. It was on a street called Pamplona Escudero, really close to the university, close to everything. It was five minutes from the university.

I later learned that that gentleman, Mr. Pamplona Escudero, had been the mayor of the city, and I'm sure he enjoyed being mayor enormously. I wondered what my mother would think about the apartment, whether she'd approve. I'm sure she wouldn't have liked it. My mother rarely liked other people's homes. I thought my mother wouldn't understand what I was doing in that apartment, why I had to live in a place like that.

It was 1983 and Guardia Civil officers were dying in Spain every day. A country where people were always dying. But having your own apartment was a reason for joy, and right now I'm dusting off all the reasons for joy I've had in my life.

I was afraid of that apartment, of that city. Fear, always fear, like a plague upon me. Fear that seeks a bride in your brain, and if it doesn't find one, it'll make one for itself; and in the end fear is wedded to despair, which is a female spirit built on deterioration and madness. And that's another fundamental part of who I am: all my life I've been dogged by the fear of going mad, fear of not being able to reason through the things that were happening to me, fear of being swept away by chaos. My mother was just like me, and my mother exasperated my father and my father would fly off the handle at my mother and I am heir to the throne of sound and fury, which is simply the desire to break things—to shatter windows, rip shirts, smash plates, break doors, kick furniture, and finally hurl yourself into the void.

God, how I love the despairing. They're the best.

15

My mother used to see the hand of the devil in everyday adversity. She often said, "The devil's in this house," when she was looking for something and couldn't find it. She'd end up yelling, "There's no way the devil's not in this house." She'd look for something that was sitting right in front of her without seeing it. I've inherited the same kind of dementia. I search for things that are right in front of me—a book or a letter or a sweater or a knife or a towel or a pair of briefs or a bank statement—without seeing them. My mother was convinced the devil was hiding things from her, that the devil was responsible for all her little setbacks. She experienced those domestic travails with a lunatic intensity. And I am her now, and the devil is just a hereditary neuronal degeneration that affects the optic nerve and produces waves of suppressed or unsteady chemical connections, and the bacteria of psychosis is incubated in that electrical deterioration of the transmission of reality, and the organic shape of intention rots in a mass of structures that are separate from the social world and I become a museum of scarcity, of silence, of solitude, of suicide, of seclusion, and of suffering.

For my mother and me, life had—has—no plot.

Nothing was happening.

16

In the early 1980s, my father used to come to Zaragoza sometimes for work. We'd get together for dinner. He'd come with some friends of his, and I felt like an alien at those meals, didn't know what to say. His friends were good people, but I didn't want to spend time with them; I found them boring and distant. But the restaurants back then had charm. There was mystery. We always met up at old restaurants—I don't know what it was about them, but they conveyed a pleasant image of Zaragoza. I later came to know the city well, but at the time I didn't have a clue about Zaragoza. There was no Google back then. My father would call me on the neighbor's phone and say, "I am your father." Because we didn't have a phone of our own in my student apartment.

He always liked doing that, saying that: "I am your father," in a theatrical voice. It was the only thing we had—that affirmation, universal in nature. And I do the same thing now with my boys when I call their cell phones: "I am your father." That always unmans them. Nobody really knows what it means, but it's unsettling, it's powerful, it seems like a foundation, like a cloud that fills the sky of your consciousness with blood, like the origin of the world. And my father used to tell me where to come meet him. He'd be eating with his friends; we'd eat well. We once ate at a restaurant on Avenida de Madrid. I'd never been there. I walked in and there was my father, along with the then mayor of Barbastro and another guy. The three of them looked happy.

They were smoking cigars and drinking carajillos. Laughing. Telling jokes. They'd had a good meal. Three happy men, sons of the same town, similar in age, children of the same life experience, product of the same streets, fruit of the same tree—and so they emitted a fraternity that was ingrained. The three of them symbolized rootedness, and rootedness is what I have today. They were rooted in a town in Aragon's highlands and in a particular way of being alive. And so they laughed and were happy, brimming with rootedness.

I invited my father to see my apartment, but he didn't come. My father never saw the places I lived in as a student. I don't know where the hell he thought I lived. He never saw the beds where I slept during those years. I don't know why. Maybe I didn't push him. Maybe the need I now feel for my father to have seen the apartments I lived in back then is a present need, one I didn't feel at the time. I didn't tell him, for example, "Dad, I want you to see where I live." And he didn't say, "I want to see your place." Apparently we were made for each other—neither of us said anything.

I make my father say it now: "I want to see your place, son." I think he didn't much care where I lived, but also, over time, he ended up not caring where he himself lived.

He diminished the importance of things.

My father was an artist of silence.

Still, he brought me a robe. He gave me a bathrobe. When I took the robe to my apartment, I started crying. He hadn't bought it, of course; my mother had. That navy blue cotton robe, thick for winter, embodied all of my mother's affection. That robe was a symbol of rootedness. And yet I had to put that robe in a strange bedroom, in a hostile place.

I cried.

I tried to keep the robe in a spot where it wouldn't physically touch anything in the room. Everything in that room was impure. I sat staring at the robe as if I were staring at absolute love, or a kingdom of love that was under threat.

I knew that my mother and I were saying goodbye. A non-verbal goodbye, wordless. The time of our lives was splitting, starting to flow along different channels.

We were moving apart.

Never again will I feel that tenderness, and it doesn't matter. I feel that now: that it doesn't matter—and that is the greatness of life. There is no reason for weeping or condemnation. What bound me to my mother was and continues to be a mystery that I may finally manage to decode an instant before my death. Or perhaps not, as the monstrosity of dying may well be the only mystery.

I'd like to stockpile that tenderness, the tenderness with which my mother helped me pack my suitcase when I was leaving Barbastro for Zaragoza back then, in the years 1980, 1981, 1982, the things that I put in the suitcase, the way she helped me with my clothes, how she packed food in glass jars, and then I stared at all of that and was overwhelmed by helplessness.

In reality, all of this has to do with poverty. It was poverty—our own impoverishment—that made me shake with fear. And I ended up calling that fear tenderness.

If we'd been rich, everything would have been better, and that's true of everything.

If my parents had had money, things would have gone better for me. But they had nothing, absolutely nothing. Admitting to poverty in Spain seems to be an immoral act, reprehensible, an affront. And yet poor is what almost all of us were.

We were poor, but of the picturesque variety.

17

I was born there, in a Spanish town called Barbastro in 1962, or so I've been told. It must have been a great year, no question, though I harbor serious doubts as to whether I was actually born in 1962. It's inevitable to have doubts about your birth date: it is the first truth that is inherited, not seen or felt or confirmed. You have to have faith that people are telling you the truth, that the numbers composing that date mean something.

You did not witness your birth. You may have witnessed other things: Your wedding, if you got married. The births of your children too. But you will not witness your death.

You won't witness either your birth or your death.

I've doubted my date of birth many times; maybe that doubt comes from my sense of the origin of my bodily and spiritual makeup, or from my sense of the way my body has collided with time, and that collision must have a date. In reality, a date is a name. The date is the name of that collision.

Everybody should doubt their birthday. The date contains no lived truth, it idiotically defines you, and you tend to grant it an importance generated not from your own intention but from social pacts that predate you. Pacts that were sealed while you weren't yet in the world or were in it without yet being born, pre-collision.

I could be the victim of a mistake; my mother had a terrible memory. I remember very little about the 1960s. My first memories are from the 1970s, except for one, which must have taken place in 1966. It's the memory of my mother pregnant with my brother. It's suffused with a sense of unreality, not a faithful recollection. We're in the kitchen and my mother is sitting in a chair, and she's dressed in this almost ethereal white, and she tells me, "Your brother is in here," and points to her belly, and she guides my hand to her belly, and I'm startled, and then I see a light that's streaming in through the utility room off the kitchen. A light that comes from the stars. Looking out the window, I see an immensity full of sweetness. This is my first memory and I don't understand it. I don't know what it is. It's a memory I'm always going back to, and what I go back to is a feeling of peace. When I'm about to die, I bet I'll feel that again.

18

I'm in the bathroom, brushing my teeth, and behind me I sense somebody tracking my footsteps. It's the remains of my dead father and mother; they cling to my loneliness, entwine themselves in my hair, their tiny ghostly molecules follow the movements of my hands and feet around the bathroom; they hold the toothbrush beside me, watch me brush my teeth, read the label on the toothpaste tube, examine the towel, touch my reflection in the mirror. When I get into bed, they linger beside me, and when I turn out the light I hear them murmuring. It's not always them, sometimes they come with sick ghosts, dirty ghosts, horrible ghosts, furious ghosts, malign or benevolent ghosts, it makes no difference—being a ghost transcends good and evil.

Ghosts of the history of Spain, which is also a ghost.

They stroke my hair as I sleep.

19

Though my parents no longer exist, I exist, and I'll be heading out in five minutes. I often repeat this gem of a phrase to myself: "I'll be heading out in five minutes." It's ambiguous; those five minutes stand in for a quantity of time that only I know. They could be five decades or five thousand years or, in fact, five minutes—or even five seconds. It's as if I were announcing my will to die whenever I choose. Since I don't care about dying, I can seize death right now or maybe fifty years from now: I'm the master of the time I have left. It ends up being a way of playing around with something that shouldn't be played with, but what else can you do with death, with something that is devoid of content and is the end of everything? And so people who are approaching death begin to incorporate it into their games, into their thoughts; they end up giving it meaning, and it doesn't mean anything—the idea of peace, of rest, may be the greatest fortune I've had. Everybody wants to rest. Everybody needs sleep. What people who are going to die worry about are those who will be left behind: doing them the least harm possible, leaving everything in order for them. Making sure everything is in order for their children and then departing, taking off. If you leave everything in order for your children, you serenely fade away—that's what it means to die at peace.

20

I'm afraid of old people. They are what I will one day be.

I'll be just another zombie in a random room in the geriatric ward of a hospital that has no name, just a number. Hospital number 7, for example. Yes, I think about aging a lot now, about how I'll no longer have value in and of myself and will be at the mercy of the rage or charity of some caretaker whose entire life will be visible to me in that moment. The gift of seeing lives—that's something I've had.

I studied with the Piarists up until seventh grade. I went to Catholic school because it was the only one around. One day in 1971 a priest called to me. He wanted me to join the school choir. I was eight years old. His name was G. Yes, there are probably still people who remember him, but not many. I went into the classroom. The sun was beaming in through the windows. I remember the cassock. A cassock over a bulging paunch. All of those priests were fat. He spoke to me fondly. Francoism was full of fucked-up priests. He started stroking my hair. Then he started to press his hands into mine. I didn't understand at all. I didn't know what was happening.

Thirty years later, I saw G.'s obituary in the town newspaper. He was dead. He used to smoke Ducados. I wasn't happy he'd died, I was pensive. I don't think he did it in the end, but I don't remember. If anything rescued me, it was the sunlight pouring into that room—it illuminated that bastard's actions and made him afraid. Maybe my brain erased everything. I'm not sure. I'm not sure how far it went. I don't remember. I can't remember. All I know is that I sometimes walk down a corridor and go into a classroom and there he is, wrapped in his cassock, and he smiles at me and the touches begin. I stare at the cassock, its garish blackness, its symbolic darkness—what does it mean to go around dressed like that? I stare at the cincture, unable to figure out its purpose; I associate it with a belt, but it's not a belt, it doesn't have a buckle or holes, it's like a decoration, but what is it decorating, and why decorate something there—maybe it has something to do with Christmas, with the birth of the son of God. Am I the son of God and that's why this man with decorations on his belly has called me in? My mind shatters, my memory screeches to a halt. I didn't know what that was, whether it was good or bad. No child knows until some time has passed. I go back to that memory again and again, trying to figure out what happened, but there's a blank. After the touches, there's a blank.

My eyes are at the level of his cincture, staring at the cincture, trying to decipher its meaning. I didn't know whether I should tell my parents, and I didn't tell them because I thought it was my fault. I thought I was the one at fault. That they'd stop loving me. That I'd been bad. That I hadn't loved them enough and that's why it happened.

The problem with evil is that if it touches you, it makes you the guilty one. That is the great mystery of evil: The victims always end up guilty of something also called evil. The victims are always excremental. People feign compassion for the victims, but deep inside they feel only contempt.

The victims are always unredeemable.

That is to say, contemptible.

People love heroes, not victims.

21

It's an afternoon in late April 2015, the twenty-ninth, and I decide to go see an exhibition about a Spanish female writer who is canonized in every sense. The exhibition is at the National Library in

Madrid. I'm starving. I've barely eaten. I walk into the exhibition rooms. There are a ton of paintings that claim to be portraits of the saint. I notice that the paintings don't show the same woman or the same face twice. It's as if they portray a great many women and at the same time none at all. Nobody knows what she looked like, nobody remembers her features. All the artists who painted her were a bunch of fakers. Her features, her eyes, the shape of her nose, her cheeks are lost forever. We don't know her face in an indisputable way. Therefore, she could have had any face, or none. Those who painted her did so based on hearsay.

There's nothing here.

I stare at her manuscripts: a frenzy of delirious ink, handwriting from hell itself. Little has been said about the materiality of writing, though it's a more relevant topic than literary influences and divine apparitions. For example, it's not the same to write on one keyboard versus another, on a laptop screen versus a large monitor, on a rectangular screen versus a square one, on a tall table versus a low one, in a chair with wheels or one without them, and so on.

Because the materiality of writing is writing. In fact, Saint Teresa wrote the way she wrote because her hand got tired of dipping her quill into the inkwell so often, hence her scrawling and chaotic and ferocious and wrathful handwriting. If she'd had a Bic ballpoint, she'd have written differently.

So her visions of God were the material visions of her writing.

Writing is a hand moving across a sheet of paper, a parchment, or a keyboard.

A hand that grows weary.

A thing gets written depending on the paper, the hand, the ballpoint, the fountain pen, or the computer or typewriter. Because literature, like everything else, is material. Literature is words etched on paper. It is physical toil. It is sweat. It is not spirit. Enough with our disdain for materiality.

Moses wrote ten commandments because he got tired of chiseling stone. He was sweaty, exhausted. There could have been fifteen, or twenty-five, but there were only ten because of the strenuous, taxing material conditions of writing on stone. All of Western history is built on idealism; nobody has stopped to consider things from another angle, especially not the simplest angle, one that takes the material realm, vain realities, into account.

I am interested in this woman, this saint. Lots of people can call her "Mother" if they like. She could be everybody's mother—what does that mean? Could she be my dead mother? Death is everywhere, and mothers too. People pray to Saint Teresa. She inspires devotion, and thus seems to be an everlasting ghost. Is her ghost better than the ghost of my mother? There are people praying to her at this very moment, confessing their grief, their misfortune, pleading for succor. And those people believe there's somebody on the other side, that the saint is listening, and in fact there's nobody listening, and that's amazing: millions of words tossed into the black hole of our brains. Is talking to my dead mother the same thing? It's not the same. My mother is here. Because I am her.

This woman who is now being remembered on the five-hundredth anniversary of her birth is dead. She is a dead woman with secular experience. Not all dead people are the same: the dead can be old too. This woman talked about love all the live-long day. She was in love, I think. And she lived in this country. I look at her biography: She was born on March 28, 1515, which is like never having been born at all. There's no way for that year to have any meaning here in 2015. Yet there are documents, and literary and artistic works, and churches and castles that suggest that those numbers—1515—must have had people in them. Five hundred years ago, in an inhospitable place called Gotarrendura, a baby was born who would be christened Teresa de Cepeda. A dumb thought occurs to me: Back then, in 1515, there was no such thing as Real Madrid and Barça, two systems of gravity, two gravitational masses in Spanish life. Maybe it's not so dumb. She was a woman who founded convents. If she were alive today, she'd have recorded music and appeared on album covers. Or she would have founded soccer teams. I myself am Saint Teresa: we are linked by pain. And by an aspiration that she called "God" and I call "X." She, at least, had a name for her aspiration, for her great desire. I have none.

Nobody knows what Saint Teresa's real face looked like. Nobody was able to take her photo. And the faces of my dead father and mother have been photographed.

I should destroy those photos so my father and mother are the same as Saint Teresa.

If Real Madrid and Barça disappeared, Spain would turn into a black hole. Spain's gravitational force is two soccer teams.

22

My mother always liked good colognes, as did my father; they passed on that partiality to me, which at bottom is merely a desire to fend off the avatar of the future rotting of our flesh. Foul odors horrify us not because they're foul (since really there's no such thing as a foul odor) but because that's what we'll produce when our flesh falls into decay's clutches.

A few days ago I was in Barbastro, the city where my parents lived and died. I thought about the interlinking actions and events, words and events, that led to my divorce. The objective fact that my mother never learned of my divorce is not a coincidence. It's as if I felt the hand of some prehistoric Great Beast manipulating my days. A diplodocus. A tyrannosaurus. A velociraptor. A stegosaurus. A gallimimus. Tears in a human fabric that was always there. Acts of an apocryphal apostle, the impossibility of purifying those acts, which makes it impossible to live in peace.

My divorce took me to places in the human soul that I never dreamed existed. It led me to a rewriting of history, to new interpretations of the discovery of the Americas, new considerations of the Industrial Revolution; it charred the time that had passed or raised it until it became a guillotine that decapitated one memory each day.

I realized it was worth living even if it was just to sit in silence. I had a hard time talking to people who hadn't known my parents—which was most of the people I encountered. People who hadn't known my parents cast a pall over my spirit.

I saw joy in terror.

When life allows you to see the marriage between terror and joy, you are ready for abundance.

Terror is seeing the fuselage of the world.

23

At seventeen I often disregarded my father's presence when I returned home; I had no idea whether my father was home or not. I had a lot to do, or so I thought, things that did not include silently contemplating my father. And now I regret not having contemplated my father's life more. Looking at his life, just that, nothing more.

Looking at my father's life—I should have spent a good long while every day doing that.

24

After my divorce, I bought a small apartment. Of course, the grim properties on offer in Spain aren't really worthy of being called apartments. The word conveys a sophistication that's alien to Spanish real estate culture. My father never saw the apartment I bought. He'd died nine years earlier—that's a long time, a really long time. He didn't see the house of my solitude. Which is to say, he didn't see my glorious present. Which is to say, he doesn't know what I've become. Which is to say, his son—the son he knew—is dead and in his place is a man from who knows where, a stranger. What would he have thought of this apartment? He probably wouldn't have understood. In the last years of his life he understood nothing at all. He wandered through life, waiting for who knows what. He complained very little, and when he did it was not about being ill but about small everyday adversities. He seemed not to remember things. As ever, he didn't talk about his father or his mother. He didn't talk about his life. My father seemed to have been born through spontaneous generation. My mother too. My mother had no past or present or future. It was as if they'd made a pact. When had they agreed to it? Had they spoken it aloud?

My mother never spoke of the past. She didn't know the past existed. My mother didn't understand time. She had no historical categories in her mind. That was a strange aesthetic creation of my mother's, as if she were consumed by a sort of historical embarrassment. Was she ashamed of her parents? My mother never reflected on her life; she acted on instinct, on instincts that masked frustration. Sometimes, when referring to her mother, she'd say "Mama," without the accent, instead of "Mamá." That way of pronouncing the word was characteristic of the villages of the Somontano. In her youth, my mother had a joyous sense of the life she wanted to achieve. I remember that when I was very young my parents used to go out almost every weekend. I imagine they were going out to dinner with friends. I'm talking the mid- and late 1960s. They'd leave me with my aunt Reme. Sometimes, if I concentrate, I can visualize the restaurants they went to. I picture white tablecloths, flan for dessert, champagne served in wide glasses, the ones known as coupes that nobody uses anymore. Now people use champagne flutes. Why don't they use those old shallow glasses to serve champagne anymore? Why do they use flutes? It probably has to do with the notion of "elegance," which is fickle and ever-changing. Coupes are also known as Pompadour glasses. And there's an intermediate glass, between the Pompadour and the flute, the so-called tulip glass. My parents used to drink champagne out of coupes in the seventh decade of the increasingly remote last century—the now-vanished coupe, which symbolized celebration and happiness.

I'll always regret having them cremated.

25

Since I've stopped drinking alcohol, I've rediscovered a man who was a stranger to me. Sometimes I scratch my hands, or pick at my cuticles, as a way of coping with the boredom and emptiness. Things happen slowly if you don't drink. Drinking was speed, and speed is the enemy of emptiness.

A divorce awakens guilt, because guilt is an exercise in high relief, it is a protruding contour on flat terrain. The life of a human being is a process of building contours that death and time will eventually smooth out. One of those contours is born of the discovery that no two human beings are alike. Thus, the desire for promiscuity. Every woman is different. And that is an assault on platonic love. At my age, I won't say that sex isn't important, but it's as if you suddenly discovered in sex an aspect that is not physical in nature, not purely libidinous. It is Eros, yes, it is a reordering of the spirit based on the desire for specific details of your beloved. It is a trajectory that bears you toward beauty. You travel from lust to beauty along a path lined with leafy trees, and those trees are your years, the years you've lived.

And so, in my life, as in so many other lives, Platonism and promiscuity were locked in battle. And that always does damage. But a divorce, under capitalism, ends up being reduced to a fight over the distribution of money. Because money is more powerful than life and death and love.

Money is the language of God.

Money is the poetry of history.

Money is the humor of the gods.

Truth is the most interesting element of literature. Recounting everything that has happened to us while we've been alive. Not as narration but as truth. Truth is a point of view that shines on its own immediately. Most people live and die without having witnessed the truth. The comical thing about the human condition is that it doesn't need truth. Truth is an adornment, a moral bauble.

A person can live without truth: truth is a prestigious form of vanity.

26

Sometimes I imagine I'm a widower instead of a divorcé. Being a widower, I think, would be worse. When you get divorced, your past becomes something that's difficult to remember or pin down or possess; in the aftermath, you have to go to the documents, photos, letters, testimonies, papers, to rebuild the past. It's like the end of a historical era. To rescue memory, you have to summon the historians. And historians are idlers, they're napping, they don't feel like working. They'd rather lounge in the sun.

Maybe guilt is a form of permanence. Maybe the enormously guilty end up, through their guilt, discerning a sort of persistence.

I once hoped that God or chance might make it possible for my death to come before my ex-wife's. In divorce, the time you've spent living together is final. A divorce after two years living together, for example, could be inconsequential. A divorce after thirty years is an entire historical era. It's like the Renaissance, or the Enlightenment, or Romanticism. The writer Alejandro Gándara told me a little while back that it takes five years to cauterize the wound of a divorce. I think he was right: five years.

I was especially wounded by the way affection crumbled. Things she used to say, full of loving kindness, float through my head. I discovered that the death of a relationship is actually the death of a secret language. A relationship that dies results in a dead language. That's what the writer Jordi Carrión said in a Facebook post: "Each couple, as they fall in love and spend time together and live together and love each other, creates a language that belongs just to the two of them. That private language, full of neologisms, inflections, semantic fields that are implicitly understood, has only two speakers. It starts to die when they split up. It dies altogether when they both find new partners, invent new languages, move past the grief that survives any death. There are millions of them, these dead languages."

My parents had a language too. I barely remember my father saying my mother's name. The way he pronounced her name, how the way he said it evolved. I do remember something wonderful: my father invented a way of whistling. That whistle was a secret sound that only my father and mother knew. A password. I can reproduce that sound; I don't remember when or how I learned it or where my father got it. They used that whistle to communicate when they were looking for each other around town, or in a store, or in a crowd, and especially in early September, when Barbastro held its town fair and people swarmed the streets, when the giant puppets and carts and musical troupes came out. I was terrified of the puppets. When my father lost sight of my mother, he'd let out that whistle, and my mother would know he was nearby. They were young then. And that sound brought them back to each other.

27

I remember when I was six or seven years old, I often had night terrors and couldn't sleep, and I'd start to cry. My mother would come to my bed and sleep next to me, or she'd stay in my bed and I'd go sleep with my father. The real mystery is that I used to pray before I went to sleep. It must have been a combination of superstition, childish fears, and the influence of my religious education. But now I know those prayers frightened off the spirits of the dead who coveted the innocent heart of a helpless little boy. I also know I've always been a little boy, and that I possess a little boy's selfishness. Little boys forced to be men will always be innocent. When I got into bed, if I knew that my father was beside me, I felt protected and my whole self relaxed. Full of peace, tranquility, and happiness, I'd fall asleep.

I was seven or eight years old and I would fall asleep by my father's side. Which is to say, by a dead man's side. Now I'm over fifty and when I go to bed, that dead man is still there.

He doesn't leave.

The past lived by any man or woman over fifty becomes an enigma. It's impossible to solve it. All you can do is fall in love with the enigma.

28

My dead father sleeps next to me and says, "Come on, come now." The dead are all alone; they want you to go with them. But where to? The place where they are doesn't exist. The dead don't know where they are. They can't name the place. But my father's corpse is all that I still hold and possess in this world. It is here, next to me. His corpse directs the great devastations of my life; his corpse governs my own; in the darkness of my corpse, his corpse's darkness urges me on; his corpse controls my corpse's light; his corpse is a teacher that shows my corpse the disconcerting joy of continuing to exist in corpse form—the Olympic realm, the Champions

League, the realm of emotions that are now without time or history, dead emotions that nevertheless aimlessly persist.

I'll be doing something and suddenly my father appears through a smell, an image, through an object.

He holds out his hand to me, as though I were a lost little boy.

29

Maybe my parents were angels, or else their deaths turned them into angels in front of me. Afterward, all the things I saw them do while they were alive came to seem miraculous. That didn't happen until my mother's death, which closed the circle.

Christianity is based on a never-ending conversation between a father and his son. The only form of enduring truth we've discovered is that one: the relationship between a father and a son. The father summons his offspring, and that is how life moves forward.

The ritual of monarchy is exactly the same: a father and a son. The ritual of twenty-first-century society is exactly the same: fathers and sons. There's nothing else. Everything vanishes except that mystery, which is the mystery of the will to be, the will for there to be someone apart from me: that mystery is the foundation of fatherhood and motherhood.

30

It may be that my parents weren't real. There are fewer and fewer people who can testify that they were. Their corpses do not exist, because they were devoured by the fire of a modern Spanish crematorium; and so the idea of resurrection becomes tricky, as does the notion that angel wings will sprout from the skeleton's shoulder blades. There are no takebacks with cremation; there is no possibility of exhuming the corpse.

But there are still some people who knew them, people willing to offer testimony. A few months ago, a woman of about seventy told me, "Your parents were the most famous beautiful couple in Barbastro—they were legendary." Yes, I'd sensed that. They were superstars back in the sixties. It's true, they were both good-looking. My father was tall and handsome. My mother was a stunning blonde when she was young. When I was a little boy I knew it, I knew it for a fact. That's why I always wanted them to take me out on walks. I wanted people to see that I was their son. When my aunt and uncle took me out instead, I was miffed because I knew they weren't as good-looking. That must have been the first time I felt a twinge of social vanity, the vanity of showing off a coveted possession. I wanted other people to envy me, respect me, flatter me, because my parents were special. I think I'm calling up a feeling that was tucked deep away in my memory, because that preening desire for people to see me holding my parents' hands disappeared a long time ago. Unearthing this memory has provoked astonishment and fear. It's as if a geologist were to suddenly witness the spectacle of the earth forming millions of years ago and discover that the birth of the planet had no meaning. Not the banality of evil, as Hannah Arendt had it, but the banality of material and memory.

They were beautiful. They were both beautiful. That's why I'm writing this book—because I'm seeing them.

I saw them back then, when they were beautiful, and I see them now that they're dead.

My parents' being so beautiful is the best thing that ever happened to me.

31

Every human being is happy at the start of life. It's a happiness born of youth, the time in which we are most supremely ignorant of annihilation. I gaze at the man in the center of the photo, lost in thought, regarding his hands, elegant, with time stopped, existence itself frozen in an echoing moment of visual delight:

It looks like he's got a cigarette in his hand and is absorbed by it, aloof from the conversations around him. There are men and women milling around. Everybody in this photo is now gone; they were—one by one—the protagonists of some hospitalized agony

or of sudden death and burial; they were all mourned, some more than others. But prior to that all of them knew my father. They were able to talk to him calmly, to become acquainted with a mystery that has always eluded me; they know the mystery, everybody who's buried in this photo. They saw him, had dealings with him. I was able to know my father only once he was already my father. If I'd known him before that, I'd have realized how unnecessary I was; I would have known a world without me. You can enjoy the world more if you're not in it. Is it on that pleasure that the angels feed?

It's a better death if nobody knows you're alive; that way you don't burden anybody with the weight of your death, with paperwork, weeping, and a funeral, with guilt and demons. The people who die best are those we never knew were alive. Life is either social or it is pure nature, and in nature there's no such thing as death.

Death is a frivolity thought up by culture and civilization.

None of the people captured in this photo were aware they were going to die. Nobody who is alive before their death is aware of that. If they are, it's only the living who see the dead who are aware of it.

I don't know what year this photo is from, I'd guess the late fifties. It came into my possession by chance; it's from a private collection, it was never at my house. My brother gave it to me, having gotten it from the owner of that private collection. My father had no desire to preserve this photo—he never even remembered it. It's a photo of the father before he is a father, the photo of a man who has no children or wife or roots; it is the photo of a man who has nothing to do with me; he didn't arrange for me to see it, never said, "I'll keep this photo for posterity, maybe for my children if I have them, which I doubt"; he's a bachelor, free from any kinship. And so I don't know who the man is, and nobody ever will.

Ultimately, this photo eludes kinship and we are both free. Every father and every son always seek the end of kinship, the breaking of those chains; it is the quest for freedom, and ultimately it is death that dissolves all kinship, all the heavy bonds of blood, however much love there is in those ties. The photo of the father before he's a father evokes a complete moment in which I am not present, and it gives me great joy not to be there. Because this man in the photo, lost in thought and staring at his hands, in a double-breasted suit with a pocket square, is not yet looking for me; his life is happening without mine.

He looks like a loner in this photo, and yet he dominates the scene. And what is he doing? He knew only in that moment; he knew what he was doing only in that moment—and what did he want then? What was the thing that could give him absolute happiness in that moment?

The father before fatherhood is a force in the world heralding a son's arrival, heralding your arrival but you haven't yet arrived, and that's the amazing bit: you haven't yet arrived and so, in this photo, there is the possibility that you never will. And that possibility is a lovely one, immensely beautiful.

Can you imagine a world in which your father exists but you do not, and nobody is even wishing for you?

A man's greatest mystery is the life of that other man who brought him into the world.

This photo was taken when I was not necessary. That's why I love this photo so much, because it contains my mystery: I do not exist, and my father there is a man who does not want to get married or have children. He isn't even considering it. He gets teased about it, the usual jokes, "Let's see who ends up reeling you in," but he shrugs them off. He reigns in the bar. It is the bar of life, it's in the center of things.

I'm not there; I'm resting.

I am trying to get back to the peace of not being.

32

Years after the photo in the bar, he found himself a wife and I was born. My father must have known the reason for my existence, since I'm his son (I am still his son even though he is no longer alive), and he took it with him to the land of the dead. We both loved the mountains: those ruined villages in the Huescan Pyrenees of a backward, inhospitable Spain, where the ruin of those villages watched over our own ruin. The snow, the high rocks, the insatiable trees, the enigmatic sun, the rivers in the valleys, the immovable mountains, an imperturbable silence, the indifference of nature—we loved it. We loved how firmly rooted the mountains were. Their "being there." In the moment. Mountains aren't a matter of *ser*, but of *estar*. Our life, too, was *estar*. My father's life was a reaffirmation of *estar* over *ser*.

We were together—and everything else proceeds from that, from our being together. I was with my father for forty-three years of my life. He hasn't been with me for a decade now, and that's the greatest moral problem of my life: the decade I've been alive without my father contemplating me.

Christ was constantly asking for his father to contemplate him. The fact that Jesus's novel has been a bestseller does not undercut my own. Everything he did in life was watched over by his father. If his father didn't contemplate his life, Christ's life was false. A father gives meaning and direction to all the industrial parks, highways, airports, shopping centers, parking lots, beltways, avenues, neighborhoods, and hotel rooms that populate the false world we inhabit.

It may be that the only human space is a Romanesque church or the family apartment—which are the same thing.

Everything was encapsulated in a name, the name of a place: Ordesa, because my father was genuinely devoted to the Pyrenean valley of Ordesa and because in Ordesa there's a beautiful and well-known mountain called Monte Perdido, the Lost Mountain.

My father didn't die—he got lost, took off. He became a lost mountain.

What he did was disappear. It was a disappearing act. I remember it full well: He wanted to leave. To escape.

He escaped from reality.

He found a door and made his exit.

33

The table I'm writing at is covered with dust. Because it's glass, the dust has a reflection, an image in the light. It's as if the items in this house have married dust. There is dust visible on the gold edges of the toaster. There are some places the dust cannot obscure; there, I can get rid of it, destroy it, erase it from the face of my house. I don't feel I have the ability or training to clean all that dust, and that makes me despair and provokes neurotic thoughts about squalor. There is even dust on the towel warmer in the bathroom, and heat and dust fuse together, like in a marriage of convenience, like those marriages of the sixteenth-century kings and queens who founded Western civilization.

I will never get used to being poor. I'm calling it poverty, but it's vulnerability. I've mixed up poverty and vulnerability; they look the same from the outside. But poverty is a moral condition, a sense of things, a sort of superfluous integrity. A refusal to participate in the plundering of the world—that's what poverty is to me. Maybe not out of goodness or ethics or any noble ideal, but out of incompetence when it comes to plunder.

Neither my father nor I plundered the world. We were, in that sense, monks in some unknown mendicant order.

34

It's been ages since I've had a drink.

I thought I wouldn't be able to stand it, but I have. There are times when I'd really like a beer, a glass of very cold white wine. Drinking was killing me; I was doing it compulsively, pursuing the end. I was reacting. Things are still rough for me now, but I'm not drinking.

I drank a lot. I ended up in the hospital twice. I'd collapse in the middle of the street and the police would come.

Every alcoholic arrives at the moment when he must choose whether to imbibe or to stay alive. The two options may rhyme, but they're completely different. And it turns out you end up loving your own life a lot, however bland and miserable it is. There are others who don't, who don't manage to get out, who die. There is death when you say yes to alcohol and death when you say no to alcohol. Anyone who's drunk a lot knows that alcohol is a tool that pries open the padlock of the world. You end up seeing everything more clearly, as long as you're able to get out of there afterward, of course.

Drinking was more important than living—it was paradise.

Drinking made the world better, and it always will.

I remember after my divorce when a bank gave me the mortgage for my apartment. I remember they asked if I was healthy and I said I was. When I left the bank, with the mortgage in place, I went to a bar next door. It was one thirty or two in the afternoon. I drank in that bar nonstop. I drank wine. I got worked up, euphoric. I left the bar and walked behind the bank and passed out right there in the plaza. Unconscious next to my mortgage papers. The police came to collect me, because somebody always calls them. I woke up in the hospital. The first thing I thought when I came to, there in a bed in the emergency room, was whether they'd take away my mortgage, whether the bank people had seen me pass out, completely hammered. That was the final straw. The episode had a humorous quality, it bore my quirky stamp, my enduring comedy, my mother's legacy—because my mother used to do things like that.

My dead mother is watching my mortal theater piece, my comic play. I don't know if my two sons will love me as much as I've loved my parents. Let there be a record of this fleeting, absurd doubt, which I'm feeling right this moment as I wander around Zaragoza. My mother loved this city because back then I was living near a shopping mall. And my mother, like me, was a shopping fiend. She adored cosmetics stores. We had more than one heated argument about it. She'd go to a cosmetics store in the mall and buy three-hundred-euro moisturizers, which my brother and I then had to pay for. My mother couldn't understand it. What had been the point of giving her children a better life if she couldn't buy herself those moisturizers? And deep down she was right. We hadn't managed to escape the lower middle class; at best, we might have moved from the lower class to the middle class.

Sometimes I think it would be preferable to be utterly destitute. Because if you're just lower class, you still have hope. Being a beggar means shutting the door in hope's face. And there is something compelling about that.

I came to, still drunk, in the emergency room at Quirón Hospital, which was where the police had taken me. I was down in the dumps, and to top it off there were some gaps in my memory. I didn't know what had happened; my only worry was whether the bank manager who'd just given me a thirty-year mortgage had seen me pass out drunk in the middle of the street two hours after the closing. I figured most likely not. I think I signed the loan a little before two in the afternoon, and I passed out around four or four something, after the bank was closed. But people in banks work hard, and they could have stayed late that day. I got tangled up in conjectures about what time the bankers had left work. The doctor who was running the emergency room treated me with contempt. I wasn't a sick patient, I was a disgusting drunk. She wanted me to leave immediately, but I couldn't stand. I was still vomiting. I looked at my vomit and it was pure wine. The nurse told me I'd vomited up a liter of wine. I thought about drinking it again, since it was resuscitated wine, real wine, perfectly good, reusable wine, like it had come out of a bottle, not a stomach. The head doctor got angry with me because I refused to leave. She said I was making a ruckus and disturbing the other patients—there were a bunch of old people around me. I told her that the World Health Organization classed alcoholism as a disease, and that she therefore needed to treat me the way one does a sick person, not a degenerate, a "sorry-ass drunk." She told me to leave, said there was nothing wrong with me, I wasn't sick.

I tried to stand up, but another wave of nausea hit me and this time I threw up not in the basin but on an old lady next to me. The doctor yelled at me. I told her it was her fault. I demanded to submit a formal complaint. I became the pariah of the emergency room. Everybody glared at me. I guess that's the kind of treatment alcoholics get in Spain. I apologized to the old lady and suddenly realized I was talking to myself. The old lady was dead. "Don't worry, she can't hear you," the nurse said. "Go on, you can leave now."

I went home and took three sedatives; I was distressed, desperate, scared, dead inside, and I fell asleep. I woke up three hours later having an indescribable panic attack, and took three more sedatives and went back to sleep.

On June 9, 2014, I stopped drinking.

35

If you're looking to stop drinking, change your location. Good and evil are the most firmly established fictions of our civilization. Good doesn't exist, and evil doesn't either. I thought about the anarchism of the heart, there where good and evil disappear and bare life returns. So I got into my car and went to the mountains. I crossed into France through the pass at Somport. French towns are stranded in time. Anyone who has driven through the villages of Urdos, Bedous, and Lescun and traveled those roads knows that those places are just the same as they were fifty years ago. There, in those Pyrenean valleys, I found an obliteration of social life, and I saw the rivers completely free of ice.

I went into a bar in Lescun and saw people drinking beer.

I went into my hotel in Canfranc and saw people drinking wine.

And I drank coffee with milk, or sparkling water. I stared at the sparkling water, the bubbles in the glass. When you don't drink, the days are longer, your thoughts are heavier, places stick in your mind, you don't forget things in hotel rooms, you don't scratch the car, you don't break the sideview mirrors when you park, you don't drop your cell phone into the toilet, you don't mix up people's faces.

I went deep into the forests. I touched life again. I traveled to Ordesa and sat contemplating the mountains. I saw clearly the mistakes I'd made in my life and I forgave myself as much as I could, but not entirely. I needed more time.

36

Growing old is our future. We disguise it with words like *dignity*, *serenity*, *integrity*, *wisdom*, but any elderly person would happily give up those words if in exchange you lopped off five years, or even five months. My mother never accepted aging. I don't know what kind of old man I'll be, and I don't really care. The best option would be to die before I become decrepit. People always die—we all end up dying. Thus do all the losers of the earth, all of the poor and illiterate, get their revenge on those who accumulated success, power, knowledge, sophistication, and wisdom.

Aging is the great equalizer.

And it's amusing to watch that spectacle. It has no moral content, much less religious; it's just an unexpected spectacle, stimulating and fascinating. Nature eliminates the predators it has haphazardly created. We are immersed in the present, with its feverish ability to make us believe that life is consistent. You have to appreciate the effort the present makes, its great civilizing zeal. It's all we have. Well, we've got other things too: almonds, I love almonds. And another even more remarkable thing: olive oil. Olive oil makes me inclined to exalt the present.

Only matter.

What I mean is that every time my mother's ghost comes to my memory, I remember olive oil, which may have been the organic substance that had the most interaction with my mother's body. My mother was always cooking. Given that she was always cooking, what was she thinking about? Flour? Bread? Eggs? Vegetables, meats, rice, sauces, fish?

No.

Olive oil.

My mother always lived her life surrounded by olive oil.

My mother passed down to me a secret worship of olive oil, never spoken aloud. I think olive oil is a wormhole, a plunging back through time that leads directly to my first ancestor, who looks at me and knows who I am. He knows that I need love. The love of somebody of my own lineage.

I don't know why I've been so disdainful about the way human beings grow old.

When I'm a ruined old man, I'll want to be loved, and then somebody will remember these words of mine. But words in a book are one thing, and the words of life are quite another, I'd argue.

They're two different truths, but both are truths: that of the book and that of life.

And together they establish a lie.

37

My mother christened the world; anything that my mother didn't name seems threatening to me.

My father created the world; anything that my father didn't sanction seems unstable and hollow.

Since I will never hear their voices again, sometimes I refuse to understand Spanish, as if the Spanish language had perished along with its dead, and is now only a dead language, like Latin.

I don't understand anybody else's Spanish because my parents' Spanish can no longer be heard in this world.

It is a kind of mourning.

38

I take an ibuprofen for my headache. Naturally, I'm convinced the headache is the symptom of a brain tumor that's growing inside my body, a killer tumor that I'll never be able to see, a tumor like a rock or a meteorite, one that encases my whole past and my whole life; a tumor that, once it's examined, tested, and studied, will reveal specific scenes and events from my life; a tumor in which human faces are visible, the faces of family, friends, coworkers, enemies, anonymous people I've crossed paths with, of cities, of random things I've experienced; a tumor that contains this book I'm writing; a tumor that might be a great work of art created using your own spirit and flesh; a tumor that might, besides killing you, offer the happy surprise that it is in fact everything you'd been seeking, longing for, and writing about; a tumor that is the Iberian Peninsula reconstituted in another country not named Spain, as if it had been created by an alternative plane of history; a tumor worthy of admiration and love, and so here I am, waiting for the tumor to manifest itself and generate a whole realm of new stories about my life, including, of course, the story in which I knock on a white door, which is the door of the head of neurology in a Madrid hospital, and behind the door there's a man seated at a table, his hands resting on the tabletop, and that man says come in and he tells me what is happening, and the man's words are included in the tumor, words that talk about it, the tumor itself, words that give external life to that bacterial or viral (same difference) mass that is going to kill me, and that tumor contains the scene where I'm sitting on the edge of the bed, thinking about what the neurologist said about this black lump that includes this scene, and it also contains the scene in which the tumor remains latched on inside my head but no longer gets any nutrients, and now it's the tumor that is forced to experience the horror of its own disappearance, since it is being kicked out of the home where it once fed.

There's a beauty in hypochondria, because all human beings,

once past the midway point in life, spend time (maybe before they fall asleep at night, or while taking the bus, or when sitting in the doctor's office) fantasizing about what kind of illness will rip them from the world. Playing make-believe, they concoct stories about their demise that range from cancer to heart attack, from sudden death to endless old age.

None of us know how we're going to die, and our squeamishness about this is melancholy. We need the tradition of *melancholy* to return to the world. It's a word nobody uses anymore. Melancholy is called obsessive-compulsive disorder now. My mother was melancholic; she spent all her life bathing in the pinkish waters of melancholic syndrome.

My mother died without realizing that she was going to die. She doesn't know she's dead. Only I know it.

She doesn't know anything.

39

When I drive, he sits right beside me. I hear the click of the passenger seat belt. I enjoy driving around Madrid. We were never in Madrid together. He would have loved being in Madrid with me, I know. I wish my father could rejoin the living so we could spend the day driving around Madrid.

My father liked Madrid. He talked about the city often—that's why I love it too. Because of him.

We wouldn't talk, if he came back and were my passenger.

At most, my father would say, "Careful, there's a guy coming up on your left," or "That's a one-way street," or "Did you see the way that maniac passed you on the right without using his turn signal," or "You're a great driver, it's nice weather out," or "I had a friend in Madrid, a tailor, but he must be dead by now, his name was Rufino."

Rufino, yes, if only I knew where he lived. So I could go to his Madrid apartment and request political asylum against death, against vulnerability.

40

I was ironing my clothes. I ironed a couple of shirts. My father had a lot of suits—I don't know where they ended up. He kept his suits in a red armoire, which probably made its way to the landfill. Why was that armoire red? I'm sure it was one of my mother's wacky ideas; she was prone to decorative delirium. But the day she decided to paint it that color must have been a happy one.

I don't know where old furniture ends up. Nor do I know what happened to my father's suits. My father loved his suits. They were his life's work. I sometimes used to open the red armoire and peer inside. The suits looked like a procession of powerful men, all on their hangers, all impeccably ironed. I would give a year of the life I've got left to see those suits again; they were the visual distillation of my father; they were my father's form of social visibility; they were the way my father showed himself to the world; they were the glory of my father's life—his youth, his maturity, his indifference; his dominion over all things, over all species; his refinement amid raw nature.

My father used to review his suits parsimoniously,

meticulously—I'm talking the 1960s and '70s here. In the Franco era, the lower middle class rose high enough to possess a suit—a white shirt and a tie, polyester pants, and a blazer.

41

In the late sixties, my father used to take us on vacation to an inn in a mountain town. The town was Jaca. He knew the inn because of his work as a traveling salesman. He said it had great food. He was eager to take us there. To be there with his family, with his loved ones in the place where he was usually alone. To bestow his discovery on us.

That's what he was doing: offering us a discovery, a victory.

It was true the inn had great food—they made an exquisite, mysterious French omelet with a flavor I've never encountered again in any other omelet. I was seven years old back then, so this happened in about 1970. The image I have of those years suggests an incorporeal distortion: I see things that shimmer, I see yellow dust, large old pieces of furniture in a liquid state, unreal bodies, smells that are healthy but dead. The smells were better in the old days, I think—not better, maybe more natural. The dining room at the inn had a nineteenth-century vibe, or that's how I remember it. The tablecloths were made of good-quality fabric, very white. The stairs leading up to the rooms were made of wood. The doors of those rooms were tall. The beds scared me. At dinner, they served a delectable flan. They used to let me go into the kitchen. I'd never been in a restaurant kitchen, and I was amazed by how big it was and how many pots and frying pans it had and how many people working. We walked around Jaca, which I thought was a beautiful place, but it didn't have a beach. I didn't understand why there wasn't a beach, since we were on vacation. My mother would take me to the public pool. There I learned to swim, swallowing a lot of water along the way. That was the golden age of the public pool. Towns with more than ten thousand residents were emancipated from their rivers.

Spain became a nation of city governments building public pools. We forgot about the rivers, which ended up serving as drainpipes instead.

That inn closed many years ago. I don't know what happened to those bright white tablecloths or the frying pans or the beds or the furniture or the cutlery or the bed linens.

Things die too.

The death of objects is important. It is the disappearance of matter, the humble matter that accompanied us and was at our side while life was happening.

42

I'm always breaking things when I try to open them. I'm convinced the devil himself creates all this packaging that's so hard to open.

So I try to avoid the whole business by throwing things straight in the garbage can. That way I don't see them. My ongoing battle is to remove things from my sight. And the garbage can is my ally in the struggle. That's why I like mine to be large. Wastebaskets are great too—they're places where you can get rid of anything that prevents you from surveying air and space without interference.

I like to fill the garbage can right up to the top.

I like getting rid of things—jars, cans, plastic, it all goes in.

I always look when there's a sale on garbage cans. I like tying the knot in the garbage bag, tightening the knot so the trash—the cast-offs—doesn't escape.

43

Irons are enigmatic. I'm staring at the iron again. My father always ironed because he wanted his suits to look a certain way. Most people don't know the value of an iron, especially not men. I learned to iron late in life. Now that I know how to use it, I like destroying the wrinkles in shirts and pants. I don't iron underwear, because nobody sees it. We don't take care of things that live in darkness. I don't iron my briefs. Not everybody irons their clothes. These days I'm always asking people whether they iron. People are perplexed by the question. Ironing is hard, especially with shirts. Jeans, on the other hand, are pretty easy to iron.

And ironing is relaxing.

You sculpt the clothing. You observe the clothing lying there inert, receiving the heat and taking on a form, a visibility, an order; you take the chaos of vicious wrinkles that the clothing has when it emerges from the washer, and you turn them into flat spaces, wide plains, a truth. You think about how your body will be enfolded in those clothes and enjoy well-being there, and there will be meaning, and even love.

I never saw my father in a wrinkled shirt. Never. Never in his life did he wear jeans. Everything was neatly ironed, always.

44

I try to get there quickly. I drive from Madrid to Zaragoza. I know the road already. It passes through a part of Spain that has a ruddy, desertlike landscape. There are large bridges, anonymous works of engineering. Who made all this? This highway, these bridges. It takes me three hours to get from Madrid to Zaragoza. I go grocery shopping at Hipercor first thing—I need to feed my kids. I choose high-quality food, but I'm nervous, nerves as wide and anonymous as the bridges I drove across.

I stand in line at the butcher counter; I buy expensive things. An old lady buys ten ounces of acorn-fed ham, and I stand studying her inexpressive face.

The woman behind the counter slices the ham and I stand staring at the leg's black hoof.

45

They're strangers now.

I've made dinner for the two of them. I tried hugging them, but everything's become an awkward ritual. I don't know where to put my face, my arms. They've gotten older, that's all.

Hugs aren't necessary—my father and I never hugged. But I keep pushing, I push to create a habit of hugging and kissing. And I'll succeed. I'm already succeeding. When my oldest was born, he had to have an operation for pyloric stenosis. He'd been in the world for fifteen days. He vomited up everything he ate. He was turning to skin and bones. I spent the whole night in anguish. His mother, my ex-wife, wept; her weeping provoked a mournful tenderness in me because I understood it. She was saying "my poor son," and it was as if those three words were being said not by her but by a whirlwind of ancestors speaking through her mouth. I thought about Pergolesi, about his *Stabat Mater*. Those three words, "my poor son," were born of the night of time, the night of motherhood. I don't know which hurt more, a mother's tenderness or the danger my son was in, or if the two things amplified each other, creating a deep river of love and tenderness and fear. But my father didn't call me the next day. I don't say this as a rebuke—I know very well that he loved his grandson. It's not a rebuke, it's a mystery.

I never get the hugs right; it's as if our bodies are unable to come together in space.

Maybe my father knew that. He knew the impossibility of embraces. That's why he didn't call to ask if his grandson was still alive. Everything turned out okay, the surgery went well, and two days later they let us take him home.

46

I grill the meat. I've spent a fortune on this sirloin; I'm scared of how much money it cost and scared they won't like it. The house is dirty and messy. The printer is on the fritz.

Vivaldi, the younger one, is very thin, but I like his slimness. Brahms, the older one, is already talking politics and doesn't tolerate much disagreement. As if I were going to waste energy arguing politics with him, when all I want is to take care of him and for him to be happy. I've decided to use these names for my boys. Noble names from the history of music. All my loved ones will be christened with the names of great composers.

Since I had my father's body burned, I don't have a place where I can go to be with him, so I've created one: this computer screen.

Burning the dead is a mistake. Not burning them is also a mistake.

This screen is the place where the body is now. The monitor is getting old; I'll have to buy another computer soon. Things don't hold up the way they used to, when a refrigerator or a television or an iron or an oven would last thirty years, and this is a secret of matter: we don't bury old appliances, but there are people in this world who've spent more time with a television or a refrigerator than they have with a human being.

There was beauty in everything.

47

Vivaldi hardly tells me anything about his life. I try to talk about school. Valdi, for short, has finished the first year of his baccalaureate. Valdi is of the opinion that public education in Spain is absurd or pointless.

I toast the bread. I've bought an excellent olive oil that reminds me of my mother, whose blood and body and soul were olive oil.

What is Valdi thinking? He is fundamentally enigmatic; so few elements of his personality bloom to the surface. He's working to fashion himself an identity; he's seventeen years old and just starting to live. Brah, Valdi, and I don't talk much. In practical terms, my role is to cook meals. The lawyer who handled my divorce said the boys were going to be great people. Good boys—and it's true.

They are good boys. They don't listen to me much, about as much as I listened to my parents. Good boys, yes—and what's more, good musicians. They are music history. Great composers of their own lives. Which composer was I to my father? My father wasn't too fond of music. My mother was, though. She loved Julio Iglesias. When Julio sang on TV, my mother would run to listen. His songs touched her heart. I was pleased when Julio Iglesias became an international sensation, because he was my mother's favorite singer.

I think that deep down she was in love with Julio Iglesias, who for her was a symbol of the kind of successful, luxurious life that she'd never enjoy.

That she never did end up enjoying.

48

I was addicted to paychecks for a long time. A very long time: more than two decades. I remember I woke up at seven thirty in the morning on September 10, 2014. I had a meeting set with my bosses at eight thirty. I was going to resign—I was getting out. I'd been teaching at secondary schools for twenty-three years, and I was through.

I didn't know how many years of life might remain to me, but I wanted to live them without that bondage. I figured it wasn't many, and I wanted to spend the few I had left contemplating my dead, doing something else, even if it was panhandling.

I'd be living off the wind now, as they say. Living off the wind—I like that expression, it's very Spanish. I remember my coworkers stared at me, convinced I was demented and possibly suicidal. Ta-ta to the paycheck. And life was reborn. I realized I'd never been free in terms of work. I felt a surge of euphoria. I was immensely proud.

I went back to my apartment and gazed out the window for a long while: Life was returning, a life that wasn't always spent being transformed into a salary, a contribution to my retirement. My hours were no longer worth anything. They were just life, life without workers' rights.

Walking, looking at the clouds, reading, sitting, being with myself in deep silence—those were my wages.

And the next day I stopped waking up early. I stopped teaching at night school. I no longer think of it as a decent job; back then, it was just yet another alienating job, even if the alienation was less obvious. Work alienation may be camouflaged, but it's still there, as acutely as it was in the nineteenth century. Schools, hospitals, universities, jails, barracks, enormous office buildings, police stations, Congress, clinics, shopping malls, churches, parishes, convents, banks, embassies, headquarters of international organizations, newspaper offices, movie theaters, bull rings, soccer stadiums, all those places where the life of the nation plays out—what are they? They are places where reality is created, the sense of ourselves as a collective, the sense of history, the celebration of the myth that we are a civilization. All those boys and girls I taught—what will have happened to them? Some of them may be gone for good. And those coworkers will also gradually die off.

Their faces are fading in my memory. They are all moving into the darkness. I vaguely remember a line from a T. S. Eliot poem in which great men enter the darkness of the vacant. Some coworkers died as soon as they retired. Chance punishes the calculators, the ones who carefully calculated their retirement. The schools harbor no memory of those bodies. Spanish high schools are charmless buildings, shoddy constructions with narrow hallways and classrooms that are cold in winter and boiling even in spring. Chalk, blackboards, the teacher's lounge, photocopies, the bell ringing at the end of class, coffee with coworkers, bad food, dirty cafeterias.

And all of it crumbling. There were no photos lining the school corridors to commemorate teachers who'd retired. There was no memory because there was nothing to remember. And those former coworkers of mine, mad with mediocrity and ordinariness, used to humiliate and disparage their students. The kids were humiliated and insulted by the teachers, mediocre people who were bitter about life. Not all of them were like that. There were teachers who loved life and tried to transmit that love to their students. That's all a teacher needs to do: teach his students to love life and to understand it, to understand life through the mind, through a joyous mind; he should teach them the meaning of words—not the history of empty words, but instead what they mean, so they can learn to use words as if they were bullets, the bullets of a legendary gunslinger.

Lovesick bullets.

But I didn't see that happening.

Teachers are much more alienated than their students. I heard the students being berated during evaluation meetings, punished for their personalities, held back in sadistic exertions of power. Oh, the sadism of teaching. The students are young kids, they're new. Spanish teachers wail and moan because their students don't know this thing or the other. I don't know, like maybe they don't know who Juan Ramón Jiménez was or how to solve integral equations or the formula for carbon dioxide and things like that. Teachers don't realize that the things they believe are important are merely a convention, a cultural construction, a collective agreement in which their students have no interest. The kids aren't insane under those drab conventions. They view those conventions the way an alien would. Nobody would criticize an alien for not knowing our clichés and superstitions about history, science, and art. Fifteen-year-olds are from another planet; they're from another place.

From them I learned a sense of freedom.

And I remember pondering how those monstrous teachers destroyed adolescence. They annihilated those kids. They enjoyed failing them. I never failed anybody. I couldn't fail anybody. Maybe at first I did fail a few kids for not knowing how to analyze sentences. Just in the beginning, of course, when you come out of university parroting the moronic things they taught you there, like relative clauses, which were my favorite: there was a flexibility in them, there were trees and flowers and skies in those subordinates. My students and I would stare at sentences with relative clauses. I recall this one:

I've read the book that you lent me yesterday.

But I almost preferred not to analyze them. We would stare at the sentence on the blackboard. Which book would that be? Who was the person who'd done the borrowing? Was the book worth reading? If you were going to borrow something, wouldn't you choose something better than a book?

We used to crack up about the direct object in sentences like this:

Juan burned the car.

Who the hell was Juan? Was it a nice car? Why burn a car? The coup de grâce was when you shifted the sentence to passive voice, because that was how to confirm that *car* was the direct object.

The car was burned by Juan.

If the inverted sentence made sense, the *car* was the direct object. We'd sit pondering, my students and I, whose car it was that Juan had burned. I thought about my car, about how if Juan burned my car, I'd fucking kill Juan.

The direct object was the proletariat of grammar: it bore the burden of everything, it bore the burden of the action of the verb.

I myself have often been a direct object, always bearing the burden of the verb, the tyranny of the verb, which is the violence of history.

I used to set out a Marxist explanation of grammar. A comical Marxism, but at least we'd crack up laughing. I'm being unfair: in fact, the teaching profession is the only loyal ally of social redemption for underprivileged Spaniards. I had incredible friends there. I observed excellent teachers, but the education system is dying—that is what I actually wanted to say, that the education system no longer works, because it's trapped in the past.

I remember all of this right now, and it's nighttime, a night that's hurtling toward dawn, and I feel a wash of euphoria and I think about the bottle of whiskey I've got stashed in the kitchen.

I can't start drinking again.

49

My mother used to get up early in the summertime to eat fruit. I can see her now.

"Now is when it's best," she'd say.

She ate San Juan pears, apricots, cherries, and watermelon. She liked summer fruit.

She'd get up at dawn to feel the cool of morning in that apartment in Barbastro, which was very hot in summer and very cold in winter because it was poorly insulated, because they'd done a bad job. Where are the builders who made it? They must be dead. And yet I can still hear them, hear their voices as they work, as they put up walls, slap down concrete, hang from the scaffolds, smoke a cigarette.

For forty summers she got up early to enjoy the cool of morning. She and those summer mornings understood each other. Seven fifteen in the morning—that was the very best time. It symbolized the joy of summer, of those mornings when I was just eleven or twelve and unfamiliar with the devastations of insomnia and could get up with her at seven in the morning and then go back to bed until nine.

And the voice returns, and it says, "Let's make a deal—do you want to keep seeing her? Do you want to see her from the present where you are? Oh, buddy, those vast currents of time, everything that leaves—you're now an expert on things that become lost, you spend your life thinking about your dead mother and your dead father, as if you were reluctant to move on to another area of the human experience, you don't want to move on, because it is among the dead that the truth dwells, and it does so luminously, not in a way that is sad or lamentable or pathetic, but with a deliberate joy even, like a jubilant conclusion that is bursting with hymns, suns, trees, and summer fruit, lots of fruit in summer that your mother is nibbling right this moment, look at her, there she is, it's June 24, 1971, and she's biting into a slice of watermelon and it's seven fifteen in the morning and you're convinced that death doesn't exist, that only immortality and the song of the summer exist, you're living the tumult of the fleetingness of everything, because everything is transitory, and you can't stand that."

Yes, the song of the summer—since the late sixties, it's clung to my skin.

My mother loved packaged potato chips and whatever song had officially been declared the song of the summer. We were so happy back then.

Matutano potato chips don't exist anymore—I think they've got another name now. My father always asked for that brand when we were at a bar.

"Make sure they're Matutano chips," he'd tell the waiter with a serene smile.

50

I come across a photo from the mid-seventies. We were little kids in the snow, listening to a ski instructor's directions, trying to learn how to sail down the slope, ringed by the inert mountains,

with the cold in our faces. In our ski gear, which was cheap stuff. I was wearing a raincoat.

The raincoat was yellow. The rich people had parkas; raincoats were poor-people clothing. I was furious that I didn't have a parka like rich people did.

A kid in the snow in his yellow raincoat.

Of all the people who were around to witness the birth of an alpine ski resort called Cerler in 1972, some number of us have grown old, and many others are already dead.

The Cerler ski resort was built in the town of the same name, located in the Pyrenees in Huesca, a province that is unknown in Spain, let alone across the world. We were amazed by those green chairlifts soaring across the mountains above the tall pines, above the cliffs of dark rock. And the powerful snow, drifting down onto the industrial pilings, the power lines, the skiers with their modern gear, the latest fiberglass skis, the automatic bindings, the hotels, the nascent tourism, the cars parked at the foot of the mountains, the newly invented ski racks on the car roofs.

Everything was a budding industry.

Everything in the world was improving; the idea of improvement is an engine of history, it is universal joy. Improvement descended on the last quarter of the twentieth century as a path toward happiness and abundance. And it was true, everything was improving: cars, communications, social justice, teaching, medicine, higher education, central heating was being extended to everybody's homes, the nightclubs and bars were getting better, and so was Spanish wine, and ski technology.

There would be no more bone fractures, the ski instructors preached, but there continued to be broken legs. The invention of automatic bindings is not celebrated in any church, yet I remember that amazing event, that advance.

Yes, and even today, with the most technologically advanced bindings on earth, there are still fractures, because the price of snow and mountains is broken bones. Those legendary names of the fledgling ski-binding industry in the 1960s—Marker, Look, Tyrolia, Salomon. In downhill skiing, the binding has a key task: it is responsible for keeping the skier's foot joined to the ski. Ski bindings contained a mystical combustion: they didn't let you fall, they kept you joined to the mountains, alongside the mountains, in a dance with the mountains.

They tied you down, that's what bindings did. They gave you gravity, rootedness. They kept you on your feet, prevented you from falling into the abyss.

For a while I kept going up to Cerler to ski, but I haven't been in a long time. I can't afford such indulgences. I left skiing to the wealthy.

I look in the bathroom mirror in the restaurants at the Cerler ski resort, six thousand feet above sea level, and I see my father.

"Hi, Dad, I'm still skiing, just like when I was a kid."

On Christmas Eve in Cerler, the sun is shining. We'd drive up in your SEAT 1430 to go skiing.

You put a ski rack on top. How much did that cost you?

Before long, a luxury hotel sprouted at the foot of the slopes. It was called the Monte Alba, but we never stayed there.

Then things went downhill for you, and we stopped going up to Cerler to ski.

Catching the snow in my hand, I catch your ashes. And that's how it will always be, until everything melts and the mountains languish.

I kept going up to ski, but things weren't like they'd been in my childhood. I went up less and less, and it cost more and more every time. I had to save for six months to ski for two days. Besides, my body can't take that kind of physical exertion anymore.

51

They got married on January 1, 1960.

I have very few material objects of theirs, few gravitations of matter, such as photos. Very few photos. One of them erased any trace, any future reach of their lives, maybe not intentionally. Neither of them thought about my future, in which I am now remembering them, in which I am alone.

I ran across this photo.

I'd never seen it before. My mother had hidden it away. What's funny is I thought I knew every nook and cranny of my mother's apartment, which was my home too. I thought I knew every drawer, but clearly that wasn't the case. My mother was hiding photos that not even my father knew existed. The level of my parents' obliviousness to their own lives is an enigma to me. An even greater enigma is that I'm the one, after their deaths, who is trying to find out who they were. The extent to which they obliterated their lives is a kind of art.

My parents were a couple of Rimbauds: they rejected memory, they didn't think about themselves. Though the two of them went unnoticed, they did produce me, and they sent me to school and I learned to write, and now I'm writing their lives. That's where they went wrong—they should have left me to wallow in the most radical and complete and irremediable illiteracy.

The fact that I can never talk to them again seems to me the most outrageous phenomenon in the universe, an incomprehensible fact, a mystery as enormous as the origin of intelligent life. The idea that they're gone keeps me up at night. Everything is unreal or inexact or blurry or misty since they left.

Photos always present the exactitude of reality; photos are the devil's art. All of Christendom would kill to have a photo of Jesus Christ. If we had a photo of Christ, we'd start believing in resurrection again.

They hid their wedding—I don't know why and now I never will. From the family record book, which was also squirreled away, I know they got married on January 1, 1960. I don't know what people were like back then, in 1960. I could watch documentaries or movies from the period. I don't see any relationship between my current person and this photo of my parents dancing.

It must have been a wonderful night.

There isn't a single photo on the face of the earth of my parents' wedding on January 1, 1960. Were any photos taken? Everybody has a photo of their wedding. Not my parents. If there was a photo, my mother destroyed it. Why? Because of style, because they both had style.

There won't be anybody who was at that wedding left; they're all under the ground.

For their honeymoon they went to the French town of Lourdes. They never told me much about that trip. My father already had his SEAT 600. I imagine the trip all the time. They had to cross the border; they would have done that at Portalet, though because it was winter—the winter of 1960—the pass was snowed over. I don't know how my father made it through that pass in a SEAT 600. Whenever I drive the French mountain roads that lead to Lourdes, I remember.

"They were here," I say.

I say it to nobody.

I'm never able to touch those shadows. Those ghosts. Where did they stay? I was going to ask my father and I can't. It seems ridiculous. You say, "Oh, I've got to ask my father about this, he'll know," and then it turns out your father's been dead for nine years. So I'll never know where they stayed in the remarkable city of Lourdes. It's a city full of handicaps, miracles, virgins, and saints, and it is also a city with lush vegetation, everything lushly green and leafy.

Why did they go there for their honeymoon?

They could have gone to Barcelona. Or Madrid. Or San Sebastián. Paris wasn't an option—they couldn't afford it. What an odd choice, one that nobody can explain to me now. Anyone who's been there will recognize that Lourdes is unforgettable, messianic, liturgical, esoteric, insane. How is it that I never asked, while I still could, why they chose to honeymoon in the place where the Virgin Mary appeared eighteen times to the shepherdess Bernadette Soubirous? The answer is obvious: I didn't ask while I could because I figured I'd ask one of these days, as if they would always be around. Maybe I was reluctant to ask them about that trip—it seems awfully personal. Anyway, one thing's clear: If you need to ask somebody something, do it now.

Don't wait for tomorrow; tomorrow is for the dead.

If I got another chance, I still wouldn't be able to ask them about their honeymoon. I didn't ask then because I knew they didn't want to talk about it.

I can imagine why they didn't want to talk about it. They didn't like the word *marriage*—that's what was really going on. Something purely instinctive.

52

January 1 was an important date in our house during my childhood, but my parents never actually told us why. My father said,

"It's our saint's day," and that was the only explanation given. On January 1 we would celebrate Saint Manuel, since the two of us shared that name. Oversaturating the date even further, Valdi, my youngest, ended up being born on January 1. The calendar has three hundred sixty-five days, yet Valdi was born the same day his grandparents were married. Was it a coincidence? If coincidence is love, then yes, it was.

Friends of my parents used to come over every January 1 from around 1965, 1966, 1967 till the mid- or late seventies. Then things changed. They changed friends. So in the eighties a different kind of friend came. I sensed the changes weren't good ones. In the early nineties, people stopped coming altogether, and the celebration shrank to the family sphere.

I was very happy that day, even if I didn't really know what was being commemorated. My father was always happy on January 1. I wonder about the friends who came to see him for thirty years.

And then stopped coming.

And the crooked walls of that apartment, which hopefully have been remodeled, are the only witnesses.

What happened to Ramiro Cruz, the first person to call them on the phone in 1968? And what of Esteban Santos? Armando Cancer? José María Gabás? Ernesto Gil? One by one they died.

I memorized the names of my father's friends because in my young mind they were all heroes. If they were friends of my father, that meant they were like him. Which meant they were the best men in the world.

They would call this number: 974310439. Back then there was no need to dial a prefix; that came later. He really liked getting calls from Ernesto Gil because he was the mayor of Barbastro. He liked it when the mayor called to wish him a happy new year and saint's day.

I remember how my father used to pick up the phone, still in his robe. They always called early. I found the calls unsettling, solemn and mysterious.

My marriage joined me to my parents in a rational or social or deductive or coherent way, but after my divorce, which coincided with the death of my mother, the last remaining witness, I developed a new relationship with my parents' lives. My divorce redirected my relationship with my dead parents. A ghostly relationship, full of enigmas and clairvoyance, emerged and settled in for good.

The spirits started coming. My father is the one who comes the most; he lies down next to me and touches my hand.

And there he is, charred.

"Why did you have me burned, son?"

I too, not long from now, will be a dead father and they'll have me burned. And Valdi and Brah will see me as a dead man.

It's a mistake to think that the dead are something sad or disheartening or depressing; no, the dead are the inclemency of the past that arrives in the present via a lovesick howl.

I believe in the dead because they loved me much more than the living do today.

They never said what had happened on January 1. They never said, "We got married that day." When I found out by chance, from the family record book, I was fascinated. I understood everything then.

53

My father's name still shows up on the internet, on an old web page for salesmen. Is there a single human being who consults that web page? Short-term total extinction is impossible; you have to wait decades, even centuries. Some company or individual might still call to retain his services. Ten years after his death, his services as an active salesman are on offer via the internet. The internet bets on immortality; it's the safest bet on immortality that human beings have available.

I sometimes go to that web page and sit staring at my father's name and the phone number next to it.

Somebody should delete it. Or better yet, somebody should add my cell phone number so that if nobody answers the landline listed, they'll call me instead, and that call won't be missed.

It must not be missed, that call expecting to find a living man where a dead one resides. That faith must not disappear. I call the number often: 974310439. That number is a liturgy.

I have often considered getting the number tattooed on my arm, and eventually I will.

I don't want to die without that number tattooed on my arm, so that death can consume it.

That number: 974310439.

54

I don't have a problem putting my father's life on display. Even though in Spain nobody is open about anything. It would do us a lot of good to write about our families without any fiction creeping in, without storifying. Just recounting what happened, or what we think happened. People conceal their progenitors' lives. When I meet somebody, I always ask about their parents—about the desire that brought that person into the world.

I love it when my friends tell me about their parents' lives. Suddenly, I'm all ears. I can picture them. I can see those parents, fighting for their children.

That fight is the most beautiful thing in the world. God, how beautiful it is.

55

One summer day in 2003 the doctors asked to talk to my mother and me.

They didn't want my father present.

The doctor gestured to two chairs so we would sit. He told us point-blank that my father had late-stage colon cancer and we needed to get used to the idea. He was an oncologist who'd clearly rehearsed for those moments, the moments when he was obliged to communicate the idea that death was drawing near, the moments of devastation. I was struck by his attitude, because in a way the man was enjoying it—not immorally, not because he got pleasure from describing death's power or divulging disaster, but because he believed he was doing his job well. It was as if he were carrying a laboratory in his head full of words that were useful for disseminating vital news. And he'd done all kinds of tests, rehearsed all sorts of words. He carried in his head the verbal articulation of world-altering news, but he wasn't a poet, he was just another madman in this world of inexhaustible beings wearing themselves out in vain.

My father died two years and some months after the doctor issued that stupid sentence. Actually, I believe my father died because he thought the oncologist's prediction was an interesting one and he didn't want to leave him with egg on his face; he died out of a sort of professional courtesy to the guy.

My father saw the oncologist's prognosis as a convenient way to exit this world on somebody else's invitation.

I don't believe in doctors, but I do believe in words. I don't think doctors know much about what we are because they are ignorant of the world of words. I do believe in drugs. Modern science has delegated to doctors the authority to catalog and prescribe drugs. Medicine is useful if it supplies drugs. That is, if it supplies what kills. Drugs are nature; they've always been there. We're not allowed to take them on a whim.

There was a silence, and I looked at the oncologist again. As my mother asked him questions, I suddenly felt sorrier about the oncologist's life than I did about my father's.

His life seemed more depressing to me than the news of my father's illness.

56

We never told my father anything, nor did he ask. My father decided to ignore his disease. His approach seemed to me a mystical one. He simply kept silent.

They operated on him several times, and he kept silent. It was as if he didn't care that they were invading his body to perform vague, routine, apathetic tasks. He didn't care that the surgeons were probing his internal organs as a way of filling their workdays, which had been meticulously agreed upon and circumscribed by the unions and the hospital administration.

While the doctors were earning their monthly paychecks, my father was dying. There was less alienation in my father's death than in the paychecks of those insubstantial individuals.

57

He used to like watching TV. I think he whiled away millions of hours in front of the television set. I've seen how television technology has evolved. Buying a TV in the sixties and seventies of the last century was a transcendental act that brought on a swell of joy and fear.

I remember the first TV that came into my house. I remember my father obsessively watching a seventies-era game show called *One, Two, Three . . . Try Again*. My father was addicted to the program, in which the contestants had to answer unexpected questions, with the mantra "One, two, three . . . try again."

My father would respond along with the contestants, and he tended to win.

He could have competed on that game show.

He never did.

He must have thought about how he'd have to take a bus; he didn't like buses, or trains either. He liked only his car, because his car was a manifestation of himself. His car was him. That's why he always parked it in the shade during the scorching summers, because my father didn't like being in the sun.

I loathed that game show, but it aired on Fridays, when we were all hanging around. We didn't have school the next day.

I don't know why you liked that program—it was awful. You

must know I hated it, all those dumb questions. My only consolation is that all the contestants and all the hosts and all the beautiful girls who were there as eye candy on that massive turd of a program are gradually dying off; you can't imagine how I suffered watching that tacky crap on TV, and you sitting there, answering questions, with those human beings reduced to a yellow smile. As I saw it, they were symbols of Spain's backwardness. And your son had already moved on to another realm of Spanish history. Luckily it's all a ghost now. The hosts have died, almost everybody has died. The relief and purification of death for those whose faces the television captured: comics, singers, presenters, all those stubbornly Spanish faces. Because the only way to surmount vulgarity in Spain is through death. I can imagine photos, housed in cheap, ostentatious frames, of those contestants on the walls of their homes, photos passed down from parents to children—it's Mom and Dad on *One, Two, Three . . . Try Again*, Mom and Dad were contestants in 1977 with Kiko Ledgard. Remember Kiko Ledgard?

Where is Kiko Ledgard buried, the legendary TV host from the mid-1970s? Did he have children? Do you remember his children? My father and I watched him every Friday. Well, actually, I watched my father watching him. I remember that out of superstition, Kiko Ledgard wore several watches on each wrist.

Those watches are somewhere out there—they were nice.

All the same, Dad, I go to this thing called YouTube now and search for those Spanish TV programs from the seventies and I watch them with inexpressible love and nostalgia because they were your programs. It's not true that I hated those programs; I only wished you'd have taken my hand and we could have gone out for a walk, that you'd spent time with me instead of spending time with them, the Spanish TV hosts, with whom I'm now spending time, on a computer screen, addicted to nostalgia, addicted to you, addicted to YouTube. Addicted to the past.

I dream that you, Mom, and I are all dressed up in brand-name clothes with gleaming shoes, and they're expecting us at the best restaurant in Paris, with views of the Seine.

I dream that we laugh and drink champagne and eat caviar and snails and Mom lights a cigarette with a gold Dupont lighter you just gave her. I dream we're rich.

I dream that you tell jokes in French; I dream that it's 1974 and the world is ours.

I dream that we never watched TV.

I dream that we were always traveling: one night in Paris, another in New York, a few days in Moscow, a few more in Buenos Aires, or Rome, or Lisbon.

I dream of world domination.

I dream that the three of us are dining in the world's finest restaurants. And we tell jokes in every language: Russian, English, Italian, Portuguese.

I dream that you buy a mansion near Lisbon. I dream that the three of us gaze out at the Atlantic together. Because I know how much you loved life.

58

The years passed, and by the late nineties my father had become addicted to cooking shows. He spent hours watching chefs making fritters or codfish or paellas on television. He'd wear this really nice green silk robe he had, put on his glasses, and sit in front of the TV to watch cooking shows.

He looked like an angel, my father did—a cheerful angel, contemplating the gastronomical organization of reality.

He was like an envoy charged with sanctifying food through the sense of sight.

There was no plot to those shows, or the plot was simply how to cook hake in the Majorcan style. I think what really fascinated him was the geographical attributions for the Spanish recipes. That each dish was cooked in accordance to custom in some particular place. Maybe deep down he imagined himself living in Majorca or Bilbao or Madrid and eating hake, codfish, or stew. He knew how to cook and he knew how to prepare those dishes himself; what he liked was seeing how other people did it.

He loved watching the joy that cooking creates. Because cooking implies future. Everything is yet to be; everything is being prepared for posterity, even if posterity is only fifteen minutes from now.

59

One day he stopped caring about his car, an old SEAT Málaga. He had always been obsessive about his car, taking care of it, keeping it in perfect condition. Then he abandoned it in a garage and stopped driving. I went to see the car, and it was covered in dust.

I told him, "Dad, the car is covered in dust."

He looked at me, and it seemed like that had gotten his attention.

"It was a good car. Do whatever you want with it," he said.

When he washed his hands of his car, I knew my father was going to die soon; I knew that was final.

It was one of the saddest moments of my life. My father was telling me goodbye by proxy, through a machine.

Instead of telling me, "We need to talk, this is over," he said, "It was a good car." My God, how beautiful. Wherever my father's spirit came from, it was graced with the gift of elegance, the gift of the unexpected, of artless originality.

Of style.

I sat down in a kitchen chair and stared at him. I got really anxious. I got really upset. In the whole universe, only I knew what those words—"Do whatever you want with it"—meant. He was telling me something devastating: "Do whatever you want with me. I am oblivious to your love."

I am oblivious to your love.

I didn't love you enough, nor you me.

We were exactly the damn same.

60

I went to see his car. My father's spirit was gusting through the entire car. His large hands on the wheel, his glasses, the empty trunk, the blanket inside the trunk to protect the trunk from who knows what (and of course my own car also has a blanket inside the trunk to protect the trunk from who knows what), the glove box with the papers all in order. My father clearly saw the mystical fusion of the Spanish lower middle class with the cars the lower middle class came to possess.

It was an industrial and political mysticism, an ancestral pairing of steel and paint with flesh and blood.

The way he left this world seems to me a superior art. He left with admirable discretion.

He was indifferent to death; he didn't think about it. He was sad about the car. It must have scared him to find that the thing that had been the object of his constant preoccupation throughout his life—and thus the foundation and meaning of that life—no longer mattered to him. It was a radical change.

They were going to die at the same time, he and his car.

The day he abandoned his car, my heart turned over.

I knew what the car meant to him. It was a bit of material rootedness in the world, a possession. My father's soul came from very far away in time, from the ancient planetary night, soul belonging to unrooted men—men living or dead, same difference—that's where my father's soul came from: souls that did not take root, that were extremely beautiful and extremely volatile.

We became invisible to my father.

My mother had panic attacks.

She was afraid of the final stages of the disease.

We were a catastrophic family, and at the same time unique.

We were constantly in and out of hospitals.

We didn't talk.

I don't understand what happened. I think a lot of the responsibility was mine. There was a dissatisfaction in me that prevented me from taking all of that on. I used to experience fits of depression in hospitals. I couldn't stand it.

My life was going badly and my father's life was simply going.

We all blamed one another. My father blamed my mother. My mother blamed me. I blamed my father. My father blamed me.

My mother blamed me. Et cetera. We were a jumble of dissatisfaction and blame.

We never got a moment of rest.

61

In fact, there was something weird about my family: nobody ever said, "We're a family." We didn't know what we were. I'm thinking back now on one terrifying Christmas Eve half a century ago—it must have been '67 or '68. My father got really angry about something to do with dinner, something that wasn't to his liking.

He smashed the dishes.

He flew into a rage, hurled the plates against the wall, the floor, like they do in the movies.

We went to bed.

There was no Christmas Eve or anything. That was all my family could think about, enveloped in an atmosphere of unconfessable sadness.

He chose Christmas Eve to smash those plates to bits.

I didn't know what was happening. I just saw the plates flying through the air. Suddenly, the plates were no longer on the table.

It was supposed to be Christmas Eve, damn it, when families were at their most respectable. I never asked about that scene, and I should have; maybe I would have understood something about my family and, thus, about my future.

How could I have asked about it? How, when it hurtled toward the unnameable, the phantasmagorical, when I wished to erase it, to discount it, when I nearly succeeded in diluting it with a thousand drops of falsehood, the drops of my tears, my distress, like that other stiff and sordid distress that Father G. caused me when I entered a light-filled classroom.

As we well know, the things we witness as children shape our later lives. Nevertheless, and this is my own view, they do so not according to any sociological or political structure, but through an atavistic spilling of blood—and in my case, they do so through the weighty science of the blessing of our destiny, since having a destiny is a blessing.

Most men have no destiny.

And it's fascinating how the past constructs a destiny in the mechanical hollows of my breathing. Because most men and women have no history. They possess lives without history. And that is beautiful too. Planet Earth is a potter's field of millions of human beings who were here but had no history, and if you have no history, it's worth wondering then whether you were ever alive.

The seasons and the decades are put in order, the hand and the rotten tooth are put in order, the bones of the hanged man are jumbled together, and in the end one can only ponder the *detestability* of God.

A detestable God whose boredom gave rise to the odyssey of men.

A son should not be there to see his mother transformed into a little girl.

62

I think my mother started crying on that fateful Christmas Eve. My mother, who used to take refuge in the kitchen pantry whenever there was a storm. My mother, who was terrified of storms.

You'd open the pantry, which was like a coffin, and there was my mother. If there's a storm, where's my mother? She would disappear. My mother would flee the world when thunder and lightning and pouring rain bore down on it.

She would hide in the kitchen pantry. That was her youth: fleeing from storms.

And I thought it was a game—I'd open the pantry door and there she'd be, rigid, girlish, statue-like, paralyzed. But her girlish face has faded from my memory, and I can remember only the decrepit old woman she became, more to her horror than to mine. She was a witness responsible for her own horror. That's why I say she was angelic; only angels can refuse to forgive themselves for the horror of decrepitude.

Decrepitude cannot be forgiven. It is *detestability* and failure. The awareness of decrepitude—that's what I'm talking about. The more aware you are of your decrepitude, the nearer you draw to the *detestability* of God.

My mother was an angel. She saw her decrepitude and rejected it, and then became a martyr, but in all of that there throbbed only her service to life. She couldn't stand mirrors, and neither could I. Mirrors are for the young. If you respect beauty, it's impossible to respect your own aging.

The kitchens of contemporary Spanish apartments don't have pantries anymore. But I've been forgetting a vital room in my parents' house, a windowless room they called "the wardrobe." It was at the end of the hall. The door stuck, so it was always hard to open. Inside were stored my father's work cases, the cases containing the samples of the textiles he sold to small businesses in the villages of Huesca, Teruel, and Lérida. And other things—there were also clothes and mysterious objects. My brother and I were forbidden to go in there. I know my mother hid artifacts of the past there, things she didn't dare throw away, though over time she did gradually get rid of them all. I never learned what was in the wardrobe. Sometimes it would come up in conversations, in sentences like "If there's space, we'll store this in the wardrobe," but it was an odd room, pointy and triangular, wallpapered with stars on a dark blue background. I think the wallpaper was the thing I found strangest. The room was wallpapered because once upon a time the entire house had been. My mother gradually changed the walls, opting for paint, for plaster, but she left the wardrobe as it had always been, since 1960. So the wardrobe was like going back in time. Wallpaper had gone out of style. The wardrobe retained its papered walls: stars in the firmament, and suitcases and clothing, and things unseen. And my huddled mother whenever storms came, either hiding in the wardrobe or hiding in the pantry; I think she preferred the pantry because the wardrobe was a dangerous place—there was a dark force in it. I loved the wardrobe; my parents' gravitational pull was concentrated there. The wallpaper fad ended. They weren't bad, those walls covered with patterned paper.

My mother became a little girl and hid whenever it stormed. Not just in the wardrobe and pantry—under the bed too. I was a little boy watching magic dissolve his mother's bonds to space and time. Suddenly, my mother wasn't there. And I'd search the house for her as summer storms swelled the sky, turned the heavens into a thousand bits of solid light. And then the two of us would be a little boy and a little girl with an undefinable, almost cursed kinship. Come, come hide here with Mom, hold Mom's hand, the world is a wicked place.

63

Our misfortune was justified.

I have always believed that.

Our misfortune was avant-garde art.

It may have been a genetic misfortune, a sort of inability to live.

My father did have good moments. When he was elected town councilor under Spain's first democratic administrations, that was a good moment. My father enjoyed that. It put him in a good mood. It was in the early eighties. I was living and studying in Zaragoza. Sometimes he'd come to Zaragoza to see me, but we were still poor. My father didn't do well with money. We were always in bad shape with money. When I was twenty, I was awarded a literary prize. And my mother took the money from that prize and polished off the entire lot. It was twenty thousand pesetas in 1982—a fortune. She spent it, and she never told me on what. She was able to cash it because the prize people sent my winnings via money order to the family home instead of to Zaragoza.

I think she spent it on bingo. My mother was a big bingo player. I remember right after I'd turned eighteen, my mother used to take me to bingo.

Both of them, my father and my mother, played bingo. Sometimes they got lucky. They went every Saturday. In the late seventies, gambling was made legal in Spain. My mother went crazy with bingo. I remember her with just one number to go for bingo, waving the card superstitiously, praying to who knows what power, mumbling strange words, invocations of chance, calling the numbers things like "pretty girl," and sometimes she'd actually win. But most of the time she lost. She'd say, "We'll play five cards and leave," and the five cards would turn into fifty.

There was no way to make money. I think that's hereditary. I'm poor too. I don't have a pot to piss in—luckily, nobody's got a pot to piss in these days. And that can be liberating. If they're smart, young people will pursue a wandering life, chaos, job insecurity, and freedom. And skilled poverty, morally deactivated poverty—that is, group poverty. It's a good solution: poverty as a collective phenomenon, pooled having-not.

The problem with poverty is that it ends up becoming destitution, and that's a moral condition.

My mother couldn't stand the tedium of life. That's why she went to swimming pools and rivers, that's why she played bingo, that's why she sunbathed, that's why she smoked.

She and the sun, practically the same thing.

64

I spoke to the oncologist who took care of my father in his final days of life. It was an irritating, agonizing conversation. She was a young doctor, very stressed. I figured she was probably in a precarious employment situation. She likely didn't earn much. Oncologists have to take care of a bunch of dying people and probably earn the same as obstetricians, who have the cheerier professional mission of bringing babies into the world. Leaving the world and coming into it, and the same salary for both.

I told the doctor to make sure my father didn't suffer in his final moments. She didn't really understand what I was saying.

She thought I was suggesting euthanasia or something like that, a sort of murder. Everything was a wash of confusion. She got angry at me; I didn't care about that anger—it was as if I were living a fiction, a delirium, a theater piece not of this world. But I made sure my father didn't suffer. I hope somebody will do the same for me: make sure I get drugged, thoroughly drugged. He spent an entire day dying. I watched him dying. I could hear breathing that sounded like a storm, a gale of long, mysterious moans. His body was consumed. But it made music. His toes had a religious look to them, like a martyred Christ, like a seventeenth-century Spanish painting, feet that were deformed but expectant. Everything was an effort to breathe. And an intelligent one. My father made booming, tragic, catastrophic noises. His throat sounded like a nest full of millions of yellow birds, shattering the walls of the air. My father became the Spanish Baroque. I understood the Spanish Baroque then, a severe art that worships death because death is the most fully achieved expression of the mystery of life.

65

Once I hit puberty, with its terrible tribulations, I rejected any physical contact with either my father or my mother. I didn't like touching them. It's not that I didn't like it—it wasn't that. The trouble was, we hadn't created that tradition. We hadn't established that ritual. I barely gave them the obligatory pecks on the cheek in greeting. And I certainly wasn't about to touch my father when he was dying. I've already noted we were a strange family—"dysfunctional," people would say now. I don't think that was either good or bad.

My father didn't even go to his mother's—my grandmother's—funeral; he didn't even phone. And my mother took care of blowing up my father's relationship with his siblings, but it doesn't matter. My father used to accuse my mother of hiding his papers. The way my mother did the housekeeping was to throw out every paper she ran across.

I remember my father banging his head against a bookcase because he couldn't find the duplicate invoice for a sale he'd made. They often shouted, but they never insulted each other. My father never insulted my mother, never ever. He would just get furious and frantic and hit things, objects—that was his rage. Whenever I walked by the bookcase after that, I'd stare at it intently: the bookcase my father banged his head against. And of course the day I emptied out the apartment, when my mother died, I stood staring at the side panel of the bookcase and stroked it for the last time. It wasn't even made of real wood. It must have been veneer or vinyl. I always thought it was wood, but no, it wasn't.

I'd forgotten the shouting. I was small, very small, almost tiny, but my puny mind leaped into action and formulated a wee question: Why didn't my mother leave my father's papers alone?

My mother was blind—that's the only reason. But it was a wounded blindness. My mother didn't understand the papers' importance. She threw everything away. She didn't keep anything. She used to throw away my comic books. My father's papers. I'd buy a comic book and the next week she'd have made it disappear. "But you already read it, what do you need it for?" she'd say. She wanted to throw away the books too, but she found that she didn't have enough figurines and other knickknacks to fill the bookcases and decided to give them a chance. And so the books were saved.

But this isn't a criticism. People are who they are, full stop.

And once everybody's dead, none of it matters, because all of the dead were great men and women; death has given them a worthy and fortunate final meaning.

Social and family life and work life and romantic life don't matter either—they're an artifice that is laid bare upon death. That's why I write this way. Because in any life there are a million mistakes added up to form that life. The mistakes are repeated again and again. Infidelity is repeated. Betrayal is repeated. Deception is repeated. And no record of the repetitions appears anywhere. Recounting what happened is fine—it's good work. Attempting to recount what happened, I mean. Maybe that's why it sears my insides to look at family photos: because photographs depict what we saw in the sunlight, what was lit by the sun and, like light, shaped men and women's lives; that's why photos are so unsettling, the most unsettling thing there is: we managed to infuse light into a piece of paper; my parents were lit by the light of the sun, and that light still persists on those faded rectangles of photographic paper, in those worn portraits.

Light, which was doomed to tumble down from the sun and ended up clashing against human bodies here in life.

Stubbornly, the photos of my parents assert that they were once alive. That distant memory of them is more important than contemporary capitalism, than the production of universal wealth.

66

My mother never liked giving kisses in greeting or shaking hands. She didn't like to touch people. I think I inherited that. Which, when you think about it, might be a genetic mandate to protect you from the infections other people carry.

When my father died, some of his friends and relatives—not many—kissed his forehead.

I did not.

Neither did my mother.

In that moment I realized that my children won't kiss mine either. That chain of frigid refusal when it comes to touching our forebears' bodies—where does it come from? There is in that frigidity, that asepsis, a high degree of inhumanity, or fear, or cowardice, or selfishness. It is a genetic proclivity. My parents dealt atrociously with the deaths of their parents—my grandparents—just as my children will deal atrociously with my death. And that seems extraordinary.

There is something there that elevates us.

A sort of aristocracy of alienation.

I did not touch my dead father's body.

I never saw his tumor—they never showed it to me, never offered to let me see the hunk of tissue that was bound to kill him.

I would have liked to hold it in my hand, hold that tumor in my hand.

What is a cancerous tumor?

It is tired wind, a general history of polluted air, crap in the diet—meaning other more unusual tumors, from processed cows and pigs and chickens and hake and lamb and swordfish and rabbits and oxen.

As an adult I didn't get close, I never touched my parents' bodies, except for the nervous formulaic cheek kisses we gave each other. They were kisses in which the devil whale splashed, a kind of awkwardness more ancient than the oceans.

At what age do you stop holding your mother's and father's hands?

67

I fondly remember how much effort my mother put, shortly before her death, into wearing red nail polish; I found it touching.

I would sit staring at her elderly hand, which still radiated a sense of beauty and memory, with those beauty-salon fingernails. My elderly mother's coquetry seemed fragile, lovable. She wanted to look nice for other people, and I found that incredible. Going around with painted nails was a gift. But even so, I never took her hand of my own free will, except when I had to help her walk—then I would take her hand.

I was grateful for that obligation, because it allowed me to hold her hand without letting go of reserve, distance, remoteness. I would hold her hand out of medical obligation, not spontaneously.

And I didn't hold my dying father's hand. Nobody showed me how. It freaked me out to do it; it scared me, with a fear that gradually reinforced my solitude. Fear of a hand, which ended up making way for the vast solitude I inhabit.

68

Cancer devoured him, but he never uttered the name of his disease. He never talked about cancer or death. We never heard the word *cancer* pass his lips. It's incredible to me that he never said that word.

He didn't ask and he didn't say it.

He was deeply anarchistic.

He never told me what or whom he thought about as he was dying.

He took that mystery with him.

He didn't even say good night.

69

He gradually disappeared—his life disappeared and his conversation disappeared, and he was silence. A man can become silence. My father, who is now silence, was already silence before—as if, knowing that he was going to be silence, he decided to be silence before silence arrived, thus teaching silence a lesson from which silence emerged infused with music.

He'd made a secret languid pact with his body, from which music was born.

The music of Johann Sebastian Bach—that was my father.

70

I know that the medicine of the future will allow the dying to carry on lengthy, complex conversations with the tumors that are going to kill them, once medicine takes a vital step that is unimaginable today: when medicine realizes that the body is a temple, a spiritual construction of the origin of the universe, when medicine is intelligent at last. Medicine is not intelligent yet; it's still merely rote, a simple verification of facts. It must yet discover the beauty and immaterial chaos of a cancerous tumor, because a cancerous tumor also contains the life drive of the body of the man who carries it inside him.

That's why my father chose silence. There was nothing to say. Medicine was empty, religion never existed, and he'd already given up his car. Human beings were already invisible; he had nothing to say to us.

He didn't say anything to me.

He didn't tell me "Goodbye."

He didn't tell me "I love you."

He didn't tell me "I loved you."

So he stayed silent.

And in that silence were all the words. Like a metaphysical boomerang, his silence contained the burning stars from the wardrobe's walls. And so I was the one who, beside the hospital bed where my father lay, sought a place to hide, and that place was the wardrobe with its walls papered with stars.

The wardrobe was our aleph, the aleph of the Spanish lower middle class that emerged in the postwar period. Wardrobes were our speculative hideout.

71

My father never told me he loved me. My mother didn't either. And I see beauty in that. I always did, as long as I was forced to pretend that my parents loved me.

Maybe they didn't love me and this book is the fiction of a wounded man. More than wounded, frightened. It isn't sad not to be loved—rather, it's terrifying.

You end up thinking that if they don't love you, it's because there's some powerful reason that justifies their lack of love.

If they don't love you, the failure is yours.

After I got married and started another family, they stopped loving me like they used to. They loved me less and less all the time. We were no longer fighting for life on the same team.

72

My father never called me on the phone and my mother called at all hours, but she was calling for reassurance. I would see their number, 974310439, on my cell phone screen. She was hounded by paranoias, the same paranoias that make me call Brah and Valdi, and they refuse to answer the phone. My sainted mother tended toward paranoia. In the late 1960s I remember how terrified she'd be whenever my father had to work, because working, in my father's case, meant traveling. She was afraid he'd get into a highway accident. So the telephone became an instrument with oracular powers. Phone calls frightened her. My mother hated long trips, especially when my father had to go make sales in Teruel—that was the longest trip. He'd be away all week, sleeping in cheap hotels, selling Catalonian textiles to the tailors and seamstresses in the villages of Teruel. Maybe when he was off on those five-day trips my father became another man. I hope that was the case. I'll never know, because he never told me anything, and he never told me "I love you."

He never told me anything that lasted longer than a minute.

I wish I could do the same.

73

The day after my father's death—that is, on December 18, 2005—the oncologist called me in. I walked into her office. She was sitting in a chair looking at her computer. It was a garlanded morning, with the Christmas holidays just around the corner. She apologized. She said she felt she'd been rude to me the day before my father's passing. She used the word *passing*, a word I despise. I almost said "a word that death and I despise." I listened to her apologies. She was talking, but it was as if she were talking from a great distance, as if she too were dead, or passed. The power of my father's death was killing her, crushing her too, as if my father were a murderer.

I think all I said was goodbye to that oncologist, who must be alive still and surely practicing in some provincial Spanish hospital, tied and bound now to a few dozen deceased, who will always be with her.

And I have no idea what haunted gifts it occurred to us to buy for that Christmas of 2005. The TV commercials, the oncologist uttering soundless words, my dead father, my mother who wanted to buy an acorn-fed ham, because my mother was losing her mind, she was totally out of it, had no idea what had happened, wanted to go Christmas shopping as if nothing had changed, and in fact deep down nothing had changed; my mother didn't understand why she suddenly had to give up the small number of inconsequential things that gave her a little bit of happiness, like doing Christmas shopping.

The poorer you are in Spain, the more you love Christmas.

74

"Why the hell would we go buy a ham when Dad is dead and we're supposed to be in mourning?"

"Your father liked acorn-fed ham," my mother said—and that was true. My father loved it, and whenever I eat acorn-fed ham I remember him and how fond of it he was.

"Poor man, he'll never get to have it again," my mother would say.

Often afterward my mother would refer to my dead father that way: "the man" or "poor man." For her, he had been reduced to his anthropological essence: a man. Not her husband, but "the man." She never said "my husband." I found it fascinating.

There was a triviality to everything that was immensely difficult to explain: that doctor's apology, my father fled from the world, the cheap Christmas decorations in the hospital corridors, the coffee machine, the interns moving old people from one place to another in a bedbound choreography, those old people's frightened faces, those faces of deep sorrow, of slow fear, of powerlessness and loss of will. Maybe it's better never to get there in the first place. The faces of the elderly are the face of a person begging younger men for mercy. And me drinking coffee that cost fifty cents. I was getting drunk on hospital-coffee-machine joe. I liked throwing the cheap little plastic cups into an enormous trash can. I liked polluting the world with garbage—it's the one luxury poor people get to enjoy. That's what poor people do: discard garbage.

Our bodies are garbage.

The entire end of my father's life is tinged with hallucination and truth.

75

My cell phone rang at three in the morning. It was the medical examiner. He told me I hadn't reported my father's pacemaker. As if I needed to report such a thing. What a bastard, calling me like that—like a registrar of death. I didn't know there was such a thing as death registration; I thought there was just property registration.

Cremation wasn't possible with a pacemaker, he told me, irritated.

I would have to sign a form authorizing them to remove the pacemaker from my father's body. Of course, they would need to perform an autopsy—in other words, another three hundred euros.

In capitalism, when a business says two extra words to you, it means there's a problem—and that means the bill is going up. The business of the dead is overwhelming, but the dead require work, and work must be paid for. The only question is the price. Capitalism's ability to turn any event into an amount of money, a price, is astonishing. The conversion of all existence into a price is the presence of poetry, since poetry is precision, like capitalism. Poetry and capitalism are the same thing.

The next day I signed the authorization. I asked if I could have the pacemaker, but everybody ignored me. They thought I was traumatized by grief. But I would have liked to keep something that had been inside my father's body, ensconced in his flesh. I imagine they must have washed or purified or disinfected the pacemaker and popped it into somebody else. Or maybe they didn't wash it and inserted it just as it was, with my father's organic remains clinging to the plastic. That pacemaker is probably still making a pace for some other poor bastard who's wandering around, happy and contented, with the device inside him.

The device going from body to body in the twilight of the world.

Since then I've felt my father's presence everywhere, as if the electricity of that pacemaker were reactivating the blood that had disappeared. I can feel it right this moment.

My father became electricity, and cloud, and bird, and song, and orange, and tangerine, and melon, and tree, and road, and soil, and water.

And I see him whenever I try to see myself.

His high laugh tumbling over the world.

His desire to turn the world to smoke and ashes. That's how ghosts are: they are forces and forms of the life that precedes ours, which is there, crowned, purified.

My father is like a tower full of corpses. I often feel him behind me when I look in the mirror.

This is you now, my father says, and then there is a deep silence.

He says just four words.

Now you are "the man," or, rather, the "poor man."

This is you now.

From his death I move on to mine, to waiting for mine. My father's death evokes my own. And when my death arrives, I will be unable to see it. When I watched my father dying, I felt terror. His death throes sucked at me. I was being carried away. Was my father the one who was dying in that hospital?

His body was falling apart.

It was like he was another man.

He was like a hero, a legend.

He was like a god.

76

I've done my best, Dad. I know you're always with me; look at this disaster of a house I live in, look at my apartment on Avenida de Ranillas. Papers are piling up, dust invades the tables, my clothing smells weird, the floors are dirty, the kitchen table is uncleared, the bed unmade—and therefore un-unmade; and the other bed, the one for my sons, who never spend the night (I wouldn't either), is covered with a jumble of clothing and papers. The jumbled clothing and its musty smell, the dust getting in the clothing, the clothing always dirty even when it's clean. I can't find anything either, and I think back on your frantic fits, you pounding your forehead against the walls, accusing my mother of throwing out your carbon copies and invoices, and here is where I'd like to take a moment, because if I can't find my belongings, it's due to my own lack of organization, and I've been thinking that maybe the same thing was happening with you, that actually nobody was throwing anything away. You were the one burying papers under more papers, unable to let go of mail or anything else. We'll never know now.

Never.

77

After the divorce, I kept the armoire that had been in the back bedroom of the house that was once mine, and now my clothing smells like acrid damp. You don't know how exasperating it is for your recently laundered clothing to end up smelling musty. It's the fault of the armoire, which I found in a dumpster a dozen years back.

Do you know what it's like to go around smelling like fermented armoire all damn day? Not to be able to afford a new armoire, after spending twenty-three years shackled to a job where all you do is shout "Everybody settle down"?

Twenty-three years teaching teenagers. And I don't have an armoire. I don't have a goddamn armoire to put my clothes in so they'll smell decent.

And my father says to me, "I told you not to get married, I told you to wait—you were too young, you had some living to do still. I told you that years ago, but you didn't listen."

You've used a lot of words today, I tell my father.

The ghost of poverty stands before me.

Smelling clean was never easy.

Historically, I mean.

If you smell clean, it's because other people are dirty—never forget that.

78

After a lot of dithering, I've bought an office chair at Hipercor, and Brah has put it together. I'm hopeless at putting things together. I never understand the instructions. I get frustrated and angry, and end up hurling it all out the window. I tried to have a conversation with the great Vivaldi. I talked to him about the future, about how he'll have to make decisions. He has a future, and I don't.

I remember when I had a future.

It's the most beautiful feeling in life, when nothing has yet begun. When the curtain has not yet risen.

I know there are people I will never see again, people who were once important in my life, and whom I'll never see again not because they're dead but because life has social rules, cultural rules, whatever—in actuality, they're political rules, atavistic laws that help to organize this thing we call civilization.

That's how humans work: there are people with whom, even though they're alive, we will never interact again, and so they attain the same status as the dead.

There is also a still greater degree of pain: realizing that you are thinking about a living person as if they were dead. That happened to me with my aunt Reme: I never went to visit her. I couldn't go visit her—I felt guilty. If I went to see her, I'd feel guilty; if I didn't go see her, I felt guilty then too, but it was more comfortable not to go see her. When she died, I was just starting a fling in Madrid. I could have gone to the funeral—I had time. I could have taken a train. But I had a date with a woman that day, and I liked that woman a lot, I was wild about her, and that night was going to be pivotal. In my head, I told my aunt Reme that. I said I wasn't going to her funeral because of lust, and that a dead person had to respect lust. I think she understood. She doesn't visit me in the night or reproach me for not attending her funeral. I think she understood how I felt. I think she understood I was in a hole and it was going to take me a while to get out, and it did take me a while to get out.

Today I would have gone to her funeral.

Human beings evolve; what was important yesterday no longer is today. I didn't go to that funeral, and when I was with that woman I was thinking about my aunt Reme's funeral, and so I pushed our relationship and our night together hard so we'd end up in bed—because if we ended up in bed, the fact that I'd skipped my aunt's funeral would make sense. All of these thoughts were happening in my head quite pragmatically, like impeccable bits of reasoning, with irrefutable logic. They were erroneous, I know that now, and stingy. It didn't seem that way at the time.

Yes, I was nuts, though on second thought maybe I wasn't so nuts. I was drinking back then, of course. I drank a lot and spent hours wandering the gleaming dunes of the paradise that drunks inhabit. To a drunk, sex is only an accessory, an embellishment to the alcohol, maybe its finest embellishment but an embellishment nevertheless. Travel, gazing at the sea, laughter, eating, entering the naked bodies of women—these are mere complements to the main event. Which is alcohol, the perfect dimension, the golden hand grasping a cup.

And now, quite simply, I find no use in the things I did back then.

When I was with that woman, I was thinking about my aunt's corpse; it was awful because I had to fake it, so I felt guilty; my brain was bleeding. If the woman had known my aunt, I wouldn't have felt so guilty. The guilt was born of strangeness. My lover was a stranger to my family, and therein lay the problem. That kind of regret has often been my companion in life. I needed my mother's approval for everything. Then I shifted that responsibility to my ex-wife. It would have been over-the-top to call my mother or my ex-wife to ask permission. But if they'd granted it to me, I would have felt better.

I sought my mother's presence everywhere. There was no escaping childhood: I was very frightened. Whose presence? I am using the term *mother* for the general mystery of life. Mother is living death. When I say "mother" I mean *Being*. I'm a primitive soul. Without my mother around, the world was a hostile place. That's why I drank so much and engaged in reckless and promiscuous sexual behavior. Even today I don't know what I was looking for. I'd need a panel of psychotherapists to figure out what I was after.

In any case, I didn't go to my aunt's funeral, one more failure to appear on my list of absences or desertions from my family members' funerals. If you don't attend the funeral of somebody who was important to you as a child, the child you once were claws at the cerebral veins of the adult you now are and stands before you with a distraught look on his face and demands an explanation; he tells you he can't sleep, can't close the damn circle of human experience.

I hope everybody's okay.

79

When I started looking for my own place during my divorce, I couldn't find anything. What I encountered were total nutjobs selling impractical apartments, completely beyond all architectural logic, totally uninhabitable. I needed to find something urgently. At the time I'd been living in a hotel for several weeks. I spent my days drinking and was completely oblivious to everything else. It was a pretty nice hotel—it cost thirty-five euros a night. They gave me a room with a balcony in the historic quarter of Zaragoza. I would take a bottle of gin and a couple of beers up to the room, and as the bottles emptied I'd start calling people on the phone. I'd call up friends, male and female alike, people in general. The next day I wouldn't remember anything. I felt deeply ashamed. I was losing everything. And my mother was already dead. We never shared a desire to talk on the phone; when she wanted to, I didn't, and once I was in the mood, she was no longer in this world. It sucks that my mother never saw the phone-addict version of me, the me who was always wanting to talk on the phone.

It's funny—the telephone is the one thing my mother and I never matched up on. Now, we would have talked for hours and hours. Our only mismatch was our desire to talk on the phone, and I say that almost completely seriously.

When she wanted to talk, I was absent. When I wanted to talk, she was dead.

The hotel was in an area full of grungy watering holes and underground clubs, so I used to go out at around one in the morning and wander the streets of San Pablo, Predicadores, Casta Álvarez, and I'd pop into some dive, almost always packed with foreigners. There would be prostitutes and partiers. I just wanted to have a few beers. We were all there completely alone; there was an overwhelming sense of unreality. One of those nights, I met the former world light welterweight boxing champion Perico Fernández, who used to roam from bar to bar along those narrow, dark, and dirty streets, there where Zaragoza is like a city from the past, as if it's been mummified. We chatted a little and I bought him a beer. I was drunk, obviously. But seeing him so wasted away, so worn-out, with his brain battered by fists and Alzheimer's, provoked a pang of sorrow and also tenderness. Sorrow and tenderness at the same time. Perico was another abandoned man, with no family, defeated, going from bar to bar, a leaden silence gathering around him. There he was at the bar; it was a filthy dive with old beer glasses. We took a photo together. I still have it. We look like a couple of angels in that photo. I was without a family, but Perico Fernández had three wives and five children. Where were his five children and three wives that night? They'd left him, of course. A smile still hung on his ruined face, a sweet, serene, indolent smile. Perico grew up in an orphanage. One thing he'd said became famous: "If my mother didn't want me, why did she have me?" He never met his mother. He was born in 1952 from a stranger's womb. That is a great mystery.

I saw him again on another night in another seedy dive that reeked of kebabs and French fries, the bar smeared with old food. He was more animated that time. The story of his life was legible in his eyes. He was so unguarded and vulnerable that he seemed like a lost little boy. He was in that place where loss has become searing plenitude. He told me he'd been world champion, and I told him, in a drunken outburst, that I was a world champion too. He laughed—he thought that was funny. A good smile, because there was goodness in his heart, that rare goodness of plain people, people who were dumped into the world and did the best they could. Perico was a village kid, with a typical Aragonese accent that in his voice became a sonorous filigree and reflected an ancient, essential, and deeply sardonic intelligence. A true son of the villages of Aragon, like no other. It was hilarious listening to him tell his life story. I remembered how in 1974 he'd won the title of world champion—I remember because I'd heard my father talking about it excitedly. Perico was a king back then. All of Spain was his betrothed. In the early seventies, Perico was universally adored. And during that period I had my father, who adored me. Both of us were on top of the world back then.

And there we both were, in 2014, both world champions. I

would end up being saved, though I didn't know it at the time, but not him. He wasn't going to be saved. He died not long after—I saw it in the papers.

Men with family die just the same as men without family do, I thought.

Maybe Perico realized that.

80

I saw apartments that were truly crappy. But I found one located on a large street whose name seemed like a sign. My father's second surname had been Arnillas. And the apartment was on Avenida de Ranillas, along the Ebro River.

I thought my father was talking to me, sending me a message. In that sense I was like Jesus Christ, whose father also sent him signs. I'm not sure what's so remarkable about Jesus's life, about the fact that he and his father chatted a lot. Generally speaking, all fathers talk to their children. Maybe Jesus of Nazareth's father seemed more interesting, more devastating, more poetic, or Jesus knew how to make him more captivating, thanks to literature.

So I ended up buying that apartment that sounded like my father's second surname. Here, flaws become apparent when it gets dark. A screw is missing from the Persian blinds, and some sort of insulation (I know it has a specific name, I should look it up in the dictionary, because everything has a name but sometimes we don't know it) has come loose from the window. Nothing was done well in this apartment. This apartment reminds me of my life.

I'm waiting for Valdi to arrive. He's gone out with friends.

81

My father was always uncomfortably hot in August. In the final years of his life he bought himself a portable air conditioner. It wasn't a big thing, but it would cool down a room, maybe half a room, not even the whole room. It was noisy. You had to stick a tube out the window. So they called somebody to cut a hole in the glass of the living room window. I never asked who made them that neat hole for the air conditioner tube. The windowpane was original to the place, 1959 glass.

When my mother died, somebody must have carried that obsolete appliance away. My brother called some guys who empty apartments for a living. I remember the refrigerator and the washing machine.

I don't remember the dishwasher because my mother never had a dishwasher. I took the plaque from the front door of the house that had my father's name on it; it was one of those plaques that people used to put on their apartment doors, a postwar custom that lasted into the late sixties and early seventies, one inherited from the liberal professions, from doctors and lawyers, that was then adopted by professionals with a lot less clout, perhaps signaling the democracy to come, or maybe just imposture. It was easy to unscrew the plaque—I thought it would be more difficult. Maybe that effortlessness meant something; it was strange that nothing broke and I successfully performed a manual task, because normally I break things.

That plaque must have been fifty years old. I've now put it on the door of my apartment on Ranillas, where it will survive the years of life that remain to me, since I have the same name as my father. The Ecuadorean super probably thought the plaque was new, that I'd just had it made. The idea that the super might think that was overwhelming. Even terrifying.

82

The plaque with my father's name has a bit of a mortuary vibe to it, since it has a black background and is made of shatterproof glass, a revolutionary material back in the 1960s. It's lasted many years. It didn't signal prosperity; it hung stranded there, like a black whale, in the middle of a door. Plaques signaled success, achievement; they declared that the family that lived behind the door had made it, had attained prosperity. The plaque that was my father's, and is now mine, didn't signal anything. It was a calligraphy exercise on the wooden door. Hence my surprise, hence why I'm so unsettled by my father's life.

I stand staring at it when I get home. Seeing it, I feel fear and sorrow. And immense nostalgia, and immense benevolence. It's the loneliest thing in the world. That plaque's journey through time seems like a Homeric journey. We are incapable of imagining what will end up happening either with people or with objects. My father never would have imagined that the plaque he ordered from who knows where (I have no idea who makes them) would end up at the apartment of his divorced son on a street that almost shares one of his names. The plaque doesn't make sense where it is now, but that senselessness is monumental.

I surround myself with cheap monuments. They are cheap and yet they have supernatural power. As if the supernatural chose to manifest itself in humility. Or as if the supernatural and humility were the same thing.

No aristocratic monuments, no VIP monuments, only ones born of the Spanish lower middle class of the 1960s, which are very beautiful, and are the mirror of my soul.

83

It will be Christmas soon. Back during my childhood, my father used to love Christmas. My father would buy a tree and turrón candies and lots of tickets for the Christmas lottery. He bought real trees, sold by a woodcutter in Barbastro's Plaza del Mercado who had all different sizes. He always bought a fir that went all the way up to the ceiling. He was a huge fan of Christmas. On the morning of December 22, he would check to see whether his lottery tickets had been lucky. Starting at ten in the morning every December 22, my father would turn on the TV and, in his stylish, slanted cursive, write down the winning numbers, which were sung by students from Madrid's San Ildefonso school.

He never won anything except the occasional refund. But I was happy watching him write down the numbers in a notebook, those numbers so painstakingly traced. He would sculpt an ornamented 5 in which the upper bar turned into a cap slanted toward the sky. His 4s and 7s came out baroque and stylized too. I liked seeing my father so focused, so festive. And then he would whistle because he'd had a good meal. I think he was profoundly happy. He felt fortunate, joyous, full of purpose.

Your father's handwriting is always important. There's no

other handwriting in the world that matters. I write almost the same as my father. Even my signature is his. I saw him sign so many times, and he'd sign with tall letters full of clouds, his name edged with curved lines, and as a whole it was the portrait of an angel's identity.

Why did he sign like that when he wasn't rich?

His signature looked like it belonged to one of Spain's prominent men. It looked like the signature of a duke, a marquis.

It was a Gothic signature, baroque. Mine is very similar, but it has fewer frills, it's more austere, more impoverished.

I fell in love with my father's signature. His love for his own name was something to see. He saw himself full of pomp, of crowns, of pride. My father's pride was cosmic in scale.

84

I'm a fan of Christmas too—I got that from him. So why did he flip out that night when he smashed the plates in a fit of fury? I imagine that's what it was—a fit of fury. Maybe he wanted to smash our faces and took it out on the plates instead. Maybe he was fed up with having a family and wanted to go back to being a handsome twenty-seven-year-old man in a double-breasted suit, free and unburdened by commitments, that man who was photographed at the ancient marble counter of a bar as he stood staring at his hands, lost in thought.

My father bought a nativity scene when I was five or six years old, or younger. I don't know how old. He bought it at a stationery shop in Barbastro whose owners are now dead and of whose business I am the only witness who still remembers. He was proud of that nativity scene. It cost a bundle. That would have been 1966. I remember how gingerly he would handle the figurines. They had a Valladolid Baroque feel to them. They weren't small. They were at least a handspan tall, maybe a bit more. My favorites were the ox and the mule.

One by one over the years the figurines broke.

My mother stored them in the wardrobe, but carelessly, because my mother ended up breaking everything. I think my mother is the one who gradually broke them. First she broke the mule. Decapitated it. My mother was always dropping things; she didn't know how to hold a thing in her hand, so everything was at risk of falling, of shattering. My father stuck the mule's head back on with superglue. But it was an injured mule. Then the ox broke. Then Saint Joseph. Saint Joseph's hand broke off. Each Christmas that nativity scene was in worse and worse shape, in relentless deterioration. The page boys took a tumble. The camels too. The Virgin and the Baby Jesus held out. But a nativity scene with only two survivors made no sense; it was practically a satanic heresy. A confraternity of cripples.

Eventually we had no nativity scene at all and my father didn't buy another because his dreams had withered and because those were hard times and my brother and I were getting older. My mother could have been more careful with the nativity scene. But my mother didn't understand the meaning of those figurines. That was the most stunning and also the most irritating thing about my mother: everything was superfluous to her, everything seemed insignificant, everything was a candidate for being discarded. For whatever reason, it didn't suit her to take care of the nativity scene. She didn't understand who the Baby Jesus was or what the Wise Men were doing there. To her, all of that was meaningless. It was a natural atheism. Her atheism was marvelous because it was inborn. She murdered that nativity scene. She murdered other things too—she murdered my comics, threw them all away. She didn't leave me a single one.

She was an exterminating hurricane.

85

I got a record player for my twelfth birthday; it was a suitcase record player, and I listened to my first records on it; I suspected that music would heal me. Back then, I felt the healing power of music—that's why I've named my sons Vivaldi and Brahms. All the names should become musicians. Wow, I'm just realizing something: I haven't given my parents names, prestigious names from music history. Maybe my father should be Gregorian and my mother Euterpe. I should find the name of a renowned composer for each person I loved, and thus fill my life story with music.

I saw them buy me the record player. I'd asked for it as a Christmas present. I saw them go into the store—it was pure chance that I happened to be there, on that street where there was a home appliance shop. I figure it was in 1974. Maybe that image of them entering that store is a boundary of memory. My father was wearing a trench coat. Why were they going into that store? My heart leaped with joy: they were going for my gift. Why was he wearing a trench coat to buy a record player? Had I requested it as a Christmas present or for getting good grades? I don't know. I only see an image: the two of them entering that store. But now I'm not sure about the trench coat.

86

My father died at seventy-five years old—will I live longer than he did? I'm convinced I'll live less time, or maybe the exact same amount: seventy-five years. But I don't think so, I think I'll go earlier.

It seems impolite to live longer than your father did. Disloyal. Blasphemous. A cosmic error. If you live longer than your father did, you stop being a son—that's what I mean.

And if you're no longer a son, you're nothing.

My father realized he was going overboard with food; he was eating too much and gaining weight. His relationship with food was out of whack. He enjoyed eating and he enjoyed living. But a person who eats too much, even if it might not seem like it, has chosen to die; ultimately, he has chosen the destruction of organs, the abuse of the intestine, the overuse of the pancreas, the liver, the stomach, the rectum, the colon. Everybody is overweight. We're used to seeing it as normal when people are fifteen pounds overweight, and we notice only when it's fifty, or eighty, or a hundred thirty. We've forgotten the gifts of hunger.

Today it's not the least bit hot. It's a perfect day for a simple question. For contemplating how much my father and mother ended up loving me.

That kind of love doesn't leave this world.

Why did you love me so much?

Is it true that you loved me, or am I making it up?

If I'm making up your love, it's a beautiful invention. If it was real, that's beautiful too. Because to bring that love out from the shadows, I have to go on a journey. The slowest journey in the world, and the most monumental.

87

A few days ago the famous actor and comedian Robin Williams died at sixty-three. Which means my father lived twelve years longer than him. Robin hanged himself with a belt. That wasn't necessary, buddy, there was no need for you to kill yourself. My father, who had nothing, lived twelve years longer than you. Twelve years is an eternity. You were rich, Robin, and you chose to die. My father was poor, and death came looking for him.

It isn't fair.

You could have left us your money—my father would have been able to find oncologists on the cutting edge of research who would have saved his life, the life you didn't want. And my father would be with me now. He would be eighty-four. There are eighty-four-year-olds who are perfectly healthy. If my father had had your money, he would have been saved.

Death is never necessary.

Because death always comes to us as a bonus or by default. There's no need to go looking for it. It makes house calls. You don't have to go anywhere to check that box. It comes to you. It's convenient. It's a good service they offer. I mean that seriously, it really is.

We pass through the world, and then we leave. We leave the world to others, who come and do what they can. Cities last much longer than we do, though of course they are refounded, transformed, or even disappear. My maternal grandfather committed suicide too, like Robin Williams just did. The despair and emptiness and spiritual nausea that lead to suicide may be the worst disease on earth.

This is the face of my grandmother, with one of her children, who's holding a cake.

Her look is full of suffering, of an internal malady akin to terror. In any case, the eyes of that woman prefigure my own and my mother's. When this photo was taken, her husband had already committed suicide and her eldest son was dead. That's why she's terrified: she has no husband, has no firstborn. She thinks it's her fault.

That woman saw one of her children die in a car accident that made her husband go mad and commit suicide, shooting himself with a hunting rifle in 1957. I'm not sure of the exact date, I'm just guessing. It could have been 1955 or 1951, I'm not sure. There were a lot of car accidents in the 1950s. I've reconstructed the facts the best I could because nobody talked and now they're all dead. There's no way to corroborate facts and dates; everybody has gone. It's as if they'd told me, "Just make it all up, we're out of here, do what you want with your past, it doesn't matter, we're no longer alive."

My grandmother's eyes contain centuries of Spanish peasantry, exhausted hands, the tang of sweat, stubbly beards, hellish summer heat, hot animal breath next to your mouth, priests saying mass, more priests saying mass, another seven hundred million priests saying mass. The great enemy of God in Spain was not the Communist Party but the Catholic Church.

Seven hundred million priests saying mass.

Her husband killed himself.

Her son died too, even earlier, and her eyes challenge the meaning of life, which is simply the meaning of the land, a nameless land, because only two cities in Spain have names and fame and prestige and wealth and success and honor and military might and economic power and universality: Madrid and Barcelona.

The other cities and towns were just abandoned hinterlands, empty places.

She, my unnamed grandmother (I'll call her Cecilia, in honor of Saint Cecilia, named the patron saint of musicians by the sixteenth-century pope Gregory XIII), is the daughter of a forgotten land, the lands of the Somontano, and I can name those lands and those villages now because I went to university—which is to say, thanks to the dictator Francisco Franco Bahamonde, who laid the foundations for Cecilia's grandchildren to learn to read and write, who laid the foundations of the Spanish middle class, who set Spain's political modernization process back several decades and did so out of ignorance and stupidity.

I write because priests taught me to write.

Seven hundred million priests.

That is a great irony of the lives of the poor in Spain: I owe more to priests than I do to the PSOE, the Spanish Socialist Workers' Party. Irony in Spain is ever a work of art.

88

Cecilia was diagnosed with cancer. My mother started avoiding her because she thought cancer might be contagious. So to me my grandmother was a total stranger. I don't remember much about her, except the photo, but her eyes are mine today. "Don't touch her," my mother told me. And if you tell that to a little boy, he'll believe his grandmother is an infectious mass of tissue, a disease-ridden rodent, a high cliff with black rocks at the bottom. But there was no ill will in my mother, only desperation. That is what has always dwelled in my mother's heart and in mine; she wanted to keep me safe from cancer because I was the thing she loved most desperately in the world. She was horrified by the mere idea that something might happen to me. It was a prehistoric, grief-stricken, claustrophobic, absorbing, and exasperated love.

My mother used to talk to her sister Reme and my father about Cecilia's inevitable death; I overheard those conversations; they were making preparations; they were studying the situation—and all of that created an atmosphere that I experienced in an odd way, because I was the king of everything and that was the joy that made up for Cecilia's imminent disappearance. I was hope and the future, and Cecilia was goodbye. We made up for each other, we were counterbalanced; my future was necessary so that her goodbye would make sense, and vice versa.

And forty-five years after all of that, the memory of those conversations held behind Cecilia's back rouses visions I didn't know my brain contained: the borders of memory are fluid. I see new things, I'm always seeing old scenes as if they were new. The gold-colored faucets with the exposed copper pipes in my aunt Reme's old house, and Cecilia, very ill, drinking a glass of water.

89

I try to think about happy moments in Cecilia's life. Maybe the day her children were born. What was her voice like? There are no recordings of that voice. What was she like as a young woman? In train or bus stations, or in airport terminals, you could walk right past your grandparents and there would be no recognition. Authentication isn't possible with the dead; our dead are anonymous beings, without iconography, without renown. If your dead rose from their graves, they would be strangers. Identification would happen only with famous dead figures—your Elvis Presleys, your Adolf Hitlers, your Marilyn Monroes and Che Guevaras—if they were resuscitated.

I wouldn't recognize my grandfathers if they came back to life, because I never saw them while they were alive, plus I don't have a single photo and no one ever told me about them. I search for them now among the dead, and my hand fills with ash and excrement, and those are the symbols and heraldic crest of the global working class: ashes and excrement. And oblivion.

That kinship does not exist.

Family does not exist.

There is nothing there—the vanity of saying "my grandfathers." I don't know who they were. I don't know what kind of life they led, whether they were tall or short, whether they were blond or dark-haired—I know nothing, not even their names. I don't know who my paternal grandfather was. And I know even less about my maternal grandfather. And now I'll never know because there's nobody to ask.

Why am I here, in the night of the world, when I cannot even grasp the first night of my world?

90

My mother used to tell me, "Don't touch her, don't touch her." Cecilia had a cancer under her black clothing, on her side. I imagined the cancer to be something white hidden in Cecilia's black clothing, the cancer like a white rat gnawing people's arms. We never talked about Cecilia's cancer. Shc is dead, but maybe her pilgrimage toward purification won't end until my death. I can also think about my death.

How long do I have left?

People don't think about that, because it can't be thought—there's no content there, nothing at all, and there's certainly no social courtesy.

Even so, there's a lurking number: five years, three days, six months, thirty years, three hours.

There's a number there, waiting to be fulfilled.

And that number will be fulfilled. We all carry that number with us. It's like one of God's bloody jokes. His fondness for numbers. My father lived seventy-five years. Numbers symbolize lives well. People make calculations when they ask the age of someone who just died.

Dying younger than twenty almost isn't dying at all—there's barely been life.

Dying younger than fifty is sad.

My father chose a mysterious number: seventy-five.

It's not very old, but it's not young either. It's like a borderland. It seems like a good number. An esoteric number. It's like a boundary. Taking one's leave before decrepitude hits, just before. But only just.

The night he died I sat thinking about that number, trying to figure out whether my father was trying to communicate something to me through that number.

All of my passwords contain 75.

There's a perfection there. He could have easily lived ten years longer, even fifteen.

Or he could have died at sixty-five, at sixty-eight, at seventy-three.

He chose a hermetic number, one full of messages, torrents of messages, a symphony of symbols.

91

Cecilia and I are walking down the street. She is completely covered, draped in veils. We walk toward a church. We go inside. There are lit candles and Cecilia tells me, "I am your grandmother." I want to remember that she said that to me, but in fact she didn't say anything. She didn't say a single word. Her confession of love is a dream in my present. And I look at her, and I see only iron veils, prisons that contain walls, funeral caskets, the dead whose living children do not speak of them.

When she was buried, on the day of her funeral, her children got together—it must have been 1967 or 1968. Maybe it was 1969, or 1970, or 1966, I'm not sure. I can only take a stab at it—nobody told me the dates, since nobody ever uttered her death date out loud again. They got together to talk about divvying up the few possessions that remained. I imagine she would have liked seeing them all together on the day she was buried. I see her children seated at a long table; there was background noise, so they had to speak up. And then, once the funeral was over, they forgot her.

My mother barely talked about her. Though I imagine she carried her in her heart. I don't know. If she carried her in her heart, she did so silently.

Oh, ghostly Cecilia, it's not that your children didn't love you—it's just that you became a wrathful or uncomfortable memory. They weren't ready to think about the dead rationally. Nobody was ready, because you lived in a Spain so poor it couldn't even keep memories warm. It was a backward country, but no historian can say why that was.

No historian has the least idea.

The Spanish enigma, they call it.

You didn't come up in conversation. I don't know anything about you because nobody told me anything. They quite wretchedly forgot you. You must have been alive once, no doubt, and things must have happened to you. When you were mentioned, on one of a very few occasions, you were like a distant shadow, wavering and insubstantial. But one of your children loved you very much.

Alberto, the youngest.

He did talk about you, his voice defenseless.

I'll call Alberto "Monteverdi" because he deserves it and that can be his good name, he who has not yet bloomed on the mountain, he who got lost on a forgotten peak and never grew up, never blossomed.

92

Monteverdi remembered you.

He would bring you up in the middle of a conversation with your children, his siblings, and would end up alone, left behind—nobody ever pursued your evocation. I would stare with a seven-year-old child's uncomprehending gaze and notice only the vehemence with which Monteverdi always said "Mama," because he never stressed the second syllable, pronouncing the word in a disconsolate monotone, and my ear registered that strangeness, which came from a primordial abandonment and emphasized how far away you were, because your name was not Mamá, the way my mother's was.

Monteverdi continued to look for you among those who were absent—he was the only one of the siblings who did so.

The others had become parents themselves, and they'd left you in peace among the departed.

But Monteverdi would say, "Do you guys remember what Mama always used to say?" And I see you now, Cecilia, looking after your children, looking after the one who needs you most, Monteverdi.

I didn't see your family, I never saw them.

I see them now, among the dead. It's enough to know that family once existed. It's enough to know I'm not making it up. That family must have existed once, and it must have been full, noble, united, robust, happy.

Because the difference between living and dead is tied to the swift, liquid movements of the rising and setting of the sun; it has to do with light and its transit over men's heads.

Monteverdi knew you were the only person who loved him. And he turned to you like a child hounded by men who never loved him. But you exited this world and left Monteverdi alone. I don't even know how old you were when you left—I don't know if you were ninety or seventy. Nor do I know how old your husband, my grandfather, was when he killed himself.

Cecilia, I never knew anything about you, not even your name—that's why I've named you after the patroness of music. Because nobody ever said your first name.

Biologically you were my grandmother, and now you may be my best ghost.

93

Nobody said your name except my uncle Monteverdi.

But there is somebody else who surpassed even you in terms of nonexistence, somebody whose name was never spoken. He was practically the Holy Spirit. It's as if Cecilia produced her seven children through divine intervention and not that of her husband. You, Cecilia, you were famous and I saw you in life. Whereas he was a black hole. My mother was the daughter of the Holy Spirit and you, Cecilia. My mother's five living siblings also had Nobody for a father.

He was unnameable, but why?

Who was that man? Because he did exist, yes—he trod the earth in sunlight, as I do now.

He produced children, so he must have existed.

I don't believe in the Holy Spirit as a sperm donor.

My grandfather was he who has no living face, and no dead

face either. He who was never seen in life, and so could never die. How can you think of somebody as dead when you never saw them alive?

We lost access to his memory because you all chose shame instead, the feeling of shame. You were ashamed that your husband and the father of your children had committed suicide. And instead of understanding and acceptance, you opted for radical forgetting. Goodbye to memory, cheap as it is. Memory, which is maintained only with the embers of the blood. Memory, which is free. There are no taxes on memory. The government doesn't charge its citizens for remembering—or maybe it does.

Because memory can be deadly. Many, many years later, I saw how people chose to erase uncomfortable people. We recall only what suits us, except me—I want to remember everything. Or we recall what has been conventionally established to be remembered, except me. I have no intention of dropping the "except me," even if it does sound vain and pompous. My memory constructs a catastrophic vision of the world, I know, but it's the one that feels true to me. You can't renounce catastrophe—it's the great superstructure of literature, the engine of evil and the engine of everything that has ever existed.

94

In that one photo of Cecilia that came down to me there's an adolescent boy, practically a child, and he's holding a cake. You can see a little of the cake in the photo, just a corner—who was going to eat that barely visible cake? What did cake taste like back then?

The boy was Alberto, my Monteverdi.

Life hadn't tackled him yet. It would go after him soon. A few years later, Monteverdi was diagnosed with tuberculosis—that was in the late fifties, maybe '57 or '58, somewhere around there.

Now, as I write, Monteverdi, too, is dead.

Predictably, I didn't go to Monteverdi's funeral. It's hard to describe Monteverdi's steep decline in his final years. Monteverdi died in 2014. I think he was born in 1940. Nobody knows. Nobody cared.

For example, Monteverdi didn't shower. He didn't wash. He was an erratic creature who wandered the city of Barbastro, every inch of it, with complete aimlessness. You would see him in the bars, in the shops, in the plazas. Monteverdi was always ebullient, enveloped in an illusory elation. There's a scene from my childhood in which Monteverdi chases after me with a knife. It was real and he was about to kill me. Monteverdi chased after me with a knife. He used to have fits of rage, or of madness. Monteverdi's sex life was a mystery too. We were all crazy, a family of lunatics. I don't know if Monteverdi suffered—I imagine he did. His life was simple. He didn't have a job. His tuberculosis forced him out of the labor market back then, in the mid-1960s.

Our family madness was also a Christmas mass. A liturgy of brotherhood.

We were very happy in the cellars of the world. Because Monteverdi always had a carnivorous smile on his face. His simplicity ended in a spear, a sharp point; that happens with beings whose basic nature has not been transformed into innocence, but instead hurtles toward deformation, anomaly, or moral convulsion. Monteverdi was anomalous, basic, but there was no goodness in his heart. There was only darkness, simple darkness, basic darkness.

The great Monteverdi never did anything in life. He got by, in the end, on a monthly pension of what would be two hundred euros today. Back in the seventies, my father used to give him his old suits. And so those suits perambulated around Barbastro on two different bodies. My father used to wear suits because he was a traveling salesman. You put a suit on anybody and he looks like somebody—that's the equalizing mystery of suits, especially back then.

Now that mystery is disappearing.

Monteverdi wore gaudy, colorful ties. To top things off, Monteverdi let his hair grow long. He looked like Jesus Christ Superstar in a necktie and glasses. Because Monte wore glasses too, the kind Paul Newman wore in *The Color of Money.* Knockoff aviators purchased at the ends of the earth.

He spoke all in a rush, full of colloquialisms that were seeking affability or approval; his speech went from delirium to tenderness, and from tenderness to the abyss.

Monte was in the abyss.

95

I haven't had a drink in a long time.

In Spain, the only help a recovering alcoholic ever receives is the kind that gets him started drinking again. In Spain, I think, there's no such thing as forgiveness for one's sins.

Ultimately, then, nobody can get away from alcohol in Spain, hence the buzz of anticipation that a Spanish recovering alcoholic rouses: Let's see how long he holds out, let's see when he starts drinking again.

It will be fun to see him fall back down.

And this time he won't get up.

And we'll cheer. We'll say, "You could see it coming."

That's the mystery of Spain that historians and men of goodwill and brilliant writers and honest intellectuals all muse about: seeing people fall down gets us hot.

We are not good to one another. When we're out and about, we seem like good people, but we stab one another when we're alone. It's something primeval: the Spaniard wants all Spaniards to die so he can possess the Iberian Peninsula alone, so he can go to Madrid and there won't be anybody there, so he can go to Seville and there won't be anybody there, so he can go to Barcelona and there won't be anybody there.

And I get it, because I'm Spanish too.

Once all his countrymen are dead, the last Spaniard will finally be happy.

96

As a little boy, I used to fantasize that my parents weren't my parents, that I was adopted. It's a sad notion—it shatters the bond, pushes you into the mechanical limbo of the stars visible in the heavens at night, into a sort of stasis of will. Being adopted was a perversion, it was a criminal reorganization of one's origin, it was a castle of corpses rotting in full view of everyone. When I was young, being adopted was stigmatized; my mother used to supply me with information about adopted kids in Barbastro; there was a moral infirmity vibrating in sentences like "That boy in your class is adopted," and that boy would become involuntary flesh with a serendipitous soul, but it was beautiful, because there was a secret there.

If you're adopted, that means your real parents didn't love you for even five minutes. You were loved by others, by parents invented by society, not by nature, which is the only truth.

I would pay astronomical sums to feel that innocence again. I used to feel an immense compassion for adopted children—they broke my heart. I would have taken them in if I could. Given them to my parents. They were the most brutal image of helplessness. Of course, all of that was happening in my head, because in reality those kids were perfectly happy.

97

My mother always bought free-range chickens back in the 1960s and '70s. A woman from a nearby village would bring them around. She brought them alive. My mother would kill them, aided by her sister Reme, who had a lot of experience and skill. Reme would come to the house to kill chickens. She'd take out the knife and slit their necks; I would watch with a certain sense of disgust, but not fear. Then they'd boil the corpse—I recall vignettes in the kitchen with billows of steam, with feathers and blood and knives. I remember the chicken's neck, slit down the throat, and the smoke.

Disgust, yes, discomfort because it smelled like blood and feathers and the kitchen was full of steam. And at what point did the other disgust arise, disgust at being in the bathroom with my father; at what point do taboos begin? A small child wants to be with his father all the time, even when his father is perched on a toilet bowl. He doesn't feel disgust. He doesn't feel revulsion. He doesn't feel any physical or emotional discomfort. Because disgust is a taboo of civilization. Disgust at one's father's excrement comes about socially in the moment of independence, of the child's social emancipation. Revulsion at their fathers' odors is necessary so that children will be able to leave. I remember seeing my father urinate and being fascinated and frightened by his penis. These are scenes from the past, and the past has less and less cachet all the time.

I remember when I was a boy somebody told me the story of a father, during the Spanish Civil War, who turned himself in to save his son's life. His son was freed and the father was shot. That's why fatherhood is so important, because it eliminates doubt—you never doubt again. You'll always give your life for your child. Everything else in the world is confusion, waffling, perplexity, selfishness, indecision, uncertainty, no nobility. That father was executed, but his son went free.

Taking the bullet for another person without a second thought—that's the greatest nobility life can offer you.

Taking the bullet for your child is the great mystery—there is no greater mystery on the face of the earth. The light of the sun dims in the face of that mystery. He will not feel the bullet enter his flesh, will not feel the loss of his future, the loss of the things he still had left to do; he will not think about himself, because he will no longer be himself but only a blessed fervor for his son, who will be alive, who will stay alive.

Giving your life for someone is not foreseen in any code of nature. It is a voluntary renunciation that upends the universe.

Fatherhood and motherhood are the only certainties.

Everything else barely exists.

98

I think it was in 1970 that the public pool opened and we stopped going down to the Vero River, the small river that flows through Barbastro.

I remember swimming in the Vero River and the Cinca River.

People swam in the rivers back then, which were full of mud and dragonflies and stones and branches in the water. And very little water.

When public pools arrived in Spain in the early 1970s, my mother was thrilled. She used to spend all day at the pool, a pool that had a dressing room, which was a cutting-edge thing, and also a soda machine, and you could watch the apparatus whir when you slotted in a five-peseta coin and retrieved refreshing beverages of the era, like Mirinda, which disappeared for some unknown reason; and it also had a guy at the door who would sternly verify that everybody entering the pool had their cards, and I remember the man's face, his corpse brushing against me right this moment, an ugly, bald man, stooped, with black eyes, a sickly face, an old man back in the 1970s, who would peer at your photo on the membership card three times to make sure nobody was tricking him and he was doing his job right, who couldn't believe that people went swimming, couldn't believe that women would put on bikinis and sunbathe and drink a Mirinda, and most certainly couldn't believe there was such a thing as the "song of the summer"—he didn't even believe in the sun.

Those pools no longer exist; they disappeared in the mid-eighties. Apartment buildings have been erected on top of them, where the children of those who used to swim now live, the children of the dead swimmers, in service to Spanish prosperity, if the province of Huesca is in Spain at all.

My father served Spanish prosperity by making sure that some Spaniards in the 1960s had a tailored suit. To me, that's heroism.

He wasn't given the medal of valor in a ceremony presided over by the king of Spain and the prime minister and the president of the Aragonese government and the captain general of the Fourth Military Region and the archbishop of Zaragoza.

No, they didn't give him that.

For whatever blessed reason, they didn't give it to him.

And they won't give it to me either, but for other reasons, different reasons, very different reasons—but also blessed.

My father and I are getting our revenge for that—him through his wife, and me through my mother.

My mother never knew that Barbastro was a town in an autonomous community called Aragon or that Aragon was a territory belonging to Spain or that Spain was a country in southern Europe.

And she failed to know it not out of ignorance, but out of divine indifference.

99

I don't remember whether my father liked flags. And my mother didn't even know Spain had a flag. My mother had no concept of political life on earth. It wasn't for her. It was useless for fulfilling her desires. My mother was as primeval as a river, a mountain, or a tree. I don't think my father ever used the word *flag* for anything. There are Spanish words that my parents never uttered. Yet it is impossible to conceive of my life without Spain because, in some sense, I love Spain. In reality, I love it because of my father, because he lived there, that's all. Because I love anything that had to do with my father. If my father had been Portuguese, I would have loved Portugal. I don't think he ever would have been lucky enough to be French or British or American.

My father always lived in Spain. He was always there, except during his military service, which he did in Africa, in the city of Melilla. When I visited Melilla a few years back, I heard the voice: "He was here when he was twenty years old, here, he was here, his whole life ahead of him; when he was here he didn't know what death was, and he didn't know you'd come to this city looking for him sixty years later; sixty years later and there are still traces of him in the air; you can still see him, smiling, with that kind smile he had that Brah has inherited and doesn't know it; Brah doesn't know and he doesn't either, you're the only one who knows and this may be the most important knowledge you've ever had, and now smile, smile because he was here."

100

There are some dead people who die with the approval of the living, and others who don't; some are deemed great men, and others are deemed depraved—but once they enter into death, any description or judgment or moral discernment is shunted aside, and only equality in the rotting of flesh remains, the rotting of flesh doesn't care about the moral good or evil that resided in the dead body. But if the living love you, you will die more at peace, and that counts for something.

After that, there's nothing.

The depraved person rots just the same as the magnanimous one does.

I don't know if carrion insects can tell the difference between good and evil; it's terrifying to think they don't notice, terrifying to think that the yellow foam and the fat turned to soap of a magnanimous corpse are the same as those of a malign corpse; that there is no distinction between good and evil through varying forms of putrefaction; that good and evil end up in the same pestilence, in the same maggots and fungi.

So maybe I did the right thing cremating them, but I don't think so.

101

My father and I are walking hand in hand through the Barbastro cemetery. It's November 1 in maybe 1968, or 1969, or 1970. My father stops in front of a wall of niches. He looks at the upper niches, which are deteriorated and have no names.

He speaks to me, says, "Your grandfather is in one of those up there." I look, but all I see are a couple of nameless niches, chipped, cracked, split, broken, like a sandstone wall, gray, far away, impossible to identify—I see only wet, dirty sand. I look at my father and with my eyes I ask him to be more specific, to tell me which niche it is. He doesn't know. He's unbothered by not knowing.

It's as if my father hadn't had a father.

It's strange.

I don't think he ever talked about his father again. It was a mystical territory. A secret territory. My father was like a CIA agent.

I would have liked to know what year my paternal grandfather died. I think my father's confession when showing me more or less the niche where my grandfather was buried was a gesture of weakness, a momentary indiscretion. Why did my father deny me any knowledge of my grandfather's life? There wasn't enough time for those revelations; we didn't think everything would end so soon. My father forgot his father. I don't know what was going on there, but something happened. Memory, I think, is a bourgeois art, and in that sense my father was profoundly anti-bourgeois. That's the vanishing point of my father's life. He dressed like the bourgeoisie, but he was brimming with subversion and some benign form of moral anarchy that led him to forget his parents. Or maybe he thought about his father every day and just didn't tell me. He thought it was better if I didn't know, because I wouldn't understand. In reality, I never knew who my father was. He was the most timid, enigmatic, silent, and elegant person I ever met in my life. Who was he? By not telling me who he was, my father was creating this book.

The corpse's stint in the tomb is not a static one. There is frenetic activity, an industrial reconversion of the matter inside the casket. The coffin is a factory. An industrial warehouse in which matter rampages downward, into the depths, because everything happens under the surface in an effort to burrow deeper in, as if seeking the heart of the planet. It may not be visible, but I perceive all that activity: the joy of a corpse that, through revolting creatures, offers sparks of life. But life is never disgusting, even if it is born in a pigsty, because the stable in Bethlehem was a pigsty too.

There is solution as well as dissolution in the world of the coffin, there is consciousness and essence—and I thwarted all of that when I had my parents' bodies cremated, thereby having myself cremated the same way, because the supreme form of life is the corpse of life, and I didn't see it.

I didn't see anything.

Skeletal remains are the mold, support, and crown of those of us who remain on earth, on its surface.

Because there is ambition and manifestation and sedition in skeletons. And I didn't see it. And there is community, because skeletons are one another's neighbors in cemeteries, and that neighborhood still fosters a kind of hope.

The hope of seeing you again, Dad, Mom.

I am nothing more than that: the hope of seeing you again.

102

It used to happen to my father too—he'd fall into these doldrums of energy. So do I. At a certain point it was no longer worth going out on his sales trips—he had to pay for gas, lodging, and meals, and he wasn't selling much. There was no point. He didn't sell much fabric and I don't sell many books—we're the same man. The obsessive notion that we're the same man is a pain I've carried inside me since before his death.

My father wasn't salaried—he had to pay his own expenses. And the commission he earned from his sales was less than what he had to shell out. His "why sell" has come down to me as "why write."

In both, the energy to act flags.

And so he opted to put on his green robe and watch TV chefs. Everything that happened to my father reverberates in me with millimetric precision. We are living the same life—with different contexts, but it's the same life. And a hidden message or irony might thrum in that communion of lives. Who is sending the message? The social and cultural trappings change, but we are the same. Sometimes that level of coincidence annihilates time, melts time and turns it liquid and unstable, and the two lives become equivalent. Nor do I want to end up being somebody other than my father—I'm terrified of having my own identity.

I'd rather be my father.

When I discover the huge, dynamic coincidences between my father's life and my own, I am not just startled but also scared—yet at the same time I feel safe, believing that there is a greater order and a greater code.

A whole life spent writing, like my father. I write poems and novels; he wrote duplicates of orders from Spanish tailors.

My father was a traveler, a traveling salesman. As am I, more or less. I write, he wrote. It doesn't matter what. We're doing the same thing. He used to call his literary work "orders and invoices." I can picture it now: he would sit at the dining room table and take out his Parker ballpoint (a gift from the company) and write everything down with almost childlike meticulousness, in his superb, ornate handwriting. My father was the one who taught me the word *calligrapher.* He told me what it meant. It was etched in my memory: *calligrapher.* The table was wonky and he had to put a shim under one leg so his handwriting didn't get jostled. I don't think my father ever had a proper table to write on.

Handwriting was important. The duplicates were yellow. Life grows yellow. Even daybreak is yellow.

103

My father never showed me how to love him. He used to hold my hand when I was a little boy and we went out into the world. Nobody ever asked him if he wanted to be a father either, if he'd really made the decision to become a father freely and without coercion.

My father copied out his duplicates, writing down everything he'd sold to the tailors in the provinces of Huesca, Lérida, and Teruel: tailors who made custom suits for men who are now dead and who may have been buried in those suits; the tailors died too and none of their children inherited the business because there was no longer a business to inherit.

He was never able to show me how to love him, but how do you do that anyway?

A number of times he was awarded certificates for being the traveler with the most sales. I'm awarded honorary degrees for my sorry stint at university in Zaragoza, the outcome of which was that I absorbed three or four facts about Lope de Vega and acquired a few skills for analyzing relative clauses: a real slam dunk of a university career. It was the same thing—what my father did and what I did. The poverty persisted; it had camouflaged itself a bit, but it was still there.

The wealthy were still other people.

Never us.

There was no way to climb aboard the gravy train. That's what Spain is for all of us, for forty-four million Spaniards: watching a million Spaniards ride the gravy train as it passes you by.

104

Yellow is a visual state of the soul. Yellow is the color that speaks of the past, of the disappearance of two families, of penury, which is the moral realm that poverty pushes you toward, of the sadness of never seeing your children, of Spain's fall into Spanish miasmas, of cars, of highways, of memories, of the cities I lived in, of the hotels I slept in—yellow speaks of all of that.

Yellow—*amarillo*—is a resonant word in Spanish.

Penury—*penuria*—is another important word.

Penuria and *amarillo* are two words that dwell together, conjoined.

I had a dream: I was going to my parents' house, and I was doing it in the future. It was the world to come. My parents' age was indeterminate, but they were definitely old. In my dream they were both alive, but in a future time, maybe 2030, or 2050, some far-off year.

The last time I saw them they were dead, not dead at the same time, but dead separated by time—my father was dead for nine years while my mother was still alive.

I've often thought about that growth, that vital progression as a dead man that my father undertook alone, his experience as a fugitive from life, his residence among the dead, his work among the dead, while my mother was among the living. It's as if he'd emigrated to the New World and was busy amassing a fortune or building a future there.

I know the things my mother did while my father was dead, but I don't know the things my father did while my mother was alive.

Nine years with each of them doing their own thing.

Never calling each other.

Nine years is a long time.

They'll have had to do a lot of catching up now. Most human beings have contact with something truly enriching, some material good offered at no cost, only once, and that's on the day they die, even if it looks like the death of a loved one.

Death, at bottom, is almost an economic boon, because nature finally sets you free. There is no longer action, or work, or effort, or salary, or success or failure; you don't have to pay rent or review bank statements or look at the electricity bill. As such, death represents the utopia of anarchism.

I entered a house with large rooms. I remember that in the dream I didn't really understand how the house was laid out; I was getting lost with all the rooms. I saw my father in the kitchen making fish soup. When I knew him in real life, in the past of that real life, my father did in fact know how to cook a delicious fish soup. It was a bouillabaisse; he was really good at making it. I stared at him the way we study someone who seems familiar. He looked up at me a few seconds, then went back to preparing the soup. Light was flooding in through the large windows of that strange house where my parents now lived. I wasn't sure whether he'd seen me. It was as if I were a shadow—and I'm alive. And as if he were real—when he's dead. I went over and saw he was putting a lot of care into preparing the soup. I was fascinated by how meticulously he was cooking it, as if he'd finally become one of those TV chefs whose programs he so enjoyed.

I noticed that my father, in the future, was hardworking, just as he had been in the past, but in the future his hard work was free of desperation and worry—that was the difference, which stunned and delighted me.

I came across another room, a bedroom. I expected to find my parents' bedroom, with a double bed; instead, there were several twin beds. My mother appeared on the scene and she had other children, but I didn't feel hurt. I couldn't see the faces of those other children, those people, those siblings who inhabited that decaying future. Nor could I see my mother clearly, but her presence was stable, as if it were diffused throughout the room, her spirit scattered or dispersed in the air. I couldn't grasp the room's size, though I could visualize the beds clearly. A lot of people were living there. Why were so many people living at my parents' house in the future when only my brother and I lived in my parents' house in the past?

It was a dream, yes, but it wasn't entirely a dream. It was a balm, a consolation, because our minds are wise, as if inside our minds there were somebody greater than us; I've sometimes had the sense that there was another person behind me, another person who will leave me on the day I die. I've thought about that person many times and even given him a name: "the engine driver."

They're dreams that seek absolution, so your body can stay alive feeling cleansed of guilt. The engine driver knows I feel guilty—he knows my unconscious condemns me for not having been around when they got old, for having moved away from Barbastro, so he presents me with merciful dreams in which my parents are still alive and I do not exist. My own nonexistence in that dream was a symbol of my condemnation, but I enjoy not existing; when I go to be judged, my fondness for nonexistence is going to exasperate the judges tasked with condemning me, as condemnation is the inevitable product of any judgment with a pedigree. Absolution is insubstantial and forgettable.

We remember only condemnation.

Absolution has no memory—that's how we human beings are.

Still, my guilt is problematic. That is the great hole in all the lives of humans who dwelled in the borderlands, those of us who hovered between good and evil.

I awoke with a sense of euphoria. I was grateful for having seen my parents again, but I saw them in a time to come, in the future, a future without me. I'd seen an illusory axis of time, an alternative plane, where my parents had started another family, to which I did not belong, in which I did not exist.

I didn't feel excluded; I didn't feel bad.

It all struck me as an inexpressible tenderness, as if I were witnessing a second chance at everything; they seemed happy, my parents did, with their other children, and I wasn't there—my absence improved my parents' lives and that made me happy. I wasn't afraid of disappearing.

I wasn't afraid of disappearing, not even deep down.

If I'd been a bad son, that stain was erased forever.

Was I a bad son?

If I was, it was out of incompetence, not intention.

A man can be an incompetent son.

Nobody is prepared to be a father, or to be a son.

I could have done more recently, of course. My sons will eventually pay me with the same coin, so my debt will be settled. Nobody owes anything here. No debts—they'll be paid with my own oblivion.

As the dream faded, I started remembering what my parents'

bedroom was like in the past—that is, the bedroom where I actually was in reality.

I will never see that bedroom again. I should list all of my parents' things that I will never see again.

I remember I felt great joy contemplating the real bedroom that existed in the past.

So, I'd seen my parents living in the future in a dream.

What will my death be like in three thousand years? The dead continue to exist, transform, endure.

The death of a human being comes and goes in time. All dead people come and go. They do different things from what they did when they were alive.

Inside death there is still a bustle of activity.

105

I was six years old and used to go to my parents' bedroom. I thought it was a spaceship. I repeat to myself once more, like a kind of psalmody, that it is completely impossible that I will ever see that bedroom again: the pale painted walls, the curtains, the bed and linens, the nightstand, an armchair, a lamp, an armoire. I see my memory while my memory sees the past.

The present that every human being inhabits turns the past into an enigma; the present is not a mystery, but as it turns into past, it will be invaded by enigma; that's why I examine the present with a magnifying glass, under a microscope, trying to see how that transformation takes place: finishing a Sunday meal with Brah and Valdi, for example, makes me want to know how my sons will remember that meal thirty years from now. And so that meal lets me see its mysteries, its spiritual apoplexy, its yellow pancreas. How will they remember these Sunday meals when I am dead, transformed into distance?

The past is furniture, hallways, houses, apartments, kitchens, beds, rugs, shirts. Shirts once worn by the dead. And afternoons—it's afternoons, especially Sunday afternoons, that produce a lull in human activity; and elemental nature returns to our eyes, and we see the air, the breeze, the empty hours.

Death thwarts the persistence of aging, and though it may seem like a foolish notion since the fantasy that a dead person can keep celebrating birthdays is absurd, the living tally up the anniversaries of the dead as if they were merely absent, so the bonds tighten and the accounting between living and dead intersects in bizarre ways, because death has no content and life without death has no end.

But I was talking about the inglorious dead, the dead who in life were not renowned or distinguished people.

Death gives an unexpected meaning to any human's life. Any new development is irrevocably halted. Any possibility of movement is shut down. Death rewards those who failed in life, those who did not feature on the front pages of newspapers, on the TV news, in photos, in iconographic fame and celebrity.

Those who were celebrated and famous in life are punished in death by outdated photos and moving images, which they can no longer escape—they are trapped inside them.

They are trapped inside the lives they led.

The anonymous dead elude the mockery of the passage of time. They were not the subject of well-remembered photographs.

They're nobody; they're wind, and the wind doesn't make a fool of itself.

Don't ever let anyone take your photo.

106

The light spills in through the windows of my apartment on Avenida de Ranillas, number 16, staircase 1, fifth floor, *B* for *Barcelona*. Inside it is the soul of my parents, who were named Bach, my father, and Wagner, my mother, since I've finally come up with names from music history for both of them. I've now turned them into music, because our deaths should be turned into music and beauty.

I managed to purchase a dishwasher; it's a no-name model, but it works. I no longer scrub dishes. It cost me two hundred fifty euros.

Mother Wagner, you never had a dishwasher. That's what the voice said when we went through your house: "Your mother didn't have a dishwasher—how is it you never bought her one?" Everybody has a dishwasher now. You could have had one since the early or mid-nineties, which is about when—I'm doing the math in my head—dishwashers became common in Spain. Of course they existed before that, I imagine starting in the late seventies or early eighties, especially in bars and restaurants, but not in people's homes. In people's homes, in the nineties. But you spent almost twenty-five years washing dishes by hand for no reason.

I remember stacks of dishes at Christmas dinners, which you washed alone; I'm seeing those dishes now, when it's too late, or the platters with bits of cannelloni stuck to them, which you had to scrub hard with the scouring pad to loosen; and those cannelloni that Johann Sebastian loved so much; and there were lots of dishes and recipes that disappeared with you; and the joy of those meals vanished too; I remember we never helped you wash, at most dried the dishes, we didn't help you at all.

We would keep sitting at the table, as if we were dukes. And now I know what that means.

Now that I'm alone, I know what it means to have a spick-and-span kitchen: it's an exhausting job, it's an art, it's something that never ends, because a kitchen is never completely clean.

You can spend your whole life keeping your kitchen clean—that's how it was for a lot of women. They lived in the kitchen; that's why I look at my kitchen on Ranillas and use it to communicate with Wagner, my mother.

If I touch my kitchen, I touch my mother's soul. If I touch all the kitchens on earth, I touch the bondage of millions of women, whose names were erased and are now music. The music of my stupefied heart.

107

I do my grocery shopping at the chain called Dia. There's a Dia next to my place on Ranillas.

I go in and it's full of people, people living in catastrophe, heirs to crisis and unemployment and nothingness. Hey, friends, buy house-brand yogurts, they don't taste the same as Danone, but they're way cheaper. I like shopping at Dia: everything is cheap and simple and obvious and edible, like my passage through this world. Everything is cheap because it's all about to expire. If you check the expiration date on what you're buying, you're surprised to discover that a lot of the products are as cheap as they are because they're almost expired. The cookies are almost expired, the fish is almost expired—that's why they lower the prices, because the products are practically corpselike. Expired cookies are like a corpse. It's unsettling to eat expired foods—it's like tossing yourself into the crematorium of the food industry. The workers who were supposed to keep an eye on the expiration dates expired too. People expire. Dying is expiring—by which I mean we've extended the concept of ending to everything around us. And ultimately the measure or transcendence of our death is not so far off from the measure and transcendence of an expired yogurt.

The expiration date is a funeral date.

Still, the dead don't expire—but the living do. Death is the place where expiration no longer makes a difference.

A one-liter bottle of Coke Zero is worth one euro: a symbolic equity that ties the measure of liquid units to monetary units. The people who shop at the Dia in my neighborhood at eleven a.m. or noon are the unemployed, the elderly, housewives, and the crazy or sick. Old women who carry the exact change in their hands and buy a can of orange soda and a bag of candy, and drop the coins on the counter, and the cashier has to count the dirty coins, damp with the sweat of the demented old lady, who's wearing a diaper and smells to high heaven. If that old woman were speaking English, we'd get to enjoy a scene of American realism, full of steely poetry, but in Spain, and in Spanish, and in a Zaragozan accent no less, we end up without steely poetry, without transcendence, without epic, without anything at all; we are left merely with the exoticism of the inferior bloodlines. But that doesn't matter. The most unsettling aspect is my tendency to relate to misfortune—not to alleviate it, but to make it mine, to place it in my heart. I place the old woman in my heart, and I love her. And I think about how that eighty-something-year-old woman was once a little girl beside a young mother. I think about that with all my might.

I've been alone all week, in my apartment.

Short trips to the kitchen, the bedroom, the bathroom, strolls around the room I'm writing in, flipping on the TV. Staring at the kitchen, the dishes, the cutlery, the coffee maker. Staring at the unmade bed in the bedroom. Looking at my calendar. Lying on the sofa. I become one with my sadness as if it issued from somebody else—that's another thing that unsettles me, crushes me, because I feel like I'm going crazy.

It's a union with everything that's gone wrong—that's what I become one with, with all misfortune, all suffering. But still I am able to become one with something infinitely superior to misfortune: I become one with the emptiness of men, of women, of trees, of streets, of dogs, of birds, of cars, of streetlamps.

108

In the wee hours I look out at the avenue and cars are no longer going by. Everybody is asleep. I have no schedule—I can go to bed whenever I feel like it, I can stay up all night, I can look out at the avenue at three in the morning; I can, if I want, go out walking along the Ebro in below-freezing temperatures at four in the morning, but I never do, because I think somebody might see me, and that thought scares me. I could walk along the river at five in the morning, but I'm afraid that might upset me, shatter my nerves. I could gaze at the waters of the Ebro at six in the morning, when the impending dawn is palpable.

No cars are traveling down Avenida de Ranillas, Actur neighborhood, city of Zaragoza, northern Spain.

People are asleep, but not me.

I want to leave.

I've bought a new mop.

I love mopping, in particular that moment when the floor suddenly gleams, and you score a victory, a triumph over filth and dirt. You achieve a purification. I mop the floor as if I were purifying souls. If only I could wash my internal organs: take out my stomach and wash it, take out my guts and wash them.

Yes, I want to get out of here.

I'll be in Madrid for a few days, and I'm looking forward to that.

I like Madrid. It's full of millions of streets and bypasses and highways and neighborhoods I don't know. I have to go to bed now. I put off going to bed too long. Years ago I had a friend in my hometown, Barbastro, who didn't go to bed until five or six in the morning.

I could call him Giuseppe Verdi.

He was twice my age—actually almost three times. He would spend his nights watching movies, immersed in an indescribable happiness, immersed in an exaltation of his private pleasures that fascinated me; I remember him in this moment, remember his long winter nights in Barbastro in the seventies and eighties, nights that Verdi spent reading and, once videos became available, watching movies till dawn. How I'd love to see him again and tell him I always admired him and that he is in my heart, that

I carry him in my heart. Actually, he was a friend of my father's, a borrowed friend, an assigned instructor. A friend of my father's who ended up being my friend too.

He was a free man, one who lived for tranquil pleasures. My father appreciated and loved him, though they were very different. I found it surprising that my father and I had a friend in common. Once, when I was a boy, Verdi gave me an envelope that contained a hundred fifty pesetas. We never talked about it in the years after, when I grew up and we became fast friends. I never told Verdi how that time when I was a kid and he gave me that gift, that abstract gift, it threw me off balance because I think it was the first time anybody gave me money. Verdi was unmarried, and he died very alone and far too soon. He had an unhappy death, or at least I didn't like the way he died. He ended up running out of reasons to live. An unmarried person's time is short. When the body loses its youth and its faculties, unmarried people are abandoned. Especially men. And especially that generation of men who were not trained in domestic life, men who didn't even know how to make a bed. Ultimately they were the victims of an upbringing that had, in theory, been preparing them for a life of privilege.

My friendship with Verdi was special because it was built on Verdi's friendship with my father; it was as if our friendship had a guarantee, a fail-safe, an indisputable collateral, and I felt secure.

I spent hundreds of hours talking to Verdi when I was sixteen or seventeen. I didn't have any friends my age, just Verdi. Later, over time, once I left for Zaragoza, we grew apart, and in the end Verdi died. And as usual, I didn't go to his funeral. I've never gone to the funerals of the people I cared about, though maybe I've never cared about anybody in this life. I can't dismiss that possibility.

Verdi is fading in my memory now. He's become as anonymous as death. There are no photos of him on the internet. I did a couple of Google searches—not a trace. Nothing. There are still a couple of entries for my father.

Bach, two entries on the internet.

Verdi, zero.

Verdi's death had a big impact on me—I didn't understand his death. I've never understood anybody's death. Verdi seemed so sure of life; he was so fiercely alive that his death turned him into a fake, a traitor in my eyes. I say this not to criticize him but to laud him. If only I could blot out the disparity between being alive and being dead, their instability and disproportionality. That is the issue: the senseless, guilty shift that goes from living movement to rigor mortis. I am flagellating my soul because I do not understand the cunning movement that goes from that which stirs and speaks to that which is immobile and mute.

If you had met Verdi, you'd understand. His death actually ends up revealing the empty fist of God smiting things. Nobody remembers him in Barbastro now. Johann Sebastian sometimes used to invite him to eat at our house.

And Wagner would make cannelloni.

There was peace and affection at those meals. Barbastro was a radiant town because of the humans who lived there, especially during the 1960s and 1970s. They were extraordinarily luminous men and women.

I talked to Verdi for hundreds of hours. We used to watch movies together. When that was happening, neither of us suspected this future from which I am writing.

If we had, we would have shot ourselves or overthrown a government—not just one, every government on earth.

Verdi was a great man, and he was happy. And the times we spent together will never come back—that's my problem. It was the seventies, when life moved more slowly so you could actually see it. The summers were endless, the evenings infinite, and the rivers unpolluted.

June would arrive in Barbastro like a god illuminating people's lives.

It was paradise. It was my paradise. They were my paradise, my father and my mother—how I loved them, how happy we were together, and how brutally we fell apart. How beautiful our life was together, and now it has all been lost. And it seems impossible.

109

I never see anybody, I never meet up with anybody for lunch or dinner, not even for coffee, when I'm here in this city, in my apartment on Ranillas. It's as if I were trying to devote myself to myself, as part of an urgent need, the need for myself, which is also their need, that of my loved ones. Who are my loved ones? There's no such thing as life's complexity—that's a trick, mere vanity. Only loved ones exist. Only love.

I don't want to meet up with anybody, because I'm with myself; I've met up with myself, my own company keeps me very busy. I'm addicted to my own company.

I see only my children, and they don't see me. I see people who don't see me. I see a photo of a little boy with half of his father's

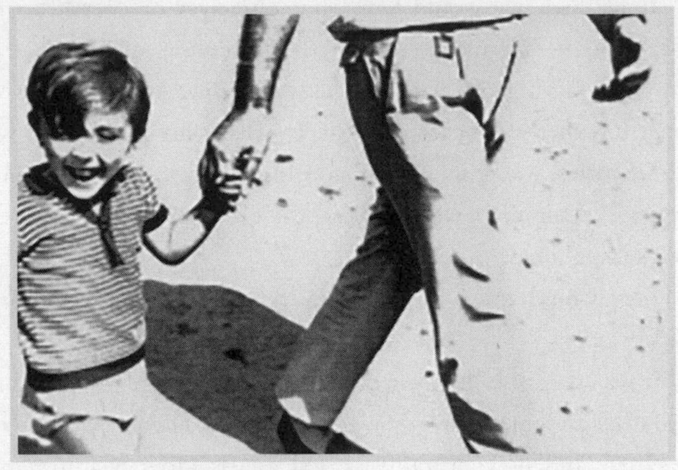

body. It's Johann Sebastian Bach and me. My open mouth and Johann Sebastian's key chain, and his shoes. I remember I liked that polo shirt—I was a flirt from a young age. I'm still in this world, but Bach left. He was already leaving when somebody took this odd and at the same time joyous photo. And allegorized that departure by visually eliminating half of his body.

Millions of fathers and sons parade through the streets of thousands of cities on the earth—it's the great parade.

The clouds muffle your passage toward complete oblivion.

110

My apartment on Ranillas is the palace of a sun king—it revels in amazement at the existence of the sun. Never in my life have I contemplated the sun in all its grandeur the way I do on these Ranillas mornings. I've pondered this because it's not just sun I see.

It's light in a communicative state, light as if made of words.

There must have been, I intuit, a cult to the sun in these lands before the Romans came, people who had the same sense as me: that the sun was coming for them.

The sun comes to see me.

And the sun is generous.

It provides you what you ask of it.

The sun's visit—the sun decides to visit some human beings, and it bares itself to them, shows them what light is. Light and the sun are a family, and their child is heat.

The friendship of the sun.

I ask the sun for my dead, that it illuminate their bodies again, and it does. The sun is God. The cult of the sun is my cult. Worship of the sun is worship of the visible. And the visible is life. If we are alive, it is because the sun floods our bodies with light, and only in light are we real and are we substantial.

The dizzying light bends into my bedroom, which has a simple bathroom. I take a shower. I've got shampoo and conditioner.

The effort of showering, that's what I think about; with the passing years, the body's effort to continue receiving the water, the awareness of everything in the damp of the shower, consuming water to wash a body that no longer deserves anything—but no body deserves anything.

There's a small room set aside for Brahms and Vivaldi, but they never sleep there. It's lovely, this little bedroom where they never sleep, where no musical genius ever sleeps. I go in and it's empty, and that emptiness seems like a being, a brother.

Empty brother. Invisible music. Light is powerful, it is will. It gives visibility to the human emptiness of this room and turns that emptiness into a black tear shed for my sons who are not here.

Brah and Valdi are exiting my life because they've gotten older, because I don't see much of them, because human beings get distracted. We get distracted.

All of this is untainted. You end up falling in love with light, just light, with the fact that light exists even if it no longer pours down on a loved one. That's the kind of light that enters my apartment on Ranillas.

I never thought I would be granted the contemplation of light.

The death of all humans is contained within that light.

111

My refrigerator is very small, but it's better that way. I don't throw anything away. I don't throw food away. Bach taught me not to throw food away. It was his most fervent political conviction: Never throw food away. And I inherited that concern. Bach used to talk about a war—that's why you shouldn't waste food. Bach was in that war, he was a little boy in that war, he'd just turned six when it started. Occasionally he'd tell me things, but not many—maybe he was interested in that war not as a historical event, but as something that simply happened.

I hang up the clean laundry to dry and then don't take it down, don't put it away in the armoire. I leave it on the rack for weeks, inside the house. I like seeing it hanging there, like those criminals who were gibbeted, strung up and left to rot, in the Middle Ages.

I tidy and clean my apartment with an adolescent moodiness

that I refuse to understand, especially at over fifty. I mop the kitchen and run the dishwasher, which is called OK. That's the brand.

It's a good name: OK.

Yesterday I was in a shopping center looking at other appliances from this unknown brand. They're the cheapest ones on the market, and they do the same thing as the most expensive ones on the market—that should pique people's interest. A two-hundred-euro OK does the same job as a twelve-hundred-euro AEG.

I weigh myself almost every day—I have a good scale, very precise. For twenty euros you can buy an excellent scale.

A scale measures the accumulation of fat in the belly, torso, face, hands, veins.

Colon cancer transformed my father into a very skinny man—it showed us his essence.

He was scared of his essence.

By the end, Bach weighed one hundred fifty-five pounds. And he was five feet, eleven inches. In the good old days, he weighed as much as two hundred.

In those final weeks, he weighed less than one fifty-five.

He got down to one forty.

I wanted to weigh him, but I didn't have anyone I could ask. I almost took my scale to the hospital to weigh him. Because of the cancer, he ended up weighing the same as he did at sixteen years old. He was moving backward in time.

He was going back to the year 1946. I looked at his emaciated frame and prayed to the fates that his thoughts and his hopes and his desires might also be those from 1946.

The devastation of illness guides you back to the origin; it sends you traveling to your adolescence.

112

Today I'll be driving to Madrid.

I like driving in my car. Stopping at bars and restaurants along the highway, where everybody is nobody. There are waiters with hazy lives—focus on them.

Yes, focus on them.

I usually stop at a roadside restaurant that has a decent set menu for eight euros. I'm waited on by an obese server. I always wonder how he makes it through eight hours of work with that load.

Another person who needs a scale.

Four skyscrapers are visible long before you get to Madrid. It's still more than forty miles to the Spanish capital, but the towers are already on the horizon. There are only four skyscrapers in Madrid—not many at all. The main beneficiaries of the proliferation of skyscrapers in cities are not the wealthy, as a large part of Spain's traditionalist left innocently believes, but the working class: the complexity of capitalism is the complexity of the universe.

We think we know a lot about capitalism, but we don't know anything. Capitalism is built on the multiplicity of our coveting. Human coveting is relentless. We've been describing our coveting for centuries, and we never manage to get a handle on it. Primeval capitalism ends up being a form of communism.

Our hearts are covetous. People want to have large apartments in the best cities, and they want second homes at the seaside, and they want full lives, and capitalism embraces us. It embraces leftists and conservatives, and they are thus united in covetousness, which drives the world forward and drives this book forward.

The R-2 is a ghost freeway; there are hardly ever any cars on it. There's no traffic because it's a toll road. It was built to ease congestion on the way into Madrid.

The R-2 is gorgeous because its solitude bears down on you; it is surrounded by desert and nameless, hopeless lands. People opt not to pay for the R-2—they take the regular highway instead, which is slow and full of on-ramps and off-ramps from secondary roads and full of speed limit signs. I hate the ones that say 80 kilometers an hour. A circle and the number 80 inside it. Or even worse: 60, because the monopoly on speed belongs to the state—which is to say, the king of Spain, which is to say, Beethoven.

In this book, Felipe VI could well be Beethoven, the king of music history. The Spanish monarchy, and Francoism before it, regulated my parents' lives and they responded with frugal indifference, with an indifference born of nature: nature in the face of history.

Spain never gave my parents anything. Not monarchist Spain or Francoist Spain.

Not a thing.

At least they were young under Franco—at least there's that. I don't like what Spain did to my parents. Spanish conservatism, always there, immovable.

More everlasting than the Burgos cathedral.

I don't like what Spain did to my parents, nor what it's doing to me. I can't do anything about my parents' alienation now—it can't be helped. All I can do is make sure it doesn't take hold of me, but it's already almost taken hold. I hope it doesn't take hold in Brah and Valdi, but it will take hold in them too. An alienation that, because my parents experienced it, becomes one with me and I end up embracing it, and I want to take off with it, in love with it.

Fall in love with the one who humiliates you.

Touching that alienation, I touch them. Their lives. Their sweet lives.

The people working the tollbooths on the R-2—who are they? Musicians from the orchestra of some small city in the former Soviet Union. I like it when our hands touch as I pay, touching human flesh. The R-2 is pretty cheap; it costs six euros, and it's not so long anyway. I'd like to work in one of those little booths. Live an honorable life like the people who grow old inside them. The R-2 workers build a whole world in those booths: they've got their Coca-Cola, their space heater, their cell phone, their sandwich, their comfy clothes. They're good people. Unpretentious. They've got husbands or wives and kids waiting for them when they get off work.

To have somebody waiting for you somewhere is the only meaning in life, the only success.

Since I've stopped drinking, everyone seems like a good person.

Since I've stopped drinking, I am stripped of pretensions.

One of these days, Beethoven will lose political control and the Republic will return to Spain, because Spain is a nation of contrasts—it's unpredictable. And every forty or fifty years Spain splits up with itself.

One of these days the lead story on the evening news will be Beethoven's head on a pike.

Watch out, my friend—even if you're the composer of the Ninth Symphony, nothing is safe in Spain.

113

I'm forced to survive in a world that requires a person to know how to do something, when I don't know how to do anything. I imagine you didn't know how to do anything either, Dad. But I think we have our reasons. When Brah and Valdi use the same word to name me that I used to name you, I see the solution to the origin of life—the problem that has vexed science forever. If we look at Christianity another way, a way that's simpler and more fundamental, not religious or solemn, we see the innocent relationship between a father and a son.

Our complete inability to attain a place in this world, Dad, to earn money, to have people take notice of us, is a kind of goodness.

You didn't want anything, and I didn't either.

When you were almost out of work, in the mid-seventies, I remember that a friend of yours who ran a bank said you deserved a good job like his. And he put you forward as a potential hire.

I was just a kid at the time, but when I heard the story that you were going to work at a bank, I knew immediately that it would never happen.

It would have been the solution to our problems.

People saw you looking so dapper, with your suit, your tie, your manners, your style, that they immediately wanted to do something for you.

You were Johann Sebastian Bach, a giant of music.

But that didn't work out for you.

Mom fantasized that you'd end up being named head of a bank.

"You're really good at dealing with people, and that's essential for being a director. You carry yourself well. I'm going to talk to the regional director right now," your friend said, downing another glass of anisette.

Maybe he did talk to somebody, sure. But I knew it was never going to happen. I was just a kid, but I had insights into the world of adults.

The notion that you were going to be named bank director stuck around for a few months of unfounded familial euphoria. You weren't named director of anything. I was never named director of anything either. That was in 1974 or 1975. The expectation that you would become bank director suffused our home, and Wagner was already wanting to buy new furniture, a new car. Wagner would have been so happy if we'd had more money. May God deliver a large helping of misery to all those cheesy people who say money doesn't buy happiness.

Up until four days ago, I thought the Spain I was born into was better than yours, but now I no longer believe history progresses all that much. Sure, we've got computers and cell phones, but Brah and Valdi hardly ever answer, and when they do we talk for thirty seconds or even less.

You grew old in a Spanish labyrinth identical to the Spanish labyrinth I'm growing old in. The values are the same. We've also added something that inhered in you and was passed down to me, something like a demoralizing diffidence when it comes to finding a place in the world, when it comes to saying, "Here I am."

The year 1980 is exactly the same as the year 2015.

Everybody wants to achieve—that's the same. Success and

money—they're the same. In the end, you spent your time watching TV. I spend mine surfing the internet, which is the same.

Our ways of sleeping and dying evolve technologically.

Neither of us had access to happiness—there was and is some phenomenon that distorts everything; of course, that inaccessibility proceeded and proceeds from a kind of sympathy with the world, with all the poor and wretched of the earth. That's why we could not, why I cannot, be happy. It would require abandoning our courtesy toward all the misfortunes on this planet and in the universe.

Have you ever noticed, Dad, the immense ruin of the universe, that loneliness as vast as our human dead, and the light you have become?

It's no coincidence that in my imagination you have assumed the mythical name of Johann Sebastian Bach, because that's the music that sketches you there among the heavenly bodies. Because you were a spirit, you started a family; and family is the presence of the immovable. You were God, music of God. You were the music of that which endures. Every man and woman wants to start a family.

It's what human beings do.

114

It's summer, and I'm at Ranillas, and bugs are drawn to the light of the computer. No matter how many I kill, I can't finish them off. They are coming for the light of my lamp, which illuminates my writing. They are disgusting creatures. Comical. When I smash them on the table, they leave a sticky but insignificant residue. They're just dirt with tiny wings. They have the great fortune that their existence is neither life nor death, but instead something that appears to be simply automatic. They flit around like dust motes with wings. None of them are alike. I look at the carcasses. Some are green, others brown, others almost black. Different sizes.

They have no family.

They aren't a family. Family is a kind of wealth. Spain is a finite set of families, and France too. None of the insects I murder is sibling to another. They are not husbands or wives, not children or parents.

They have no social structure.

They're just flying shit.

115

My apartment on Ranillas is full of dust. The grime is neverending. Valdi complains there's no overhead light. Valdi comes by when he feels like it. He doesn't smile. The great composers of music history don't smile. This is a disaster. But the disaster is taking place only inside me. Valdi doesn't see it, because teenagers don't see anybody, not even themselves. They have a good relationship with life, actually. They don't even realize they're alive; they're being carried along.

I found out a couple of days ago that the city government changed the name of my street—it's no longer Avenida de Ranillas.

Is that you, Johann Sebastian, sending me a message from among the dead? Does this change mean I need to leave Zaragoza for good? Your second surname was Arnillas. That's why I came to live on this street, because it was your name with two letters switched around. I think you're trying to tell me something.

When I learned about the name change, I felt powerless. I cursed whoever had made that decision. I could have beaten him to death—it was an insult to my father. I flopped onto the bed on Ranillas and tried to weep with rage, but I couldn't squeeze out a single tear—it's an inability to cry that destroys men over fifty. We can't cry anymore, we're deficient in potassium and manganese, the tear ducts are parched. Instead of crying, we drown in grief. The name of my street had been changed, your last name, and you yourself were fading once more.

You weren't sending me a message. They'd just changed a street name, the same way they change sidewalks, streetlights, buses, benches, statues.

There was never any message.

It was all happening inside my head.

Only in my head.

116

I have to put my tongue between my teeth to keep them from grinding together. My tongue between my upper jaw and my lower jaw. I went to the dentist because one of my molars was aching.

"It's not a cavity," the dentist said, "it's trauma. You have to make sure not to clench your teeth. It's nerves—it's a psychological issue, stress, anxiety. It probably happens when you're asleep. You grind your jaws against each other."

He made a face. Clenched his teeth.

So I put my tongue between my teeth. I paid the dentist two hundred euros.

Two hundred euros' worth of nerves. I focus too much on money for the simple reason that I don't have much of it. I wonder whether I'd focus on it so much if I had a lot. In any case, people internalize the idea of the value of money without realizing that money ends up being destructive or turning you into a crazy person. We all fall into the money trap. And we all end up seeing money as the definitive and accurate way to measure things. It's like the ultimate step toward objectivity. Money comes from our zeal for objectivity. Zeal for knowing for certain. Money is solidity; losing it drives us nuts; not earning it makes us morons; money is supreme truthfulness, and it's where our species attains its greatest weightiness, its gravity.

"I don't know, maybe it's a hidden cavity," I said.

"Not a chance, I would have spotted it. There's no cavity," the dentist said.

I go back to my apartment on Ranillas, which isn't called that anymore, and see a TV report about political corruption. A list of accusations directed at politicians: lying, fraud, bribery, money laundering, influence peddling, misappropriation of public funds, membership in criminal organizations, and so on.

Spanish politicians are sinking, becoming victims of absurdity—all they care about is buying themselves houses and cars and luxury trips and rooms in six-star hotels. They're full of emptiness.

They're obsessed with wealth, the accumulation of wealth. It's impossible for them to spend all the money they're accumulating. But that makes no difference—it's the accumulation itself they're after. They like sitting in armchairs and watching their bank accounts swell, mainly in Switzerland, which is what El Dorado is called these days.

It's an arithmetic enjoyment, the pleasure of doing mathematical operations. And as such it resembles a childish game of addition and subtraction. It's a battle against boredom: you've got to do something in life, something measurable. They don't notice that they're stealing. And then they're found out and end up ensnared in lengthy trials from which they tend to emerge relatively unscathed, even if their reputations are in the toilet. They're oblivious to their crimes, and that may be the most interesting aspect, that annihilation of insight, where reaching an elevated position in the social hierarchy inevitably also means becoming exempt from other people's judgment, the covering over of all mirrors, the gift of impunity and silence.

And suddenly the silence is broken and the mirror is laid bare, and they're accused of corruption, and in that accusation they see only injustice and ingratitude.

You hear the way their flesh is rotting. You sense how they will be transformed into cornered, broken, furious creatures once they end up in prison—though they're never there for long, maybe a few days or a few months. Never very long, and then everything is forgotten. Forgetting works in favor of all human actions, good and bad alike.

Spanish political corruption makes me forget the corruption of my parents' flesh and my own.

There's a social function to political corruption, a cathartic function, which ought to count as a mitigating factor. People forget about their own miseries when they see an accused politician on TV. Politicians' corruption distracts us from our own moral corruptions.

On the daily news, I see one of those politicians leaving prison, and his daughters are there to meet him.

Full of hope, his daughters have gone to meet him. Despite everything, his daughters are there. They love him all the same—he's their father. Nothing and nobody can destroy that. There's somebody waiting for him. They won't rebuke him. They won't frown. They won't say, "We came because we had no choice." They won't complain. They'll give him two kisses in greeting and smile. I envy that man. Nobody would wait for me.

My mother took me to the dentist when I was a kid: my canine was emerging above my first premolar; the canine had no space, it was perched on top of the premolar. The dentist gave me a retainer and said if I didn't wear it, I'd look like Count Dracula when I was older. My father never went to the dentist. My father had a gold tooth. He got it when he was young.

I had forgotten about my father's gold tooth. When I was a kid, my father's mouth was full of light because of that tooth, which seemed mysterious to me and even a little scary. To little-boy me, my father was the man with the golden smile. My father's luminous mouth was an enigma that accentuated his heroic, supernatural origins.

When my father's body was cremated, did the gold tooth melt? At what temperature does gold melt? Should I check that out on Wikipedia, and what would I gain from finding the answer? Did the medical examiner who performed the autopsy on my father remove his pacemaker but keep the tooth for himself? Did he resell it afterward, and how much did he get? Did he offer a package deal: Gold tooth and pacemaker? Gold and heart?

My father had a golden heart.

117

I'm on a train and I have just opened my bag to see what's inside. I have a toiletry kit, a comb, and some keys. I remember how my father's kit aged. It never occurred to me to give him a new one during those last years. He carried a battered kit, practically falling apart, with his things inside it, with his mystery. It was an older style of toiletry kit, with a compartment for a bar of soap and another for a shaving brush. Who knows how many years he'd had it—his whole life, probably. My father was loyal to objects; it was his way of being respectful toward inanimate beings. He wouldn't have been excited if I'd given him a new one. I got a whiff of what was in my travel bag: it was the smell of loneliness. I sniff my belongings to find out something more about myself and about the person who put me into the world.

Nothing outlines a human being's loneliness better than his toiletry kit. I remember my mother's handbags. How alone she must have felt in her final years. All together we build a rough road to solitude. My father used to say I was a lot like my mother. I never asked him why. What I wanted was to be like him. I think I'm not like either of them—therein lies the abyss of procreation, in the development of different selves.

No child is like anybody else, not the father or the mother, not aunts and uncles or grandparents, nobody; we never understood that.

A child is a new self.

And he is alone.

We tend to say a child is like the father, or an aunt, or a

grandmother, to avoid grappling with the unavoidable: that the child will end up being a solitary man or an equally solitary woman.

That he'll end up dying alone.

It's our way of conjuring the future.

118

It's the summer of 1970. We're at the beach, in Cambrils. Late July. I'm a little kid, fascinated by European tourism. We're staying at a hotel called the Don Juan. I'm obsessed with the cars of the Germans, the Swiss, the French. I ask my father what the letters *CH* that appear on some of the license plates mean. My father tells me, *Confédération Helvétique.* Years later I understood, when in high school I translated *Julius Caesar* and the Helvetians appeared in those pages.

Cambrils is a fishing village in the province of Tarragona. My father heard about the Don Juan from a taxi driver in Barbastro. I was afraid of that taxi driver, the perpetual cigar dangling from his mouth. He was a large man with a prominent belly and fat lips that stuck out like they'd been glued onto his face. Every time I saw him on the streets of Barbastro, I'd think, That's the man who told my father about the Don Juan hotel.

It seemed like there was a fellowship of men who traveled for a living, a sort of association in which they swapped useful information. My father was a traveling salesman and that man was a taxi driver—they did basically the same thing.

The men who traveled the Spanish highways of the 1970s founded that association.

"You can eat well for fifty pesetas here," they'd say.

"This one's a good place to sleep, clean sheets and warm rooms for sixty pesetas, and they serve a good breakfast," they'd say.

That's what I thought.

A sort of booking.com (a mutual aid society) for people who earned their living in that world.

Johann Sebastian is happy at the beach. He's made friends with the owner of a snack bar who cooks him a potato omelet at midmorning. I can see him eating that omelet, I can see him right now, forty-five years later, the yellow color of the egg mixed with the potato. There's a kindly sun beaming down on all of Spain.

My father has a SEAT 1430. It's in the shade, parked under an auspicious eucalyptus tree.

There are songs by the Dúo Dinámico playing, songs that extol the virtues of the Spanish summertime. My father is listening to them in July 1970, on a beach in Cambrils.

119

I inherited that gift from Wagner. She had it too, but she didn't cultivate it. She used to see the dead. Wagner saw the dead, but she completely ignored them. That's how she was. Possessed of a divine indifference, which refused to contemplate anything that did not serve to fulfill her desires, however marvelous it might be.

I'm in my apartment on Ranillas, pondering my few possessions: a painting, some books, the TV, the curtains, the sofa. I've been conned over and over again, because that's what life has become: one scam after another, scams that snatch away the time you've got to live.

If you get conned it's because you're alive; the day people stop conning you, it will mean not that the world has improved, but that you've croaked.

Wagner and Johann Sebastian never let themselves get conned. They got pissed. In the end, the two illustrious musicians became geezers who went against the grain: dodecaphonists, avant-garde musicians who were shocked by the prices in grocery stores, two secretive retirees who bought things on sale.

There is nobody behind these assaults on life—no businesses or corporations, not even the devil.

Nobody.

Just an enormous void, which we all serve.

Nobody is waiting for me anywhere, and that's what my life has come to: I have to learn to walk down the street, through the cities, wherever I happen to be, knowing that nobody is waiting for me at the end of the journey.

Nobody is going to be worrying about whether I make it.

You walk differently when that's the case.

You can tell by the way a person walks whether there's somebody waiting for them.

All families take their leave of this earth.

Fathers, children, grandparents—families say goodbye.

Millions of family scenes disappear in that moment. I find young fathers who step up as parents immensely moving: they adore their children, but their children will forget them.

My heart is like a black tree full of yellow birds that screech and drill my martyred flesh. I understand martyrdom: martyrdom means ripping off one's flesh to become more naked; martyrdom is a desire for catastrophic nakedness.

120

My father was an inveterate card player. For twenty years he played every day whenever he wasn't traveling. He used to smile as he headed out to his games. They started at three in the afternoon, and he always arrived right on time. We had to eat lunch at two on the dot so he could make the three o'clock game, held in a popular club in Barbastro called the Peña Taurina, which had a mounted bull's head on its main wall. As a kid I used to stare at that head with commingled fear and empathy. My father was an expert at two games; his favorite was take-two, and then tute. He used to play from three until seven in the evening. Sometimes, when I was really young, I would watch him play. He would get upset with his fellow players. He was strict and inflexible and always right. They played for coffee and a glass of cognac. A Torres 5—that was the cognac.

Cards were his paradise. He played for the pleasure of chance. Never for money.

I think playing take-two made him infinitely happy. That must have been in the summer of 1969 or 1970 or 1971. And at seven he would come home to fetch my mother and they'd go out to the bars to have something to eat and chat with people.

During that period my father's life was marked by intense happiness. I remember his shirts. I remember the key ring he carried and his watch. It was a Citizen, purchased in a watch shop called La Isla de Cuba, run by a mother and son. My parents were friends with this mother and her son. Mother and son were mysterious, as mysterious as the name of their watch shop, and I don't think they sold very many watches, though I couldn't swear to it. One day they disappeared from Barbastro, as if by magic. And their watch shop disappeared along with them, its time among the living come to an end. Now there's another business there, and there were many others before this one and after La Isla de Cuba closed, which must have been in about 1980, I figure. Businesses come and go—some last a year, others a hundred, others three months, others six years, nobody knows, and where there once was a watch shop there is now a bar or a shoe store or a bakery or just an empty storefront. I loved and respected my father's watch. It was like the watch of a god—that's where my devotion to watches came from, from the love I felt for my father's Citizen. I would see its steel chain, the face, the hands, the clasp, and it all seemed marvelous, unattainable. My father was unattainable—he always was unattainable for me.

As a boy, I could never understand why he liked take-two so much, why he spent so much time playing cards—I thought he owed me that time. He was a famous player around town. Much feared, since he always won and if he didn't win it was everybody else's fault.

It was everybody else's fault—that was a recurring theme in my childhood. In the face of any obstacle or adversity, my father would blame other people, especially my mother. I don't know where the hell that attitude came from. My father would blame my mother for any misfortune, and my mother gradually learned to manipulate the facts on her own behalf, and as a result we would all be dragged into an emotional labyrinth that led to sadness and despair.

My father used to fly into rages in his forties; the decade between forty and fifty was his furious period. After that he calmed down. He calmed down the most after seventy. Something happened to him at the casino where he used to hang out, the Peña Taurina. He must have gotten pissed off at somebody, and stopped going. Instead he started going to the small bar attached to the Argensola movie theater. That seemed like a bad sign. It was the beginning of his decline as a take-two player. In the mid-1980s he stopped playing cards and started watching TV. He never said why he stopped playing cards. Another mystery I'll never solve. They make my heart ache, these mysteries of the past that I'll never be able to figure out. It seems to me that there are wonders contained within them that will remain concealed forever.

He reigned supreme as a take-two player from 1968 to 1974. Then everything changed; the golden age ended.

He used to sit placidly, looking intently at his cards, making mathematical calculations about the game's odds, and he'd sit near the Peña Taurina's open balcony, and the June-afternoon breeze would tickle his face, the breezes of 1970, when the world was still good and there was peace in his heart and joy in mine. And he'd study his opponents' faces and analyze their weaknesses and keep an eye out for teammates' possible mistakes. He was after perfection—he was always seeking it in that thing he did well, and he did it his way.

I don't think any of the players from back then are still alive, the ones who sat and played against my father in the Peña Taurina, a casino that also held dances. There was a small stage for the band. My father would order me a Coke and I'd sit down to watch him dance with my mother and later they'd buy me a croquette, but I never liked them.

One day the Peña Taurina acquired a pinball machine. And

my father became obsessed with that machine. As did I—I would have been just eight.

It was a ritual of ours.

We'd show up at the Peña Taurina on Saturdays around noon. My father would order me a Coke and the two of us would start playing pinball.

We were very happy. My father tended to jostle the machine hard whenever he was on the controls, and that would cause the machine to short out and shut down automatically, and you'd lose the ball.

Those silvery balls—my father would yank on the controls to fire them into the highest regions of the machine, the highest regions of the world and of life, and he'd watch the ball fly up and I'd be standing on a chair because I was still really short.

Those chairs are etched in my memory. It's like I can still see them right now, 1970 chairs.

God, my father loved playing pinball. We were both enthralled by the silvery ball's descent, the colors, the lights, the sounds—waiting for it to arrive, with our finger on the button. My father loved getting an extra ball.

So did I.

We both loved playing. Whenever we spotted a pinball machine in a bar, my father and I would head inside. We'd play in silence, communicating through gestures. It was a ritual. A forty-year-old man in wordless complicity with his eight-year-old son.

I think those were the moments of greatest communion we shared, when we played pinball.

We were father and son back then, in a way we would never be again.

We played really well.

We formed a single being, fusing together.

We were love.

But we never talked about it, we never said it.

Never.

121

I'd been drinking the night before. I woke up when the telephone on my nightstand rang; I was in a bed in the Gran Hotel in Barbastro. They were calling up from reception because my cell phone was turned off. It was my brother. And it was ten in the morning on May 24, 2014, a Saturday.

"Your mom is dead."

He didn't say, "Mom is dead." And as a matter of fact I think he was quite accurate in saying "Your mom is dead" and not "Mom is dead."

What a strange family we were. I got out of bed, stunned, scared, with the aftermath of alcohol terrorizing the erratic circulation of my blood. I stood staring vaguely around the room. I got dressed and skipped breakfast. I headed to my mother's house, where my brother was.

I went into the bedroom and there she was, dead. She was in bed—she'd died in her sleep, or that's what someone said.

The collapse of a historical era. With her, everything was disappearing, including me. I saw myself saying goodbye to myself.

Exactly: the end of a historical era. Goodbye to the Renaissance or goodbye to the Baroque or goodbye to the Enlightenment or the Russian Revolution or the Civil War or the Romans or any civilization worthy of memory.

An era was ending. A queen had died.

There the queen was, her head on the pillow. She wasn't talking anymore. Her new-fledged silence seemed like a miracle.

The queen lived very much by herself, and my brother and I didn't visit much. Especially not me—I went very little. My brother went a lot more. He knew how to take care of her. That's why, in just recompense, I know my sons won't come see me either, when I become an old man, a moribund monarch whose death will also bring an entire historical era to a close.

For the past few years, my mother had slept in the bedroom that used to belong to my brother and me. I never asked her why she changed rooms. She decided not to sleep in the bedroom she'd shared with my father. I don't know why she did that. And I'll go to the grave without knowing. But there must have been a reason, and I'm sure it was an intense one.

Because my mother was intense.

Maybe my father was appearing to her at night, and my mother sensed that his apparition wouldn't visit the room that had been ours, her children's, because my father's ghost would respect that space.

That must have been the reason.

I used to hear my parents from my room when they got home late and went to bed; they used to talk before they fell asleep. I'd hear them talking through the wall—already as a child I was suffering from insomnia, a childish insomnia full of terrors and fear of the dark. I would hear the elevator, the keys in the door, I'd hear what they were chatting about before falling asleep. They were relaxed. It soothed me to hear their voices. They would talk about the people they'd been out with. They were communicating, endeavoring to become a single self—that's what they were doing.

They were striving to progress, just like every married couple that's ever been. Marriage is a mutual aid society. It is building a fortress made of kinship and economics. They used to talk about that, how they were becoming one, a patrimonial fusion. They talked tenderly, and I heard it all. They would describe and assess what they'd seen. They'd talk about what their friends had been wearing, how their friends' lives were going, and how the meal had been, whether it had been a good one, about how much each couple had owed when the check arrived, the appropriateness or inappropriateness of somebody's comment, the new car so-and-so was going to buy, what they were going to do next weekend.

They talked.

They were trying to understand and accept each other, and from that understanding and acceptance came marriage, a walking through life together.

122

In Barbastro my mother was a pioneer when it came to sunbathing. She sunbathed everywhere. She taught it. And she converted some of her female friends to that religion whose liturgy centered on a simple rite: sunbathing. When June arrived, she was already down by the river, sunbathing with her friends. She spent the entire summer sunbathing. She'd get really black, as if she were changing her race. And she liked it when people said that—"You're so black." They didn't say "You're tan"; back then, in Spain, you'd say "You're so black"—because the past, too, is a ritual of words and a way of saying them. When fear arrives, people start speaking with another accent, another pronunciation.

My nostalgia is nostalgia for a particular way of speaking Spanish. My nostalgia is nostalgia for a world without fear. My mother's friends, too, are dead or about to die. Nobody's asked me about my mother for a long time. I don't hear her name said out loud. I don't hear her voice. I don't remember her voice. If I heard her voice again, maybe then I'd believe in the beauty of the world.

Now I feel the old heat of 1969, and my mother sunbathing in the garden of the house of a friend of hers, younger than her, unmarried. Her name was Almudena, and she lived with her parents. They had a backyard with beautiful trees. There were plants and flowers. And there my mother and Almudena would sunbathe, and I'd be with them. Almudena was a teacher and graded tests while she sunbathed. That house and yard no longer exist; there was a large kitchen, and you walked out into the backyard from the kitchen, and the backyard was full of light, ample and calm, and protected by a wall—nobody could see you sunbathing. As far as I was concerned, it was paradise. My father bought me an Orbea bicycle and I learned how to balance on two wheels in that backyard. I would fall and scrape my legs. Almudena and my mother kept an eye on my progress with the Orbea. Once I crashed into a tree and broke a planter. Why do I remember that house so well? It was one story, with an old-fashioned living room, and the kitchen was large and emanated beauty and peace.

I liked Almudena because she was very beautiful—I was attracted to her and had fantasies about her. She was gorgeous. It annoyed me when she treated me like a kid or ignored me. My wee vanity felt injured. And she must have been really young back then—I figure she would have been twenty-two or twenty-three at most. My mother had younger friends, which was a bonus for me. Almudena was my math teacher—she taught me division. I had no idea what division was, I just liked looking at her. I looked at her while she taught me at the Piarist school and I looked at her while she sunbathed in a bikini with my mother. Everybody said she was very beautiful. The boys in my class would comment on it: "The teacher is so pretty." And I hid my secret, my privilege, the gift of being able to see her sunbathing almost naked. But I hated those strange mathematical operations. Division seemed impossibly complicated. There were rules, you had to learn the rules that governed the world: the rules of division, multiplication, addition, and subtraction.

Almudena's face is fixed in my memory. She doesn't age, hasn't changed at all—she remains immutable, halted in time, lit by the sun and my roaring blood.

Almudena's mother grew a lot of flowers. The three of them would start talking about flowers, and I didn't get what there was to say about flowers. But mostly what they did was smear their bodies with sun lotions, which were a new thing, very modern, and drink beer with lemon soda, and smoke. And they'd drink an entire porrón of wine and laugh and were happy. Nivea, in a round blue tub, with its cold, white cream, featured prominently in our summers. And I'd be sitting there watching the sun set over the trees and the flowers and the bicycles. The sunset may have been the only thing that mattered. It was back then that I learned to love the month of June. My mother taught me to love that month, which is special; that garden was a celebration of the month of June, because June heralds summer—it's sunny out, but the rot of summer has not yet begun. When July comes, the hemorrhage begins, still invisible. August is the month in which summer's sepsis, its wound, its laborious transit through the atmosphere, becomes visible—on men's faces, in the branches of the pitiless trees as it dies.

The death of summer is appalling. My mother saw the end of summer as a tragic event, a sacrilege. Who would dare kill summer? She hated it when unpleasant weather arrived. She believed in the sun. She was heretical, living according to the rites of the sun. She was obsessed with light and sunbathing. As she saw it, the sun and being alive were one and the same. She loved summer. She loved how it got dark late, really late. The sun's presence was the only thing she considered worthy of contemplation; though she wasn't aware of it, her love for sunshine and summer was an ancient legacy passed down from Mediterranean culture. I've never met anybody as Mediterranean as my mother. In fact, she loved the Mediterranean Sea, whereas she didn't like the Cantabrian or the Atlantic. I knew that the Mediterranean was a special sea because of my mother's love for it.

Being at the Mediterranean was her paradise.

The Mediterranean was her only homeland.

123

I go back once more to that morning, the morning of May 24, 2014. I stood staring at the room where my brother and I slept as children. With my eyes I scanned the walls and the armoire until I reached my mother's dead face. The headboard of the bed was blue. My mother had all the headboards painted blue. The armoire was blue too.

I opened the armoire and was unable to recall its interior. It had been mine during my childhood and early adolescence, but I didn't remember keeping my clothing there. From the armoire I looked at the bed again. The woman who'd been taking care of my mother had come into the room. She was a woman of about forty-five. A good woman, with a big heart, from Bulgaria. She was crying over my mother. We never really found out what her name was. Her name was Bulgarian—we called her Ani. But I don't think that was actually her name. We'd taken her Bulgarian name and Hispanicized it, and she was fine with it. She was blond, tall and stocky, with a serene, cheerful face. She still had some trouble with Spanish. My mother had loved her a lot. I was stunned to see her crying. Ani was upset, and her weeping was genuine. Why was she crying—it wasn't her mother. Why was she crying—I was the one who was supposed to cry and wasn't. Was my mother sending me a message through Ani's tears—was she reminding me that I didn't love her the way she'd wanted me to? That's what I thought. I thought my mother would keep talking to me from beyond death. I thought we would talk now in a way we hadn't before.

I envied Ani's ability to cry for somebody who wasn't her mother. I can't cry, not a single tear, but if my capacity for suffering could be measured in tears, all of Spain would be submerged and its citizens would irretrievably drown. The Iberian Peninsula would be flooded, and Madrid's four skyscrapers would be buried beneath the waters.

So, goodness did exist. There it was, telling me how far from it I dwelled.

Ani was holding my mother's hand. I stared at the two hands, one living and the other dead. And the dead hand seemed like it was now at peace, and the living hand, touching the dead hand with its goodness, assailed death. As if death didn't exist.

I looked at the room again. So my mother had died in the bedroom where her two sons grew up, where the two vital elements that shaped her existence hadn't slept for a long time. I looked at the space of that room, trying to find a door in the air. She'd had it painted blue because she thought her two sons were blue. She died in our bedroom, and there was another powerful message in that. She took shelter there, in our room, which was turning before my eyes into a sacred space, a tomb.

We were blue for many years. Until their eighteenth birthdays, children are blue. With time, though, everything turns yellow.

Blue children become yellow children.

The blue was still there. The blue came back for a few seconds and overwhelmed the color yellow. The two old beds where her children once slept looked like two boats sailing from life to death, beds that had seemed indestructible to me as a boy—and that color blue at the foot of the bed, on the legs and headboard, acquired a purity that seared my eyes.

I stared at how well painted they were. How that paint had held up for fifty years. It was strange, that endurance. There wasn't a scratch, a single tiny bare spot. Why did everything look freshly painted when those beds were half a century old?

I opened the blue armoire again, knowing it was the last time I'd open it, knowing I'd never see that armoire again. And the troops and artillery and cavalry and light of the old days came rushing out, and I saw myself choosing a shirt when I was thirteen, studying myself in the mirror, wondering whether I'd impress the girl I liked. And I looked toward where my dead mother lay and found a tempest of time and annihilation—I wasn't prepared for that contrast.

Dying is practically the least of one's worries.

It was the last time I saw you, Mom, and I knew that from then on I would be completely alone in life, the way you were, when I didn't notice or didn't want to notice.

You were leaving me just as I had left you.

I was turning into you, and in that way you would endure and conquer death.

I should have taken dozens of photos of that room. I should have photographed the whole house so nothing would ever be lost. One day I will no longer clearly remember that house where we loved one another so much, and once I can't remember it, I'll go mad. I believe in your passions. Your passions are mine now. And your passions were worth it. I wish I had those photos, though. Your passions, Mom, your obsession with life—you passed them down to me. I have them seething here in my heart.

124

The brother of my dead mother, my uncle Alberto Vidal, dies on March 11, 2014, at the age of seventy-three.

In this book, I've been calling my uncle Alberto Monteverdi.

Monteverdi had a bit of a reputation in Barbastro, our town, his and mine, though he'd been born in a much smaller one, called Ponzano, where my mother was also born, practically a village.

They're burying him there, in Ponzano. I can't go to the funeral, of course. I never go to funerals. That's been my life: avoiding funerals. And so I don't know what his grave looks like, or his niche. I don't know if there are flowers. I don't know anything.

As a teenager, back in the fifties, Monteverdi was diagnosed with tuberculosis. They sent him to a hospital in Logroño, a postwar structure. There they sawed out one of his lungs, and shipped him back to Barbastro. That's what I heard as a kid, that "they sawed out one of his lungs." The word *saw* is what I heard. A carpenter's word.

He was missing a lung.

He was the youngest of seven siblings.

My aunt Reme took him in. He lived with her and her husband for more than fifty years. It's a story of personal sacrifice, of my aunt's love for her brother. It's a story of goodness. And he experienced all of it with one lung missing, with less air in his throat, with that frailty of insufficient air within the body.

After my aunt Reme died, he lived on a couple years longer.

Living without one lung is a legendary thing, a revolutionary thing.

My mother, when I was a boy, used to leave me at my aunt Reme's house on the weekends, and there I got to know the bizarre and unpleasant personality of my uncle Alberto, the great Monteverdi. I would have been seven or eight when he threatened to stab me with a knife. It was a good knife. I can see it now, forty-five years later, with a clarity that is diabolical and yet not devoid of sweetness. I can see it right in front of my eyes, the way Michael Strogoff saw his. I can remember all the important knives in my life. That one had been sharpened so many times that the blade edge was no longer straight, it was very rusty, and the handle was cracked. It was a praiseworthy knife. We talked glowingly about how well it cut. It had been passed down by my uncle's family—it was a patrimonial knife, forged in the late nineteenth century. It was completely black, though not a dirty blackness, but an honorable, noble one. They would trace a sign of the cross on the bread and then that knife would cut it into slices, a spongy bread, with a fat crumb, a festive, late-sixties bread.

He chased me with the knife through my aunt's apartment, an apartment with a very long hallway and a window that looked out into an air shaft halfway down the hall. An apartment that whenever I remember it makes me want to cry, because I realize now that I was happy in that apartment. I could reconstruct it inch by inch. I could make a meticulous blueprint. It was charming but a little gloomy, and I loved how old it was. It was built during the Spanish Civil War, in 1937, with materials gathered from the rubble after the bombings. But previously there had been a farmhouse. The spirits of the unsaved Spanish peasantry seemed to dwell in the place—there were spirits everywhere, and those spirits seized possession of my uncle's heart.

"I'm going to cut your throat," he yelled.

It was my aunt Reme's husband who stopped my uncle Alberto. He grabbed him by the arm, twisted it, and forced him to drop the knife to the floor. I know other things happened. Madness has flourished wherever I've gone. My uncle Monteverdi was pretty nuts. And I'm pretty nuts too. I know he chased me with the knife, and he was cursing. I shit on God, he said. Johann Sebastian never cursed. Monteverdi did, often and with gusto. Johann Sebastian never did. There are two types of men: those who curse and those who don't. Those who curse are generally hopeless, and they suffer as if condemned to it. So do those who don't curse.

There are also two types of music: the kind that sings and the kind that condemns.

The same thing happens to me with Monteverdi that happens

with G., the priest who fondled me: there's a short circuit in my memory. There's a blank imposed by my will to survive. I know he tried to stab me with that knife. I don't remember exactly what set him off—I must have repeated something that someone else had said about him, something about his being helpless or useless. I said aloud cruel words I'd heard about him. Because words matter in families, unlike in society at large. And he went crazy, and he tried to kill me, when actually he should have killed one of his siblings. My uncle Mauricio, the oldest (I'll call him Handel), used to say Monteverdi was good for nothing. He expressed no compassion for him. He didn't care that he was missing a lung. There was primeval resentment and calamity in those Huesca towns.

Those towns I fell in love with.

125

Handel took his leave too, before seventy-three, I'm pretty sure—I think he was sixty-nine, suggesting that life continues to employ comedy as a medium for self-expression. I think I repeated out loud things that Handel had whispered about Monteverdi. I'd heard Handel say that Monteverdi was a disaster, something like that, and I divulged it. I had no idea what was going on. I didn't understand anything. I was the typical little kid who sticks his foot in it by uttering some family shame or secret in public. A despairing man tried to stab me with a knife.

Monteverdi didn't speak to Handel.

They didn't get along.

Monte thought Handel should have helped him out in life,

that's what a big brother is supposed to do. Handel had a tough life too—I think he had a terrible loneliness he carried around with him. I remember his mustache and his large head, perched atop a rail-thin body. He smoked a lot, three packs a day. Dark tobacco. I don't know where he came from. I think we were and are a breed close to the missing link, but there's a triumph of the life force in that too.

Handel looked like a demon, with very close-cropped hair, like a soldier, and he was an eccentric man. His favorite thing was killing wild boar. He was a consummate hunter. The two of us went hunting once. Or rather we went waiting. We had to wait for the boar to show up. When one appeared, he shot it between the eyes with a slug. He got it in the head. He had a smoke while he watched it in its death throes. He left it there for the rats to eat, because it was old, it was an old, sick boar, with tough, sinewy meat, and we took off in the car, down roads that were windy and parched and cold that November night.

And the moon up above illuminated the boar's body and Handel sank into an arid silence, and he started smoking and staring off into the distance, that distance you see in the Somontano, a mix of emptiness and a foretaste of the blackness and ugliness of the night we will all become.

I tried to turn on the car radio, but I couldn't find a station. All we heard was static.

126

Monteverdi looked like a demon too, except he let his hair grow out, and he was also an eccentric man.

The two were brothers by blood, but above all they were brothers in eccentricity: one with his hair buzzed off, the other with a mane.

Now that I remember, they both had a mustache. Handel had a tiny one, and Monteverdi's was lush.

The old Barbastro knew Monteverdi well. The new generations, though, not so much.

But the old Barbastro respected him and understood him and loved him. It understood him because, deep down, Monteverdi was a natural product of that land, those streets, those plazas, that way of being in the world.

Monteverdi talked a lot, all in a rush. He always said hi the same way: "How goes it, son?" The way he intoned the question was odd, picturesque, as if in uttering it he were revealing a secret cult of madness, of distraction. Yes, distraction was Monte's crowning feature. He'd start chattering away in disconnected sentences, sentences piled one on top of the other—it was a verbal display that contained something alien to the domain of the living. Recently I've begun talking a lot too: both of us yammering on to make sure the other person doesn't have time to judge us, to keep their thoughts occupied and prevent them from seeing us through the lens of silence and realizing that we're totally nuts and past our prime. That we've been through so much that all we have left is the tic of syllables.

The camouflage of the battered man, yes, but also the camouflage of the man in love.

A few years back I ran into him on the street and he showed me the cell phone he'd bought. We exchanged numbers.

We looked at each other's cell phones sadly.

I never called him—why would I.

His appearance was utter catastrophe: he wore old suits with flowery ties, and he smelled bad. At the end of his life, he stank. It was an innovative catastrophe, though, one with artistic intention.

You couldn't get within ten feet of him.

He never showered.

He smelled foul. Pure avant-garde art. His stench was renowned. All of Barbastro knew the trail of his nauseating odor.

He lived together peacefully with his premature stench of death.

The infernal odor of his body was his Beatrice. It was a way of distinguishing himself from other people. And it was a way of erecting a fortress around his body, an unbreachable wall behind which solitude was hermetically shielded, as a mother would protect her baby.

His solitude was his baby, his sole and beloved child.

He protected his baby with fetor, the way animals do, like skunks, whose stink can reach up to ten feet. Exactly the distance that Alberto Vidal's stench reached, ten feet. That stench also had a certain political impertinence—it was a political force, the apotheosis of the rejection of any social decorum. It was an exaltation of sterility.

He lived with his sister Reme and his brother-in-law Herminio, a good man. Anyone else would have complained.

They wouldn't have agreed to it.

Living with his wife's brother his whole life—Herminio did that.

A room set aside for Monteverdi, always.

The three of them settled down in an old house on Calle de San Hipólito. And they loved one another. Sure, they argued from time to time, but they loved one another a lot. Herminio's goodness was biblical in scale. He may have been the best man I ever knew in my life. Herminio loved my aunt Reme. He put her up on a pedestal. They were in love, and they stayed in love the whole time. I was oblivious to that miracle. I'm oblivious to all the wonderful things I saw in my family. I should have paid attention to that love. Herminio adored his wife.

Then my cousin was born. So there were four of them: a husband and a wife and a daughter and a brother-in-law, living together for decades. A mystery. Because there was beauty in that unforeseen mutuality of four human beings. If I think about it now, I can't understand it. I can't wrap my head around how two men lived together for fifty years with their only bond being by marriage. Who would Herminio be in the history of music? Pergolesi perhaps; who less than the composer of *Stabat Mater*?

My uncle Alberto's bedroom was cold and damp and always had to be aired out a lot, but it had its charm. I never set foot inside it—I wasn't allowed. I caught a glimpse sometimes when it was being aired out. There was an armoire and a simple bed. There was a table. I think the best part was the window. The square shape of the room gave it a religious heft. What I wouldn't give right now to return to that forbidden room. It must have been a room of vulnerability, in that trance in which vulnerability turns liquid and permeates the walls, the floor, the furniture, the air. That solitude must persist there, muffled within those four walls, if they still exist.

He never got a job. He never got married. He never had a girlfriend. Nobody knew him to have female friends, but he must have had them. He must have fallen in love at some point. If I knew the name of a woman he'd been in love with and if I knew she was still alive, I'd call her to talk about him. That would be a miracle.

Since he'd had tuberculosis, he always used his own plate and glass and cutlery. I was a little kid, and I would stare at his plate and his glass and his cutlery as if they were something forbidden, filthy, malign, dangerous.

I was scared of his plate.

Terrified of his glass.

They were the unknown, the abyss.

His own napkin too, always with a funereal ribbon around it.

My father used to give him his old suits.

And so there went my uncle Monteverdi, in Johann Sebastian's old suits, strolling through Barbastro. They were big on him, because Johann Sebastian was tall, but my uncle didn't care. He looked like Cantinflas. Lower-class Spaniards in suits—such a cliché. Monteverdi loved imitating the way Cantinflas talked.

After my father's death, Monteverdi kept wearing my father's oversize suits around Barbastro.

Whenever I ran into him on the street, I was reminded of my father in the seventies, because the suits were from that period, long out of style, the double-breasted suits that people wore back then and absolutely nobody wears now.

Alberto Vidal walked the length and breadth of Barbastro, garbed in a double-breasted suit à la Al Capone. He was always everywhere. Always walked, in a town where nobody walked. He seemed ubiquitous.

He invented the stroll.

My uncle Alberto Vidal had odd friends who died or disappeared or were wiped out or never existed at all. I met a few of those friends, and I would have liked to know what those friendships were like—they were so inconsistent, I think, that out of necessity they must have been pure and good, simple, elemental.

Elemental friendships—that's how I think of them. I never knew where those friends lived. I remember the face of one of them—his face was flat and wide like the cab of a Pegaso truck. Such nonexistence can't be described.

In the early eighties, my uncle Herminio scrimped and scraped and managed to purchase a small apartment in a co-op building on the edge of town. And so they moved there, now down to three again, because my cousin went off to make her own way in life. Monteverdi had his room in the new place. They gave him a small job managing the co-op apartments, and people always said how well he did his job and how happy the neighbors were.

He still wore old suits with outlandish ties, like a gangster. You can be very poor and wear a suit. A poor man with style—we had a lot of those in my family. Monteverdi extended the life of my father's suits and brought them to the brink of eternity. My father was dead, but his seventies-era suits were alive and well on the streets of Barbastro. I found that beautiful. Epic, even.

My aunt died and the two of them kept living there on their own in that apartment, two old men with no real family relationship. There they stayed, Pergolesi and Monteverdi, talking about the music of their lives, keenly feeling the absence of the link that bound them together for fifty years: my aunt Reme, whom I'd like to call Maria Callas, since unfortunately there aren't any towering women in classical music history. I think it was more than fifty years. Maybe sixty. Pergolesi and Monteverdi had a civil bond, named Maria Callas, but the source of that bond had disappeared. Somebody should write an anthropological treatise examining that kind of civil bond, where it comes from, in what dark abode of history it was forged.

And now Alberto Vidal is dead.

The great Monteverdi is dead.

Once more I remember that time he chased me through that apartment on Calle de San Hipólito, brandishing a knife to cut my throat, the throat of an eight-year-old kid, that old knife, with its wooden handle gnawed by the ghosts of war and famine.

Don't worry, Alberto Vidal, you set a trend during the seventies and eighties in Barbastro. A trend that only I noticed, but that doesn't matter.

And you will rise from among the dead.

I wish you had stabbed me in the throat with that knife. We would have ended with me in the ground and you in the garrote.

And though the laws of men condemn and denigrate those sorts of endings, they're not so bad: the grave and the severed neck.

Those are our origins, and this new historic opportunity that the modern era offers us, this opportunity to become something or somebody, this opportunity to have a job and a pension and social security—we will always fail to take advantage of it. We come from the trees, the rivers, the fields, the cliffs.

Our world has always been barns, poverty, stink, alienation, disease, catastrophe.

We are composers of the music of oblivion.

It makes no difference to us whether God exists or not.

If God or whoever offered us paradise, within four days, with you and me in there, we'd turn it into a pigsty.

And if God gets mad at us for turning his paradise into a sewer, what is he going to do? Kill us again? Send us back to hell?

Oh, believe me, Alberto Vidal, we are God's punishment. God

is back, by the way, since humanity hasn't managed to find anything better. So laugh from your grave, now that spring is coming, because you died just before spring, which is the great season of those of us who were always here, previously, long before history existed.

Laugh, Alberto Vidal, and wash your hair and dab on cologne.

Remember that you were dirty, remember you had style.

Remember you were alone—you were the man who was most alone in the universe.

As an adult, nobody loved you. Not even me, your nephew. As a boy, you were loved by Cecilia, your mother, whom you called upon unheeded. And I do see it as a supernatural experience, the experience of those who wander this world without anybody loving them. There is a tough, poisonous sort of freedom in it. There is an invocation of the power of chaotic matter, prior to the human order, because matter is alone. Having lived without having been loved is not a failure.

It is a gift.

The bloody gift.

There's more that's visible—you can see the meaning of unconstrained matter. Human beings have to seek a culmination, we need things not to happen by chance. We look for an underlying intention. We want to be here for a reason. For our lives to accomplish at least one goal. But the existence of God is as much a falsehood as the existence of goodness in humans.

Many people today think that if they've been useful and honest with their fellow humans, they've found meaning. It helps you die with a certain tranquility. But there's an emptiness there as well. Honesty, too, is an ontological fraud.

It doesn't matter if you have no idea what the word *ontological* means, because it isn't anything.

That dense emptiness is amazing. Seeing it, the way I see it. The way you saw it, Monte.

And believe me, Monteverdi, your path is the heroes' path.

"How goes it, son?"

127

In my apartment on Ranillas again. Well, the street's called José Atarés now, not Ranillas anymore, but I'll always call it that because of my father.

When I'm away, when I'm traveling, Brah and Valdi come to this apartment and use it as if it were the home of someone who's disappeared. Being disappeared isn't so bad, though.

When I'm around, they hardly ever visit.

Their lives are still marked by the disruption of divorce, the moral iconography of which requires victims and villains. They don't remember my parents, their grandparents. They don't realize that their grandparents are here in this apartment. They don't see them, but they're here. They don't know what it means to be hopeless and alone. Many people will leave this world without knowing what it means to be hopeless. Most of the people I've met in my life don't know it and never will.

In a kind of exaltation of my despair, I bought cheap frames at Fotoprix and hung them on my walls with photos of my parents and me and Brah and Valdi. It was really cheesy, but I liked it. My mother used to do the same thing. She'd buy cheap frames and put in photos of Brah and Valdi, never of herself.

Since I had more photos than I did frames, I just stuck the rest on the wall with colored tape—it didn't look bad. I was trying to build my new home. When I got divorced, I lost my home. When my parents died, I lost my home. Now I rebuild homes through the chaos of photography, papering Ranillas with photos, some of them printed out from my computer in black-and-white.

I'm going to change the locks, I tell myself in a fit of fury that fades within ten minutes. It would be a way to remind them that the house matters, that the house is alive. But I don't do it—deep down I like it that they come by, even if they do it when I'm not around.

Lonelier every day, childless too, and nothing happens. It must be the law of life. I wish I didn't care so much. If they're okay, if my sons are okay, it doesn't make a difference. Life is this dark room. It makes no difference. But it bugs me when they leave the lights on, like they did last time, because I'm the one who pays the electric bill. Me: The father who in abandoning was abandoned. The disappeared father. The father beneath the waters. I never left the lights on at my parents' house.

No, I didn't leave the lights on.

I forget it all within ten minutes.

And so it goes. Occasionally we eat together in this bare-bones apartment. Life is waiting for them, and forty years from now they'll start looking for me. I hope they find my love. If only I could protect them till the final instant of eternity. I think I can do it. I'll always be beside them. I'll always love them. Like I was always loved by my father. They will look for those twenty-minute lunches, and this apartment; they will look for my face.

And they won't find it, because I'll be dead. But I'll be watching over them all the same.

128

I brought Brah and Valdi presents from my last trip. They saw them, said they loved them, and left them behind at my place.

I've got them right here: inert, unvalued, pathetic. They symbolize the disappearance of a home. And thus, the disappearance of love. We never tell the whole truth, because if we did we'd shatter the universe, which functions on the back of what is reasonable, bearable.

What are those gifts doing on the bed in the little room where nobody ever sleeps?

I lie down on the bed in the big room. I get up from the bed and go back to the little room, and I stare at the presents I brought my sons, which are there, on top of the little bed, abandoned, the abandonment of the gifts melding with the abandonment of the little bed, their solitudes melding into a single vast solitude that splits your heart and your life in two.

I'm not sad they forgot the gifts, just surprised, maybe because I've moved beyond sadness, or traded sadness for surprise, and because I love my kids I don't care what they do with me or my gifts. But a father also has a survival instinct, because he's human. The low esteem for my gifts could even produce panic; I've felt more panic in my life than I have sadness. After all, panic comes from guilt, whereas sadness comes from itself. Which is to say, if they left the gifts behind, it's because it's my fault. Sometimes it seems to me that my guilt is vaster than the universe. It could compete in size with the abyss of the heavens. Guilt is one of the golden enigmas. Obviously I'm not talking about the guilt fostered by religion, particularly Catholicism, but about primordial guilt, guilt as a symptom of gravity and as an alliance with the earth and with existence, Kafka's guilt—that kind.

Guilt is a powerful mechanism for activating material progress and civilization because guilt creates "moral fiber," and morals and ethics are the bulwarks of reality. Without guilt, we wouldn't have computers or space flight. Without guilt, Marxism wouldn't have existed. Without guilt, our skulls would be empty. Without guilt, we'd be ants.

My mother used to give me cologne. I never forgot the bottles at her house. But deep down I didn't want her to give me anything. She was obsessed with giving me expensive colognes she couldn't afford. She was obsessed with my birthday. Maybe my sons left their gifts behind because deep down I didn't want my mother to give me anything. The more parallels I discover, the more sacred life and memory seem.

I study the photos of my parents hanging in the frames I bought at Fotoprix. They're the world's cheapest frames. Fotoprix is putting up a good fight against the prices in the Chinese-owned shops. Those shops don't have heating or air-conditioning and Fotoprix does. All the immigrants and the poor go there or to the Chinese-owned shops to buy frames to house the faces of their family members and loved ones.

The business of cheap frames for family photos is booming. When you frame your memories and your loved ones in two-euro frames, you turn your past into tenderness in miniature.

129

On Tuesday, March 24, 2015, a Germanwings jet crashed in the French Alps. A hundred fifty people died. All the world's TV networks tried to be compassionate. Nobody knew how to be compassionate on TV. Tragedies last a couple of weeks, then gradually disappear. Within a few years, these lines I'm writing now will be distant history. Maybe that's why I'm writing them, aware of the inexpressible flavor of all the things that happen to us. What perception of the end, of their bodies' destruction, did the passengers on that Germanwings flight have?

How did they die, from the impact or in the blaze afterward?

Understanding death is as necessary as presenting all the technical details that we see in the media. Nobody talks about how the body of a fourteen-year-old boy shatters when it's hurled against the sheet metal and fire and plastic and iron of an Airbus at 500 miles an hour. What is it like? Do the internal organs burn? How does the central nervous system perceive skin being seared by heat? How does a person's emotional intelligence evaluate the destruction of the body?

What is suffering; how far does it go?

There were fourteen-year-olds on board.

And what does it feel like? Yeah, how does it feel? They must have thought about their mothers three seconds before the end, and they must have actually seen them, seen them in their essence, in what they are—mothers are love. They think about their mothers and their mothers aren't thinking about them because they won't learn about the accident for a few hours still and in the moment of their children's deaths they are working or grocery shopping or talking on the phone or driving a car. Because telepathic communication is a lie, it's a fiction, that whole myth about how you can say a supernatural goodbye to your loved ones when death arrives unexpectedly, fatefully, tragically.

Love doesn't exist in nature.

Is instantaneous death a real thing? Oh, the great metaphor of instant, painless death, the kind that proponents of the death penalty are after. Know this: Instantaneous death doesn't exist. For a very simple reason: Because life is powerful, life is ever powerful and robust. Life never leaves peacefully. We always die with unspeakable, insurmountable, inhuman, indecent pain. Because life is the triumph of ancient resistance against the enemies of life.

When you're a father, like me, you're the father of all the children in the world, not just your own. That's how this fatherhood business works.

Everything else is politics.

That's how I love Brah and Valdi.

130

I buy things, things I think I need, but I return them afterward. Once I've returned them, I buy them again. I've done that with two small appliances: a scale and a toaster. The funny thing is I used the toaster. I'm alone in my apartment on Ranillas and I'm thinking about my mother. She was a chaotic shopper too—despair transferred to home appliances.

I remember once she bought an electric knife. It was when

they first came on the market, in the mid-seventies. Electric knives never caught on and they stopped making them. My mother was possessive. She didn't want me to get married. And a few months before her death, she made a fateful phone call to what was my home at the time. And I wasn't there. And my mother told the woman who today is my ex-wife but wasn't at the time, "He should have gotten back by now—he left here at five." At most, I should have been back by seven.

And it was ten at night when I walked in the door.

But the worst part was that my mother made that call right as I was going up in the elevator—I even heard the parting words in the conversation between my mother and the woman who was then my wife. If I'd arrived three minutes earlier, my mother wouldn't have set into motion what probably would have been set into motion anyway, but not right at that moment and not because of her.

Most especially, not because of her. That's the crux of it, the whole thing.

I tried to see the complex handiwork of fate there, as if events weren't governed by chance. I suppose we need to believe in magical thinking, because it is fundamentally human to imagine that intention and reason exist in events and that there is an art of fate. We don't resign ourselves to chance. We want the terrible things that happen in our lives to have a supernatural dimension. Though now, after a certain amount of time has passed, we see only an irony of fate.

On the other hand, terrible events are decisive when it comes to recounting, narrating our lives.

Without terrible events, or events, period—actions, something that happens—our life has no story or plot, and so it doesn't exist.

My mother never found out. I didn't tell her. I didn't tell her that her phone call had turned my life upside down. Her phone call exposed an infidelity. Obviously it was only a matter of time, because I was stuck in an endless series of marital infidelities, which were destroying me and drowning me in alcohol. And my marriage was dying, though I refused to accept it because I was scared, terrified of being left to fend for myself.

After my mother's call, I went down to the bar, devastated, decapitated, and ordered a gin and tonic, and by the time the second gin and tonic came, I was gradually feeling calmer. That's what alcohol does when it hits the bloodstream: everything starts to shine again. In the hands of the waitress at the bar downstairs from our old home who was serving me gin and tonics, I saw my mother's fingers. And the third gin and tonic produced in me a poisonous, unproductive joy.

I was entering the labyrinth of fate, which uses people's faces as a transfiguration of its own strength, which swaps their faces for entertainment, which scrambles reality a bit. I thought how I would never be young again. I had to leave what had up to that point been my home, because of a phone call from my mother. A furious comedy. And Brah came down to the bar and said, "Dad, I'm going to live with you," but later he changed his mind. I was touched by Brah's words. That "Dad, I'm going to live with you" is the most beautiful thing I've ever heard. I'll always remember it. It contained an infinite tenderness. I think I'll die still hearing those words, which were never followed by corresponding events, which is for the best. Events aren't clear either. The past doesn't exist, though I still recall with eyes raised to heaven the energy that the third gin and tonic delivered to my bloodstream. I see beauty everywhere now. It wasn't such a big deal anyway. It was a common story. The story of thousands of Spaniards, thousands of human beings. Though there are Spaniards (many more men than women) who decide not to get divorced so they won't lose their library, or the beach condo, or the TV set, or the clean change of clothes in the drawer, things like that. Because distress has the strangest faces you can imagine. As it happens, I did end up losing my library, and I really miss it. But they were just books. And books aren't life, only a decoration for it, and little more than that.

131

I would have liked my mother to know that she was the one who kicked off my divorce with her phone call. It's a strange enigma that she died without knowing it. As a result, she knew me in only two mental states: single, under her control; and married, under the control of another woman, who was also her. She missed the third: divorced, without control. Which is to say, without her. Whereas I was the center of her entire life, and at the same time she was the one who gave my existence bulk and heft, this third state is akin to the final truth of my existence, a state of raucous freedom, of trembling vulnerability, because I can't live without the instructive presence of that woman, who was a goddess, who generated my flesh in her womb—and she can learn about this state only as a ghost, which she's doing.

A Stone Age goddess reincarnated over and over—that was my mother.

And in the end she's no longer around. Not even her transformations live on. Maybe that's what she was doing—showing me her complete death, not just that of her body but also the death of all its ramifications, leaving me exposed to inclement freedom, thus telling me, "At last you are alone, because only my death could have given you the freedom you desired and feared so much—let's see how many years you manage to live or survive in this world without me and my metaphors, without me and my intricate bifurcations, my expansions, my perpetuations in your wife, your work, your kids, your house, your library, and the air you breathe."

Because my whole life had been an outsize image of my mother. She had reigned over me. My whole life was Freudian, matriarchal feudalism. If something went wrong when I was a child, it was my mother's fault. If something went wrong when I was forty, it was the fault of my ex-wife—my mother's proxy. Maybe that's why my adulteries and infidelities affected not my ex-wife, but my mother.

My mother ruled my life, and she ruled it well. None of it matters. The remit of my mother's rule was not my happiness but my survival. Matriarchy's remit is that the progeny endure. That was what her good rule consisted of. I could have been happy thanks to her rule but then died at forty. No, she chose to make sure my life lasted, she chose my preservation as a living self: I know this now, where I didn't before; when the phone call came, I didn't know this yet. I realized it later.

Ancient witch who pondered her son's prattling at night, who plotted against oxidation, entropy, the fraying of her son's flesh, and who destroyed her son's spirit under the sweet light of matriarchy, more ancient than Greece, more ancient than history, forged in prehistory, which was where my mother's spirit came from.

It was ironic, terribly ironic: a phone call to make sure I was all right, and it was that call that turned my life into a living hell.

She called for my own good and her call brought me ill.

If we could see each other again, what would we say? I'd have to tell her everything that's happened since she left, and I wouldn't know where to start. If she came back, I'd have to explain that her home no longer exists, and neither does her son.

132

My mother's final years were awful, but they also contained an unexpected illumination of our lives. Her final years taught me many things. And sometimes we almost managed to be together. We had the occasional moment of peace, where we could be mother and son, without any other task. Maybe we managed to be mother and son without her actually being a widow and me a man without a father. Maybe we never overcame the gravitational pull of my father's death, the darkness his departure subsumed us in. Maybe his departure weakened the bond between mother and son. Maybe he was the greatest force in our lives.

She didn't know how to be alone and used to call on the phone constantly, the way I now call Valdi and Brah, and they pay about as much attention to me as I did to her, or so it seems to me, perhaps moved by guilt or by my eagerness to receive messages from the dead.

She told me that once: "I hope your boys pay as much attention to you as you do to me." I knew what she meant, you bet I knew what she meant. She had the gift of the most secret certainties.

Well, she was right. She predicted things. That's how she was. She had the gift of divination, but she didn't care. My mother knew she was right, because she ended up knowing everything, though I don't think she was ever consciously aware that she knew everything. People strive their whole lives to manage to know something, with sacrifice and hard work, and my mother knew everything by divine whisper.

But it doesn't matter. I think I've improved the species a little. My father, for his part, never called me. My father never phoned because he was too busy watching TV, watching his moribund chefs with their recipes for cadaverous retirees, the kind of people who sit down to watch TV at ten in the morning, as I've started doing myself in recent months.

At the end of her life, nobody could stand my mother. Not even her. She would grind anything that crossed her path to bits.

The great grinder—that was her. A remarkable woman. Full of a wild love for life, too much love.

She would get mixed up.

She'd be disappointed.

She'd get her hopes up again.

And then she made that crucial call. She thought her calls were harmless. I could die laughing.

Dear Mother, with your unhealthy obsession with calling me on the phone at all hours, you wrecked or transformed my life: I'm still not sure whether it was a wrecking or a transformation, and the funny thing is that I've gradually stopped caring which it was. What would you have thought if you'd known? Maybe you did know. Maybe your hand, picking up the telephone, was compelled by an unknown power. Maybe you wanted to do that. Maybe it was your last memorable act on this earth.

My existence marches toward intrigue, which seems to have a sort of gravity. People need to realize that life contains intrigue, machinations, conspiracies. There are actions whose meaning is unknown. My mother died along with my marriage, and so the deaths of my mother and my marriage are fused into a single death. There's an intrigue there that I can ponder. There is a blind intentionality in those plots; there is manipulation and resolve.

But who is behind the scheme?

Doubtless God himself.

Who else?

Chance?

No.

Neither God nor chance.

Time is behind it.

133

My mother was a punk. She flummoxed her doctors. She used to change her birth date at will. She even changed it at the civil registry office. I have my mother's documents with altered dates. Her national ID card gives 1933 as her birth year. But the family record book says 1932, and a birth certificate says 1934. The days change too: in one document she was born on April 7, in another on December 2, in another on October 22. A similar thing happens with her second surname. She would change it. She created phonic variations. I never knew what my mother's second surname was. Sometimes it was Rin, or Ris, or Ríu, or Ríun.

My mother didn't like to be called anything. She didn't believe in having a name. She didn't want to be subject to a name. This resistance wasn't ideological—it was instinctive.

She was pure instinct, that atavistic gift. And that's what I inherited from her: instinct, a sort of resonance that allows you to see the origin of things.

Having no choice about the matter, she accepted the officialness of her first surname, but she did whatever she wanted with the second. She mangled her second surname. Her mind rejected the names of things. She had trouble saying certain words, but it wasn't because she lacked a basic education—she'd gone to school, at least until she was fourteen. To her, words weren't important in and of themselves; what she cared about were the things that words disguised. Real things mattered to her. The phonic costumes of real things were flimsy and overly complicated.

When the Spanish legislature passed the Law of Dependence, aimed at helping my mother and other elderly people unable to take care of themselves—my mother needed a caregiver because of severe mobility issues—she changed its name and started calling it the Law of Independence. It was a funny mix-up, ironically evoking the nineteenth century, when Spain managed to expel Napoleon in what we call the War of Independence. That confusion of names contained an irony about the totality of our knowledge; it reminded me of when my students used to confuse Quevedo with Góngora, or Lope de Vega with Galdós, and I would be amazed—far from tearing my hair out, I saw there a new place from which things could be contemplated, the unexpected emptiness of culture and words and human reality.

No, I will never condemn those mistakes, because they're not mistakes, just indifference, lack of motivation, another form of intelligence. So whenever I was asked, during some bureaucratic process, for my mother's full name, I would do what she did: I'd say Ríu or Rin, and I'd leave it up to the understanding of the person asking, as she used to.

The dead must be sick of my mother already. They'll be hoping she's the first one resurrected.

People don't realize how fun it is to change your birth date or your last name. It's not a game, not some sort of whim; it's a defiance of human laws. It is also a way of seeking out vulnerability, of exposing oneself to the elements. Ultimately, it was her disaffection with the laws of social reality that shaped my mother's outlook.

I've inherited that disaffection. Meticulous human laws are—as they were to my mother—irrelevant to me. Everything that civilization has built is irrelevant to me. This isn't arrogance, quite the contrary; nor is it a disdainful apathy; rather, it is pain. You reach indifference via pain, emptiness, a lack of gravity.

Like my mother, I've been left here alone to worship the sun, that sun that enters my apartment on Ranillas each morning and shatters my eyes.

The sun leaves us blind to everything that is not the sun. We will look at the sun together again one day.

The truth is always in constant transformation—that's why it's so hard to tell it, to point to it. Or instead, it is always fleeing. The important thing is to reflect its endless movement, its irregular and uncomplicated metamorphosis.

No, Mom, we will never look at the sun together again. Millions of years will pass and we still won't have seen each other.

That June sun you loved so much.

134

At long last somebody's come to see me. It's Brah. Full of optimism, I make him dinner: sausage, potatoes, and eggs. I bought a good sausage, with wild mushrooms in it, a fancy, expensive sausage. I peel potatoes. I fry potatoes, with fresh olive oil. I hate to reuse olive oil; my mother never did. Brah has just spent four days with his friends on vacation in the mountains; he hasn't visited for two months. But whatever, it doesn't matter.

He eats while watching TV.

We watch TV.

What would we do without TV.

I suggest we go to the movies once he's finished. Tell him there's a movie out that looks good. He says he doesn't feel like it, he's meeting up with his friends. When he leaves my house, I ask if I can go with him for a little while. I've been cooped up inside all day and I'd like to stretch my legs. The suggestion makes him uncomfortable.

He says no, he's going alone.

And he leaves.

I gather up the dirty dishes, fill the dishwasher. I'm happy I was able to buy a new dishwasher and that it works well; I scrub the kitchen and sit down to watch TV. I discover bread crumbs on the floor of the TV room. I go back to the kitchen and stand staring at my OK-brand dishwasher.

And I think, Lucky thing I've got the dishwasher—it seems like it solves everything. It's a sort of humble revelation from God himself.

Its noise keeps me company.

Wagner, in her final years, would have been kept company by the noise of the refrigerator, since she didn't have a dishwasher.

Johann Sebastian, in his final years, was kept company by the noise of the television, because he never went to the movies. Why would he go to the movies, when he himself was the history of film? He was the screen and the actors' faces, gnawed by time, on the yellowed screen.

My mother knew perfectly well that everything would be repeated. She made dinners and lunches. I make dinners and lunches. Mine aren't as good, of course, because she knew how to cook. In that return, in that repetition of twin acts, there is a maddening ecstasy. And so she is coming, my mother, through her prediction. She's not coming to tell me, "Your children treat you the way you treated me," no, she's not coming to tell me that; she's found a road back to me. She's coming to tell me this: "I'll always love you, I'm still here."

And that is the portent.

The portent is that she already knew, when she was alive, that the road back existed—she was already aware of it.

It's the road of witchcraft, a primitive road.

When a few years ago she said to me, "Careful, if you don't come to see me, your children will do the same thing to you," what she was really saying was, "When I'm dead, I'll come back to you down that road, a road lined with leafy trees and June light, with the murmur of the rivers nearby. When I'm dead I'll still be with you through our solitudes, yours and mine. The road—see there, it's a sunny road, the road of the dead." Every time Brah and Valdi don't come for dinner with me, Wagner returns to me down that road, all deceased, all decayed, all corpse, with the yellowing orchestra of the eternal return of the same thing.

My mother was Nietzschean to her core. That's why she's called Wagner.

Wagner tells me: You'll use that road too, tell Brah and Valdi about it, it's time for you to mention the road. It's our family's great road, the one that allows the dead to be with the living.

I'm not going to do it—it's not yet time, I tell my mother, to show them the road I'll travel to return to them after I'm dead.

Wagner tells me: It is so time, you don't have any time left.

But Brah decides to sleep over, which makes me extremely happy, which ends quickly. He wakes up in a bad mood. I give him a kiss, which makes him uncomfortable or maybe just seems ridiculous to him.

Brah leaves for the other house, his mother's house, which is also mine, even if I no longer have any right to that house, because he's got a bigger bed there. I offer him coffee and cookies; he rejects them with a sour, scornful expression on his face. It says, Shut up, shut up already, I've done enough just spending the night in that awful bed of yours.

Wagner says: He's building the road, it's a wide, flowery road that you will use to return to be with him for good, just as you were building it every time you failed to kiss me or hold my hand or come to visit—it's the same road, the same return.

The eternal return of crumbling motherhood and fatherhood, the same thing ever returning.

I sit staring at the rejected cookies. I stare at them like an idiot. I'd bought them with so much optimism. They're the most defenseless cookies on the planet. My mother, too, must have optimistically bought things for me, things I didn't see, which at the time seemed insignificant, and that insignificance glides through time and has been slumbering for forty years and now reappears and settles down by my side. That's how my mother talks to me, that's the form my mother's ghost has chosen to talk to me: the Wagnerian road opens before me once more.

She dreamed it up.

My parents spent their lives planning and designing and inventing uneasy roads to reach me so that I wouldn't be alone, roads that led from their death to their son's life.

Ranillas and Arnillas was another road.

My divorce, yet another.

My hopelessness, the sunniest one of all.

It's as if a yellow circle—always yellow—were being completed. And my son's son will fail to appreciate the things my son lovingly gives him. It's a labyrinth where we communicate beyond disappearance, through misunderstanding. As if misunderstanding were a mathematical equation that destroys the physics of death.

And Brah leaves.

He hasn't even made his bed.

He left it all rumpled.

I start making the bed.

The bed, too, is defenseless.

135

I live next to the river, since Ranillas runs along the Ebro. People who live next to a river live longer. I get in the elevator and head down to the garage. The elevator has a distinctive smell—it's not a bad smell, it's hygienic, it smells like industrial cleaner, but it's a foreign smell, unnatural, it smells like nobody, humanity's degree zero. The garage is below river level. It makes me feel like I'm scuba diving. My garage is underwater; it's a submarine.

When I came to live on Ranillas I was the only human being living in the building, a hulking thing with sixteen apartments; it was one of the great real-estate luxuries I've enjoyed in my life. I found it amazing that the elevator was always on my floor, and amazing to know that nobody was around for three floors above and four below. I also found it a little terrifying.

I never had to wait for the elevator. People waste so much of their lives waiting for elevators. So much of their lives. Months, if you add it all up.

I felt like a prince, like a government minister. When I went to bed, I was aware of doing so in an empty building, as if I were an astronaut reposing in deep space, as if I were Christopher Columbus in the New World. I think it was my father who arranged all of this—he set it up. He wanted my life to fuse with the empty building. My father arranged it; it had to have been him, through the coincidence of names, who told me to choose this street, because this street was him.

It had to have been him, I tell myself. It had to have been him, stepping out from among the dead and blowing me a kiss.

I think very few people in this world will ever get to enjoy not having to wait for the elevator—they'll never know what it feels like, but I did for several months.

It was always there, on my floor.

That immediacy of ascent and descent opened up a mystical path in my perception of my new home. Because if I went out into the street, when I came back the elevator would always be on the ground floor. I was the only one who used it. And it knew it. There wasn't any noise either. I could blast my music at three in the morning. And I did. I would turn up the volume on my Pioneer stereo as loud as my ears could bear.

The building's beauty lay in its abstract solitude, which was a concrete symbol of my parents' departure. They left so elegantly, saying goodbye without saying it. I can see them so well in death, and on Ranillas, their lives conjured up by the electronics industry: the Siemens elevator, the Pioneer stereo.

136

Then, gradually, neighbors appeared as the apartments were sold one by one, after the developer was forced to adjust the asking price to match the market. The price dropped by more than forty percent, which was how I was able to buy one—I was the first person to take the plunge. And it was completely by chance. That price cut coincided with my own urgent need to find a new home after my divorce. The apartments needed to be remodeled, since they were unfinished inside. All I did was put down flooring and create a bathroom. I installed an AC4-grade floor that somebody recommended; I learned about the different categories of laminate. And some Romanian workers made me a bathroom. I was concerned the shower partition was too low, that the water would spray out, but it turned out fine. I spent several days researching the height of shower partitions. I discussed the ideal height of a partition with the Romanian workers. We stood staring at the partition as if contemplating a riddle. For me the Romanian workers were a riddle too, but they enjoyed an easy camaraderie that I admired, since I was feeling very lonely. One of them smoked and would toss the butts in the toilet; I had to say something to him. He stopped doing it, but the rebuke rubbed him the wrong way. They ate enormous sandwiches.

And so within four days I'd moved in and started living in my apartment on Ranillas. The other neighbors did extensive renovations and put in fancy new kitchens. In any case, the wonderful part was living alone in an apartment building for more than three months. It was as if nobody wanted to live there. I felt as if I'd moved into a spaceship that was orbiting in deep space. But if you live in an eight-story building all by yourself for three months, you learn the language of that building, and you realize that houses are alive. The history of the building was also a history of loneliness. Construction had been completed in 2008, right as the Spanish real estate bubble burst, so the apartments remained unsold until they decided to lower the prices in 2014. The apartments, the staircases, the walls, the elevator went six years without anybody around. The elevator was sad. I think that elevator was grateful for my presence. I fantasized about that sort of thing a lot. I remember nothing worked except the washing machine. It was a new washing machine, an intact Corberó, but it had been out on a balcony for six years, exposed to the elements, without anyone ever hooking it up. That virgin washing machine had never washed anything in its life, and that seemed like a great mystery to me. The first time I hooked it up I assumed it wouldn't work. The person who'd sold me the apartment said he doubted it worked. But it did. The washing machine worked—it was like I was bringing it back to life. How many years can an appliance's machinery last without being used?

The last washing machines my mother had were cheap brands.

My mother had faith in those no-name washing machines, as did I. If she'd been alive, we could have talked on the phone about washing machines, but it was too late. We could have even lived together. If God had given her another year of life, we would have lived together.

The past cannot be remodeled, or maybe it can.

137

I'm trying to improve this apartment, where everything is of questionable quality. Things break. The kitchen faucet is poorly installed, and the sink too, so it splashes, and I have to go around with a rag wiping up drops of water everywhere. I bought an aerator for the faucet, but it barely made a difference.

What other neighbors did was change out the kitchen completely, and the bathroom and the front door, and buy high-quality appliances. That's why they took so long to move in. What the neighbors did became a mantra reminding me that I always screw things up.

They moved forward with their improvements objectively, confidently, and I did not. And in that mistake, which is stunning and shameful when compared with my neighbors' good judgment, is a confirmation of my lineage and my fate. My brain was of inferior moral fiber, I figured.

Putting in a new kitchen and throwing out the one that came with the apartment—that's what I should have done. But unfortunately I didn't, because I didn't have the money.

That's why I went for the aerator instead, which cost four euros and ninety cents.

I now see, through my kitchen, my mother's kitchen in the apartment in Barbastro; I realize now that she was always cleaning, and I know significant events took place in that kitchen, events I don't really dare to see, I don't want to see them, but my memory dredges up a scene in which my mother is lying on the kitchen floor and crying, I can't see anything else. I just want it to end. For her to stop crying and get back up. And my mother writhes on the floor. And my father isn't around. It happened in the kitchen, maybe in 1967. They'd argued. My father slammed out of the apartment. I don't know what they were arguing about. I get the feeling they assumed I was too young to record the scene in my memory, but they were wrong.

I remember my mother barely rinsed the dishes, while I hold them under the faucet a long time, trying to wash away the soap for good.

138

I just went grocery shopping at Carrefour with my son Valdi. It was after a long holiday weekend, so the store was full of people—full of zombies, really. I was looking for something to do with Valdi—something to do together, I mean—and all I came up with was grocery shopping. Whenever I run an errand with Valdi or Brah, it feels like an earlier time is returning, an era prior to the collapse of the family we used to be, and it feels like that to them too, but we know it's just an illusion, the illusion that the past is coming back. The time before the divorce can never return. Valdi, Brah, and I are aware of that impossibility, yet it contains a scenery that is both terrifying and revelatory. We are full of revelations; I notice them more than my sons do.

In everything the three of us do together, there are reverberations of the things we used to do when there were four of us.

It isn't nostalgia or remorse or guilt. It's something I cannot name. It's inspiration. It's melancholy. Good melancholy.

I thought it would be nice to go shopping together, but that crowd of zombies made me fume. I would have liked to have held his hand, Valdi's hand. I remember how, some eight years ago now, he was taking guitar lessons. And the guitar was bigger than he was. I remember how, six years ago, he was taking Ping-Pong lessons. He even competed in national Ping-Pong championships. Valdi was a total genius with a Ping-Pong paddle in his hand. Valdi doesn't know it, but he carries within him an ancient goodness, a gift that precedes history, and the best mysteries of things gleam within that gift. Valdi's goodness is like the monolith in Stanley Kubrick's movie *2001*.

I adore Valdi. I always have, ever since he was born. Johann Sebastian was smitten with Valdi too, even if he hadn't been excited about becoming a grandfather. Johann Sebastian didn't pay much attention when Brah and Valdi arrived. He didn't act like a grandfather. He didn't like being called that. Deep down, he didn't like being called a father either.

He never found a family category he felt comfortable in. Johann Sebastian stared at baby Valdi with skeptical astonishment: Who's this? Where'd he come from? And baby Valdi made lots of creative noises with his tongue, which Johann Sebastian praised loudly. He was amused by those sonic metaphors.

They're like the undersea wrecks of World War II battleships: baby Valdi and grandfather Johann Sebastian.

My hands shook as I grabbed things: a container of milk, a tray with a piece of chicken, a sponge cake. You can learn everything about a person from the food he buys at the grocery store. There were bulk lentils. I break things when I try to take them out of their containers. My mother always did too. She had no patience. I don't either. She broke things. I break things. We try to open the container and are unable to, and for us that is a frightening and exasperating and infuriating injustice. My mother used to talk about failure as the devil's work, whereas I talk about impatience and how primitive man never should have left the cave.

"The devil must be here in this house," my mother would shout.

I would have been about twelve or thirteen when I grabbed a dictionary of my father's and hurled it to the floor. I was looking for the meaning of a word and couldn't find it. I got angry. I didn't understand how that dictionary worked. As it lay on the floor, I gave the book a fierce kick that cracked its spine. After a while, when my rage subsided, I opened the volume again and realized that it was a Spanish-French/French-Spanish dictionary. At that, I felt a huge wave of tenderness for the book. Plus, it was my father's book. I tried to mend the injury to the poor dictionary's spine.

I inherited that blindness from my mother.

We both had erratic moods.

Neither of us could open bags. We broke everything. Everything tumbled from our hands. My mother used to hack open containers of milk with a big knife. We didn't understand the mechanical laws that govern things.

I can never get plastic grocery bags open. The cashier has to help.

I kept thinking the better of everything I was putting in the shopping cart. I put things in and then took them out, and Valdi saw the horrifying chaos that ruled his father's actions. I abandoned an orange-flavored chocolate bar next to the cauliflower after suddenly second-guessing my selection of that unnecessary sweet. There were so many people in the store that we were running into one another with our carts. We were running into one another with our shopping carts. I sense the end of this civilization, that's what I mean. I sense that this world is going to end. I was sliding into a fit of uncontrollable rage, and it felt good to run into other people's carts. I was losing it.

I was agitated.

And then I was throwing things.

I picked up a hunk of cheese and hurled it at a frozen hake. I opened a box of frozen rolls and glared at them. That would be the entirety of my contribution to the revolution: creating a bit of private chaos in a supermarket—in other words, making life miserable for the poor kid earning six hundred euros a month whose job it is to keep the products in order.

My mother passed down impatience and superstition.

The ubiquitous background noise of my parents' lives drives me crazy.

My mother was always breaking containers. She dropped things. Our clumsiness was the product of the newly developed hands and inept fingers of the first hominids. My mother had no patience in supermarkets. She didn't understand checkout lines. She didn't understand how the aisles were set up. She would be overcome by rebelliousness and blank fury. As am I.

139

We headed back to Ranillas. Valdi stayed with me a while longer and then left. I took a shower. I came out of the shower and dried off with the red towel. And I recalled the bathroom in my mother's house. We had a tiny bathtub in that old apartment—my mother never wanted or was able to remodel it. It was a built-in bathtub that was merely symbolic; it was impossible to wash in it. My mother used to bathe us once a week. The water heater never worked well, it didn't heat enough water, so my mother would heat the water in pots on the stove.

The water heater had a brand name—Orbegozo.

They were basic baths, with very little water. It was almost ridiculous—the water didn't even come up to your ankles. My mother would dry us off with a huge red towel. When she died, I found that towel in an armoire. It had survived almost fifty years. I was amazed that it still existed—I didn't realize a towel could live so long. I took it with me. It was so well preserved. . . . Was it high quality at work? Or was it a miracle?

It was like my family's Shroud of Turin.

Over the years, lime gradually clogged the hot water faucet. I no longer lived with my parents by then.

I don't know how they got by. I never asked. I don't know how they managed to shower. Maybe they didn't. Maybe God himself anointed their weary bodies with the gift of clean smells, the smells of people who have entered the realm where there is no decay.

Now that towel is in my wet hands. I often stare at it, trying to ask it things, yes, ask the towel things. And it responds—the towel talks to me: "They're the ones you should have asked, and you had the chance, but you didn't know how to go about it, you didn't know, you didn't know what words to use."

I dry myself with that towel.

It's still soft; the fibers are just as fine as they were that very first day my mother used it on my body, the body of a six-year-old boy. We could never shower because of that tiny bathtub and the showerhead clogged by mineral deposits so only a slender trickle of water came out, drops that were tired of being water.

Nobody realized how deeply that can mark you.

My mother didn't care. But what the hell was she thinking when she decided not to do anything about it?

My mother ruined the original design of her house, which was modern and pleasant and made sense. She made foolish changes. She designed a huge dining room that she never let anybody go into, so it always looked like something out of a magazine.

It was her dream.

And in the meantime, we couldn't shower.

My mother nurtured a dining room and my father nurtured a car. She wanted to impress her friends with that room. Her friends, who all took off. By the end of her life my mother didn't have many friends left. She changed friends all the time.

In the last years of her life, she had some bizarre friends.

I don't know where in the world she found them. She sold things. She sold good furniture or gave it away. Hers was a colossal misrule, firmly exercised for fifty years. My mother was in power for fifty years, longer than Francisco Franco.

Francisco Franco and my mother—they could have danced a waltz together.

My mother never knew who the hell Francisco Franco was. That thrills me—it makes me adore my mother.

That's the punkest thing there is.

All my mother cared about was Julio Iglesias, Julio Iglesias's wives and sons and daughters and father, and Julio Iglesias's songs. When I hear Julio Iglesias's voice, I think of her.

140

She once introduced me to those final friends of hers. They were people on society's margins. The affluent, bourgeois friends she'd had in the seventies abandoned her when things started going sideways for my father. She could have gotten rid of that disconcerting dining room then, since its only purpose was to be shown off to the rich friends who left, who disappeared when my father's luck as a traveling salesman ran out and he became a poor man. The truth is that my father did well economically for only six or seven years—I don't think it was even a decade. During that period, my parents became friends with well-to-do couples. I imagine they had the illusion that they were prospering, but they never reached the level of those people, because those people always had a lot of money and my parents did not.

Hell, she could have dismantled the dining room and installed a shower so we could bathe properly. She lived her life confused, tormented, and she didn't know it; she was a monumental hooligan. She was a woman governed by impulses, utterly lacking in foresight. So we lived in shambles, but we had a splendid dining room to sit in. Because we were waiting for her petit-bourgeois friends who no longer visited, who would never visit again. It was only when I left that house at eighteen that I learned what a proper shower was.

They stopped visiting in the late seventies, those glamorous friends of hers. My mother's social capital collapsed. During the few years my father was doing well, my mother managed to cloak herself in a social class that ended up expelling her from its bosom. And the bathroom went unremodeled. My mother was pursuing social esteem, which was fleeting, and I am pursuing literary esteem, which is also fleeting. That's why I say there's no difference between my mother's fantasies and mine.

We are both victims of Spain, of the desire for prosperity—material prosperity and intellectual prosperity are the same thing. She screwed things up, and I'm screwing things up too.

But it's beautiful that we're so alike. And if we've both failed, that's even more beautiful. It is love. We're together again. Maybe she planned it this way. So my failure has been worth it: it guides me to her, and with her is where I want to be forever.

141

I first saw those coiffed, jewel-draped women when I was ten or twelve. They were about forty or so. There was a gorgeous blonde who became a widow and then disappeared. She was voluptuous and set off erotic longings in me. She was a little younger than my mother, maybe four or five years younger. I once had to go to her house for my mother and she appeared at the door in a towel, freshly showered. I remember that my parents went to her husband's funeral after he died suddenly. I can see him now. He was shorter than his wife, and that seemed incredible to me.

The history of my parents' friends is tangled and labyrinthine. They all seem like ghosts now. They died over the years, gradually.

One would be gone one day, another the following year.

They're all dead.

My father is dead and so are his friends.

I don't know if they were friends.

I don't think any friends came to see my father on his deathbed. That seems to me an unorthodox sort of freedom. And as I've said before, at the end of her life my mother had unusual friends—I don't know what happened to them. They were poor women, widows or never married. I have no idea where they came from; they were straight out of a fantastical history of Spain. Badly dressed and unkempt. Seventy-year-old punks, that's what they were. My mother had strange pacts with things. She had dark regions, cellars that only she entered. And my father, at the end of his life, achieved a level of idleness that was next to saintliness—not a religious sainthood but the kind born of the suppleness that the morning breeze gave his freshly shaven face, the superfluity of silence, and the sun's echoes reverberating in his wrinkled eyes; the saintliness or bliss of a man who has renounced memory, his mother, his son, and any sort of permanence; the exemplarity of his remote indifference; an indifference like that of the universe, which exists, but in silence, in secret; or like that of the sea, which has existed for millennia, an existence that was always sunk in darkness and invisibility, until humans brought it to light, looked at it, but to no avail.

My father knew instinctively that people grant you the gift of being looked at, but it's flawed, illusory, tending toward vanity. Yes, that's where my father went: to a place where any form of vanity is indeterminate or insolent or improper.

He shed all vanity.

That is true freedom—and beggardom.

I remember my father's friends. I'd love to phone the ones who are still alive. I don't know what they'd say. It's amazing how at the end of life there's nothing to say. People don't even want to make the effort to remember. Because remembering means burning brain cells in vain.

Because remembering is malignant.

No famous musician friend came to visit when Johann Sebastian left this world. It was as if he never had friends in his life. How immensely alone he departed. No old friends came to say goodbye. That's how Johann Sebastian wanted it. He didn't feel like thinking about that. He was preparing for something that had no sound.

He didn't want to see anybody, that's the truth. He didn't want to waste time on the illusion of friendship. He didn't want to recite ceremonious words, words that were social and polite and amicable. He had quashed the myth of social esteem as the only confirmation of existence, the only confirmation that a person is alive.

He didn't want to be with anyone but himself.

There was only solitude in him.

There was only me, his son, whom he loved so much and still loves, even in death.

142

It's a July morning in 1969. I'm almost seven. The whole family is riding in a four-door SEAT 850. We're on a short summer vacation, and we're in the mountains. We just passed through the town of Broto. There were tourists and hikers along the road—hikers with backpacks, eating sandwiches wrapped in aluminum foil, which is a novelty, having just been introduced to the Spanish market. Everything is joy and jubilation, because going to the mountains when it's hot during the summer is a viceless bacchanal. My father is driving the SEAT 850 and talking about a wonderful place. He's been talking about it since we left Barbastro. And he talked about it before we left too. The place is called Ordesa, and it's a mountain valley.

It's got to be around here, I tell Valdi and Brah. Right here. I've stopped the car and am looking for the exact spot where, forty-six years ago, my father got a flat tire in the SEAT 850 as we were entering the Ordesa Valley. I think how I need to ask my mother where it happened. But I can't ask her anymore. She'll settle the question. But she's dead. It hits me once more. That's how it always is.

The truth is, she hardly remembered anything. She didn't even remember her husband. She focused her attention on things she considered to be profoundly alive. She concentrated on Valdi and Brah that way. She saw them as kings of life and time, perched on that untouchable throne where my brother and I once sat. She went from adoring her husband to adoring her sons, and from adoring her sons to adoring her grandsons, always attentive to anything that prolonged and extended her own existence in the undefined realm of life on earth. That's how she was—a fierce instinct that it was impossible to blame. My mother was pure nature—that's why she had no memory, she had only present, the way nature does. Wherever she is, she will adore Brah's and Valdi's children, and she will be with them, like a huge tree that is also invisible. In the perpetuity of her blood she will persist, because I knew her, and I know full well that she had no end. My mother was infinite. My mother was the present. The power of her instincts guides her to my presence. Her presence in my presence becomes presence in my present children, and in becoming present in my present children, she heralds her presence in my children's children once they someday become present.

The person I should have asked where the SEAT 850 got a flat, where exactly on that stretch it took place, was my father, since he was driving.

I'd opted not to inform Valdi and Brah that my objective in choosing Ordesa as the destination for our three-day summer holiday was to recall the spot where a tire went flat forty-six years earlier, so they must have been caught off guard when I stopped the car on a straight stretch of road that climbs up toward Ordesa from the village of Torla and started looking for it. That stretch is steadfast. The road hasn't been widened or redone, it's exactly the same; it may have been paved nine or ten times in fifty years, but that's all. It's narrow and lined with tall trees. Beside the road is an old hotel. I tried to reserve a room there, but it was full. It doesn't have many rooms, I'd guess maybe twenty or twenty-five at most; no wonder it's full, given that it's summer, high season. And even if the hotel is full, that doesn't mar the landscape, which remains intact.

The hotel is in a prime spot; its location may explain why the road is unchanged from fifty years ago. I remember that after staring at the deflated tire crumpled against the ground, its vigor gone, I looked straight ahead with my child eyes and saw the hotel rising up like a mirage, as if it had come out of nowhere, and then I saw my father's obstinate face as he stared at the tire and opened the trunk, getting ready to change it.

I was conscious of my life. For the first time I was conscious that time was beginning.

I remember the flat only hazily; I don't know exactly how things ended up shaking out. I remember the white SEAT 850 well, and I remember the spot. My father loved Ordesa. Because in Ordesa suddenly all of life's alienations fade away beside the splendor of the mountains, the trees, and the river. I search for the spot with the flashlight of memory. Valdi and Brah have no idea what I'm doing. Cars whiz by. I sniff the road like a hunting dog. I examine the stones.

It's Ordesa.

Here is where he got a flat, around here. And I feel his presence. He pulled out a spare from the trunk. He is with me. He was young—whistling, smiling, despite the flat tire. It was his kingdom, his valley and his mountain, his homeland. I got out of the car and stood gazing at the mountains, and that hotel appeared, the one I called a few days back for a room and found that there wasn't a vacancy.

But everything has disappeared.

That's how I know God doesn't exist; if he did, he'd have given me a triple room in that hotel, for my two boys and me, and I would have had all the time in the world to search for a flat tire. But there weren't any rooms—they were all full.

Everything was future back then, when the flat happened.

Everything is past now, when I search for the flat, the most fantastical or absurd search in the world. But life is absurd, which is why it's so beautiful.

The Ordesa Valley is still there—it doesn't change, hasn't changed in the past fifty million years. It's exactly the same, just as it was created during the Tertiary Period. After fifty million years of being alone, it was declared a national park on August 16, 1918, and mountain climbers began arriving to ascend Monte Perdido's 11,007-foot height.

There's nobody up there.

143

They didn't always love me. They loved me to death when I was a boy, but after I left home they started growing apart from me, and once I got married they might have stopped loving me, stopped loving me in that way I'd never find again.

I've called Brah and Valdi, but they aren't answering the phone. I look at myself in the bathroom mirror and see that my hair has gotten shaggy. I'm seized with the urge to cut it. It's the same urge my mother used to get when she handed herself over to the hairdressers—my mother was always wanting to go to the salon. She was never satisfied with the hairstyles they gave her. As a boy, I accompanied her. She went to a salon on the second floor of a building on a narrow street in Barbastro. I was surprised by that, my childish brain unable to process such a transformation—I didn't understand how an apartment could turn into a hair salon. The salon even had a kitchen with an old sink, kitchen implements, a table, and cupboards. While she got her hair cut,

I'd be left in a room with used toys that I found unsettling—as toys I'd never played with before, they were alluring, but I was also repelled by them since other children had already played with them.

My mother, whenever she was depressed and sad, would start messing with her hair. She would stare into the mirror and say she hated her hair. Then she'd go to the salon. She was never happy with the result. She was looking for absolution at the hair salon, an elevation of the self; she was looking for lost joy. She changed hairdressers a million times. She was looking for salon utopia. She spent her life looking for *the* salon, the great truth of her hair. But her hair was aging, that's all.

There wasn't a salon in the world that could help my mother.

If she came back to life right now, she'd ask to go to the salon. Even if she came back as a corpse, as a skeleton without flesh or skin, she'd ask to go to the salon.

But she's at the final salon now, the one at the end of the world.

144

My father always liked to be neatly groomed. He didn't even leave the house if it was windy, because it would mess up his hair.

My father started gaining a little weight, and he was self-conscious about it. He often asked if he was fat. He was seeking our judgment. He liked to eat. It was a unique relationship with the world: taking it in through food.

Either you eat or you screw, or both. Both things seek bodily combustion. Every human being is seeking satiety.

He used to comb his hair—he took forever to comb his hair. A complex job that required great attention. He employed all his techniques to make sure his hair came out right. I would watch him as if he were a god or an ancient hero.

I remember that comb, which gradually became covered with a dark substance, collecting layers of grease, and eventually turned white, then went from white to yellow; it stained the toiletry kit where it lived, it became a symbol of my father's masculine identity, it let me know that my father was home, that he was back.

My father was a category error in the Spanish society he inhabited; he verged on an imaginary dukedom when, having been keeping accounts in the inert whorls of his brain, he decided he had enough money to have the barber come to the house on Sundays to cut his hair.

He refused to go to the barbershop.

I took it for granted that it was normal, but in fact it was quite unusual. It would happen on Sundays. A barber would come to our house. It was a luxury my father indulged in. How much did he pay that traveling barber?

I loved that: my father refused to go to the barber, while my mother visited every salon around.

I thought it was weird that he made the barber do house calls. Why was that? He never set foot in a barbershop. My father never set foot in a barbershop, just as he never set foot in a church unless it was for a funeral. And in that case he'd arrive late, barely go inside, hover by the church door, by the baptismal font, near the cold water, to make sure the demented, incompetent God of men didn't notice him.

He won't be at my funeral. My father won't be able to come to my funeral; for me, that failure to appear is symbolic of how the meaning of life has vanished, how we have stumbled into the end of everything. He should fight off the shadows, come out from among the dead, the way they say Jesus did, and show up at my funeral and say something. Say a few words, the way people do at American funerals.

My head hurts so much right now. I'm hooked on ibuprofen, which takes away the pain, but not as much as it used to. Drugs lose their power.

My mother's headaches were legendary at my house, as were her liver pains.

She used to shriek with pain and beg for morphine.

Along with my mother's liver spasms, another awful memory comes to me: I'm walking next to my father, holding his hand—it must be 1968, or 1969, or 1970. That was my absolute favorite thing: walking down the street with my father. I was a seven-year-old boy showing off his father, because I knew he was a tall, handsome, elegant man. We went down the street and walked by a beautiful woman. We stopped. They looked at each other. There was a moment of tension. A smile slowly blooming on both faces, me staring up at them like somebody watching the clouds go by. My father didn't say hi, and she didn't either.

Afterward my father looked at me. He gave a small smile and said, "If I hadn't married your mother, that woman just now would have been your mother."

145

We link different eras together. I knew people who lived until 1975 or 1976 or 1977, and then those people died; in the same way that they were linked to previous decades, and they knew and also didn't know what to do with those people they knew and saw die in 1945 or 1946 or 1947, and those people who made it to 1945 were linked to people who passed on in 1912 or 1913 or 1914, and the chain keeps spooling out, and there will be somebody in 2051 or 2052 or 2053 who remembers me as a witness to an era, witness to 2014 or 2015. Connection is coupled with melancholy and uncertainty—the latter of which comes from realizing that you've failed to accumulate much knowledge about the nature of life. And so we have only matter, objects: houses, photos, stones, statues, streets, things like that. Spiritual ideas are poisonous melancholy, balls of burning antimatter. Matter, on the other hand, still retains some amount of knowledge.

We link eras, as if our bodies were the message.

Our body is the message, and it is also the unifying thread that moves from one era to the next.

Matter still retains a space, it keeps old time captive within a space. Thus, again, for the umpteenth time, how wrong I was in deciding to cremate my parents. Graves are a place where we can commemorate something that no longer has time but does have space, even if it's just a space for bones.

Bones are important because they're a type of matter that lasts.

That old Spanish expression comes to mind just now, the one that says, *No tiene donde caerse muerto,* which is equivalent to "He doesn't have a pot to piss in" but literally means "He doesn't have a place to drop dead in." It's a genius expression, and it defines an era: my era, the great era of real estate speculation. Because of this era, historians will be studying us in another hundred years.

It's important to find oneself a space, a place to drop dead in. My father used to watch TV from one corner of the aging couch at home; it was a complicated corner, constructed through lots of letting go of the things of this world.

He sat not in the middle of the couch but in one corner, as if seeking a refuge, a hideout. Something akin to desertion, and the TV in front of him. He would perch on the edge of the couch, where the couch ends, on the cliff of the couch, waiting to fall, because the fall would give him invisibility.

Why didn't he sit in the middle of the couch?

I never saw my father lying sprawled on the floor, the way my kids saw me. They saw me lying on the floor, on the doormat. I managed to make it to the doormat, and that's where I fell. I almost made it. I was in a stupor, and I'd pissed myself. A little farther and I'd have been spared the shame, but I fell outside the front door. I almost made it—only a few feet to go.

I'm there now too: in one corner of a seat, a chair, a sofa, pressed against the armrest as if it were a protective barrier. A couch in front of a TV set, and the TV offered a look at other people's lives, people who'd opted for movement, for activity. They were humans who were changing the world, or at least trying: they were on TV. I don't think my father envied the people he saw on television in the least; I don't think he coveted their lives or their jobs or their popularity. He'd deserted from the world's army of coveters, and I'd like to desert too. But he watched them with curiosity, as if all the things on TV were distracting him from terrible things.

He was a deserter—my father was a deserter. He spent his final years contemplating his desertion and trying to figure out what he'd deserted. That's happening to me now: I don't know what I've deserted. All of Kafka's oeuvre is seeking the same thing: What have I deserted? Where did I start out from? Where am I going now?

Through television, he was trying to figure out what he'd deserted. As my father saw it, the people on TV weren't deserters. If he managed to figure out who they served, maybe then he'd understand the origin of his desertion. He scrutinized, lurked, descried some message on the TV. He gazed at the TV the way a priest gazes at the altar. He saw the devilish complexity of life on TV.

He saw the world go dim on TV.

Sometimes I get the feeling, in the solitude of Ranillas, in the wee hours of morning, that my father is about to appear on the screen of my TV, a small, cheap twenty-one-inch LG, that I'm going to see my father's old age, that he's going to assert himself on-screen.

The green robe, the glasses, on the corner of the couch, taking up as little space as possible. And not actually there at all. He didn't hear anything when he watched TV. He didn't hear us, of course, but he didn't hear what they said on TV either. I never knew who he was hearing.

Who was he hearing, if he wasn't hearing us or the people on TV?

He never wanted to go to bed. He never wanted to stop watching TV. If he was watching TV, that meant life was continuing.

I liked watching TV with him. We watched TV together for more than forty years.

It's the best thing you can do with a loved one: watch TV together. It's like watching the universe. Contemplating the universe through television is what life has given us. It might not be much of a gift. Trifling though it is, we milk it for all it's worth.

We could have held hands, but that would have interfered with our concentrating on the images.

Hundreds of programs went by: series, movies, newscasts, documentaries, game shows, debates, bulletins; years went by, lustrums, decades.

Everything was there, on TV.

It was as if we were watching over the world through the screen. A pair of watchmen. My father was the master, I the disciple. We watched over life: the sea, the stars, the hills, the waterfalls, the whales, the elephants, the high peaks, the snow, the winds.

Ordesa.

146

At the moment I'm watching over the apartment on Ranillas. I'm contemplating the layer of dust that's accumulated on the house telephone I took from my mother's place when she died. When I picked up the receiver, I got dust all over my hand. The buttons are covered with dust. I never use this phone. I use a cordless one I bought at MediaMarkt; its instruction booklet is covered with dust and lying under a bookcase, which is also covered with dust. I keep this telephone as if it were a sculpture, a memento of my mother. It's the phone she used to call me on. She knew a ton of phone numbers by heart. We used to joke about that. My father would test her; he'd ask her for phone numbers and she knew them all. She would memorize the phone numbers and dial them on this instrument sitting in front of me, covered with dust. It's strange to inherit a telephone. It occurs to me that I'm building a chapel. The voice is telling me that now: "Ranillas is a chapel—

you've hung photos and papers on the walls, the paintings your uncle did, that uncle you haven't talked about, your father's brother, whereas you have talked about Monteverdi, your mother's brother. Now talk about your father's brother, call him Rachmaninoff, call him Rachma."

Rachma was the younger brother of Johann Sebastian, my father. He was a painter, and I've got two paintings of his in the chapel on Ranillas, painted in the late 1950s. Rachma painted a ballerina in 1958.

The date is at the bottom of the painting. I always stare at that date, painted in red below Rachma's signature. A date when I wasn't in the world or even expected, nor had my father met the woman who would be my mother. I imagine my father and his brother in 1958. My father was twenty-eight, and Rachma twenty-four. There was no sign of the future to come when Rachma painted this painting. They lived together at home with their mother, my grandmother. Nobody ever talked to me about that house or that period. But it must have been a good one. I know which house it was—somebody told me. Not them. Not my father. But I can picture it. I can picture the two brothers' beds.

I rescued the 1958 ballerina when I cleaned out my dead mother's apartment. When I die, Rachma's ballerina will begin another journey. She will end up in an antique shop somewhere, and maybe somebody will buy her. Rachma's ballerina has started moving now, after being motionless for almost sixty years, hanging on the same wall. When I leave this world, she'll have no value to Valdi and Brah.

Rachmaninoff's ballerina has value only to me. I saw very little of Rachmaninoff in life. He lived in Galicia. He'd been sent to Galicia. He did the same work as my father, traveling salesman. They both worked for the same Catalonian company.

They had the same job and represented that Catalonian company in different regions. Bach was a salesman in Aragon; Rachma, a salesman in Galicia. The Catalonian bourgeoisie got rich while the two of them went from town to town (Aragonese towns for my father, Galician towns for my uncle) peddling fabrics from Sabadell and Barcelona, where the wealthy lived, the privileged classes for whom Bach and Rachma worked on commission, a paltry commission. There was no industry in either Aragon or Galicia. All the industry was in Barcelona. Their bosses will be dead now, and their bosses' bosses. Bach's and Rachma's names will no longer appear in any file—everything will have been shredded. Sometimes a secretary from the textile company my father worked for would call. That secretary must be dead too. And her grandchildren won't have any idea what work their grandmother did or which people she used to call from the company offices.

We don't know which of the dead our own dead knew.

The two brothers never saw each other again. And Wagner

didn't do much to make sure they did. I made a trip to Galicia in about 2002, and I phoned him. He called me Manolito, as if I were a child. I was forty years old. I didn't understand much of that conversation with Rachma; the rushed way he talked reminded me of Monteverdi.

I barely got a word in during that jumbled conversation. Rachma didn't let me. But he didn't say anything important either. He talked about things that didn't matter. He hadn't seen me in thirty years. Who the hell was calling him? It was the oldest son of his older brother, who was also the oldest.

Birthright founded the things of this world, in a blaze of light.

Over time, I've discovered that my entire family was made of air. There wasn't anybody there. Go visit your cousin, Rachma told me. I was calling Rachma from Pontevedra and he was in Lugo. My cousin, for her part, was in Combarro.

There was a time when my father used to talk about Combarro, and lovely memories of that little seaside town stack up in my mind, memories from when I was six or seven years old: the narrow streets, the pile granaries, the sea, the Ría de Pontevedra, the smell, the intense ocean smell of the Galician rías.

My father was happy there, in Combarro, with Rachma. The two of them used to go out for beer in the bars of Combarro. Late seventies, with the future still bright. Because Rachma had the virtue of popularity. Rachma's Galician friends. But also his friends from Barbastro, who still remember him, even though it's been more than fifty years since he left Barbastro, and three or four since he died.

Rachma's memory has faded in Barbastro, sure, but people

still remember him. A few, very few, remember him. Because everybody leaves.

But in that summer of 2002, I spoke to him on the telephone.

147

"There were many things he couldn't say," the voice says, "because your call was made of sadness itself. Yes, Rachma faked it well, and I'm not saying it didn't make sense for you to call him; you wanted to find out about your uncle, whom you hadn't seen in thirty years—it was 2002 when you phoned him. You hadn't spoken to him since 1972. Jesus, you hadn't seen him in thirty years. Did he remember he hadn't seen you since 1972? The bad thing is, you didn't see him again after that call either. But that was because by then your father's brother no longer existed on the earth; that's how Rachma found out you were asking about a dead man. You have a thing for asking about the dead. You're always asking the same question: Why are you dead? You basically ask that question of everything that exists and is going to die or has already died. You like speaking Spanish, speaking in Spanish, because Spanish is useful for talking to the dead. You pronounce the syllables, shout the Spanish syllables so they'll clutch at the human beings they represent. Why are you dead, why are you no longer with us, why can't I call you anywhere? Those are your questions. So Rachma seemed only vaguely pleased by your call, and you were disappointed by that—but it was Rachma's voice, a voice from your childhood, and in your childhood there lurked a dark incident, and a never-expressed gratitude, and that was the real and profound reason you'd wanted to talk to Rachma."

148

Rachma came from Lugo to Barbastro around 1972 or so. He wanted to see his hometown again. He'd left in the early sixties. He showed up in a brand-new car. He'd bought a Simca 1200. The two brothers had made it.

Johann Sebastian had a SEAT 124 purchased in 1970. And Rachma had bought a Simca 1200. The engines had the same number of cylinders. The two brothers had big dreams, the vigor of youth. They decided to race. I think Rachma won. Yes, they raced from Barbastro to the little town of Castejón. That's nine miles. That road doesn't exist anymore—a new highway was built many years ago, and it no longer goes through Castejón. Rachma wanted to show his older brother that the Simca went faster than the SEAT. My father embraced Spain through the SEATs he bought over his entire life. He was loyal to Spain via the SEAT. I am moved by that loyalty. When I saw the movie *Gran Torino*, in which Clint Eastwood's loyalty to the Ford is a form of loyalty to the United States, I felt gratified—I felt that my father hadn't been mistaken with the SEAT. He wouldn't have dreamed of buying a Renault or a Simca. In fact, I think SEAT was synonymous with cars for him. That's why he didn't really understand Rachma's race, or Rachma's car. As he saw it, Rachma, by not owning a SEAT, was declining to be Spanish.

I don't know who my grandfather was or what his name was, when he was born or died, but he would have liked seeing the two brothers with their big dreams. But he was dead, buried in an anonymous niche in the Barbastro cemetery.

My grandfather was a niche adrift. I don't even know where my grandmother is buried. Not in the cemetery, but in the city. What did my grandfather think of his sons? Was he proud of them? Did he kiss them? Did they make his heart swell the way Brah and Valdi do mine? Will my love for Brah and Valdi be lost the same way my grandfather's love for Bach and Rachma was? I can't rescue my paternal grandfather from anywhere; I can't even make him up. I don't even know what year he died. Who was he? Would he have loved me? Would he have held my hand when I was small? He didn't see my birth—he didn't even get to imagine it. Any part of my family that didn't touch me or intuit me or guess at me seems supernaturally pure. Because the memory I have of Bach and Wagner and Monte and Rachma has become something superhuman. I carry that memory inside me like a pulse of dark joy. There's nothing left: not a watch, or a ring, or a pen, or a photo.

I don't know where Rachma is buried either. My cousin called one day to let me know. Rachma passed at seventy-four, a year younger than Johann Sebastian. They went more than thirty years without seeing each other, but they loved each other. Rachma thought Bach had a rigid personality. And it's true, my father tended toward moral inflexibility, but that helped him live—that inflexibility was like an automatic pilot. It oriented his life. Rachma was different, and his voice soon took on a Galician accent.

They loved each other without seeing each other. They were brothers. My father carried him within, in his heart. He carried Rachma within, his little brother, whom he never talked about. I know he loved him a lot, but he never said it.

Rachma became Galician. It was as if he'd been born in Galicia, but he was born in Barbastro. Rachma was very different from Johann Sebastian. For starters, Johann Sebastian was taller. Rachma was slender and charismatic. And to top things off, Rachma got divorced. That was surprising. My father never said anything about Rachma's divorce. He passed no judgment. It seemed like Rachma's life was full of emotions. He also won the lottery. I think it was three million pesetas in the mid-seventies. He got a new car—dumped the Simca 1200 and bought a Chrysler 180, a car that was a major step up. But something happened between them. I'll never know what it was—nobody will. Maybe absolutely nothing and they just decided to celebrate their birthdays on their own. Or something like that. Later, through acquaintances, we heard Rachma was drinking. I imagined his life as a divorcé. I imagined him living alone in an apartment in Lugo, on a narrow street, and going down to the bar below his house at night to have a cognac and talk to the bartender awhile. I don't know why I invented that life for him. I think it was in the mid-eighties when I came up with it. The odd thing is I envied him that life. I don't think human nature's cut out for long-term marriage. I'm glad Rachma was able to realize that. I imagine that's what happened. Men accept long-term marriages because they stop believing in youth.

I think after his divorce he must have become another man. Rachma must have said no to the symbolic ordering of reality that undergirds long-term marriage, which is a nightmare, which is captivity. Sure, the people in those marriages smile and the smiles even look real. I don't think marriages are worth it; I know it's an exaggerated claim, but renouncing one's passions is an exaggerated version of reasonable sacrifice. Some anthropologists say monogamy isn't natural. The endless parade of infidelities between men and women, of painful misunderstandings, is the by-product of imposed monogamy.

Long-term marriages were invented, perhaps, by ecclesiastical capitalism.

There are no certainties.

I just woke up on Ranillas, and light, life's stepsister, is here. Light seems like a character, like someone saying to me, "I'm light, you're the child of light, see how I give things materiality, because things exist through light."

I stare up at the sky.

So Rachma is paving the way for me. It's as if God himself were sending me messages through my parents' brothers.

Monteverdi said, "Catastrophe and solitude and failure."

Rachmaninoff said, "Divorce and Chrysler 180 and Galicia."

Both messages are good because life, which we serve, burns in both of them. The only sin a man can commit is to stop serving life. And it's not a major sin, more of a minor failing.

149

A man may eventually end up falling in love with his own life. That's what's happening to me; it's been happening for a few months now. My soul is returning to the intoxicated zones of infatuation. Intoxication is something you have from birth. The part I couldn't imagine was this reconciliation with myself. Maybe that's what Rachma discovered: that he was much better off alone than with a family. Because maybe in the end the thing that ends up being destroyed is loneliness. And maybe in the end you find that the only human being who isn't a total asshole is yourself.

Maybe that is the pinnacle of identity: oneself being sufficient in all things. If you throw a party, an immensely important guest shows up, and that guest is you; if you get married, you're madly in love with your spouse because your spouse is you; if you die and come back to life and see God, you're immensely perplexed because you're seeing your own face. And it's funny that I'm the one saying this fantastical thing—me, who can't even be alone for fifteen minutes, for the length of a fifteen-minute taxi ride.

150

I just drove from Ranillas to Madrid. I traveled by night. It's Good Friday. I started driving at eight in the evening, when all the Holy Week processions begin throughout Spain. I'd never spent a Good Friday driving before. I feel something akin to liberation. It's as if I've gone AWOL from the history of Spain. While all of Spain is praying, I'm traveling in my car from Zaragoza to Madrid. I accelerate. And there's nobody on the road.

I've always had a fantasy that I'll fulfill at some point: heading out on the road one Christmas Eve at nine p.m., just as the TV is rebroadcasting the king's speech. And driving down Spain's national highways and byways until midnight or one. Those three hours of glorious silence, of leaving Spanish territory and reentering nature.

I was thinking about Rachma as I drove. When Bach died, my

cousin sent flowers to the funeral. When Rachma died, I didn't send flowers. I don't attend burials and I don't even send flowers: Always shirking my obligations, always failing my family. Always guilty.

Rachma talked with me when Johann Sebastian died. Johann Sebastian was his older brother. It was a conversation of little substance. He asked about a ghost from his youth and I told him how the most important person in my life had become a ghost. He kept calling me Manolito.

That was beautiful. Except that Manolito was dead too.

But we no longer had anything to say to each other, because there comes a time when we all pay. We pay for having been disloyal to the idea of family, which gives substance to man on earth.

Without family, you're a dog without a pack. Solitary dogs get abused, strung up on abandoned walls by the roadside; dogs get strung up on any crumbling wall with rebar sticking out, because their solitude sets a bad example.

I'm no longer satisfied by the company of humans. I love humans, but I have no desire to be with them. It's like I've discovered the Rachma constellation. It's like having understood that solitude is a law of physics and matter, a law that infatuates. It's the law of the mountains. The law of Ordesa. The fog swaddling the peaks. The mountains.

151

It's a summer morning in 1970: Rachma and Bach are walking down the Galician beach of La Lanzada, near Combarro. There's wind, there's sun, an enormous expanse of sea and sand. It is paradise, but it is only my memory. The sea looks at the siblings. The sea is my grandfather—he looks at them, sending them waves, sending them wind, silence, solitude, gratitude, sending them fervor.

The two brothers are close, scions of the lands of northern Spain, despite how different they are. And that beach at La Lanzada, five miles long, now flows into my heart.

I've got that image in my head: the two of them strolling down the beach, beside the too-blue sea, beside the too-high sun.

Even the least favored classes of history demand a legendary destiny—they want fine words, a bit of poetry.

Later the brothers go to a fishermen's bar and eat king crab and velvet crab and scampi and drink Galician wine. Rachma has met a gorgeous woman. He's married a very beautiful woman. He went to Galicia to work and married a local woman there. And she's an exotic beauty, with red hair. I never heard anything about their engagement, but I assume that my father did know, and whatever he knew is now lost. Nor do I know anything about what Bach, Rachma, and their wives did when they were young: I imagine dinners with friends, laughter, youth, a trip here or there, parties, dances, and now nothing.

Parties and dances and dinners and the four of them together.

My devotion to Rachma is specific and dates back to 1972, when he showed up in Barbastro in his Simca 1200. He was ebullient, happy to see his hometown again. He insisted that he wanted to give his nephew a gift. I don't know how many times Rachma had seen me in his life; it can't have been many, seven or eight, maybe ten at most. So it was an important occasion. Rachma and I went to a store that was—still is—in downtown Barbastro. It was called Almacenes Roberto. Rachma wanted to buy me a nice toy. I felt excited and confused at the same time, because it wasn't Christmas but somebody was giving me a present the way the Wise Men did.

There was an employee at the toy store, a guy in his early twenties, who offered to show me all the toys. Rachma left me in the employee's care while he went off to say hi to an old friend and let him know he was in Barbastro, so I took my time choosing the toy I liked best.

The employee was a tall, sweaty man, quiet, fat, pale. He led me by the hand down to the basement, where there were a lot of toys in storage. He showed me a number of them.

And here again things go black, just like with Father G.

His sweaty hands touch my body and try to caress me. He touches me. Fondles me. He tries to kiss me on the mouth. I feel shame, an irrational shame. And guilt.

But this time is different. What I hadn't been able to tell my father, I told Rachma. It was easy to tell Rachma, or rather he was able to see it, he was able to guess, and all I had to do was confirm it. And Rachma flew into a rage. Rachma looked for that guy, he was ready to punch him in the face.

Rachma wanted to kill that guy.

I never felt so protected.

I invoke that protection now in the face of the mystery of death.

That guy was a bastard.

Rachma defended me and took away my guilt. It wasn't my fault. That certainty that I wasn't to blame served me later in life—it was useful many times. Rachma asserted it in his actions. They were defending me, in the end. I remember how forceful he seemed, talking with the owner of the establishment, unafraid of any power on earth, unafraid of the consequences, unafraid because he was defending me. Before you can defend somebody, you have to be sure of yourself. Bach lacked Rachma's confidence. That confidence is the most valuable treasure our bodies and minds can possess. I hope Brah and Valdi inherit it—it is in our blood, because Rachma had it.

Thank you, Rachmaninoff, your music is playing once more in my weary heart.

Your defense of my life comes back to me tonight on this Good Friday forty-five years later. Ultimately, it wasn't my fault.

152

I'm in Barbastro, taking out money from an ATM. The machine spits out brand-new bills, smooth, unwrinkled, sharp-edged, just off the press, recently emerged from the mint. My father loved new bills. I wish my father could know right now that I remember, I remember that detail. Whenever he went to take out money from the bank—years before ATMs appeared—he'd ask the teller for new bills. The teller would always be surprised by the request. The voice tells me, "He's trying to communicate with you, he's talking to you through those bills, you remember his smile—he'd get one-hundred- or five-hundred-peseta bills, brand-new, and he liked it when they weren't wrinkled, they were worth more if they were new. His smile, his smile is contained in those bills." Just like him, I like for my bills to be new. It's as if somebody made them just for you, somebody thought about you, somebody made sure you were carrying these marvelous postcards in your wallet with drawings and the faces of eminent people, not the debased artifact known as money—that's why my father wanted new bills.

He didn't want money.

He wanted pristine postcards.

And that's why I want new bills too. I'm not looking to spend them; I want to experience the sensation of having Spain itself writing to me. Sending me greetings, a love telegram.

Bills freshly emerged from a nineteenth-century mint.

They're not yet infected with the epidemic of misery. Nobody has touched them with pain. They haven't humiliated anybody. They haven't been flaunted at anybody as a weapon. They haven't bought anything yet. The hand of the miserable, the corrupt, the murderous, the poor, the defeated, the finished, the abominable has not touched them.

They're like babes in paradise, those bills.

That's what my father was after.

That's why he wanted them new.

See, I even remember that. Everything you did for me is sacred now. Everything I saw you do for me is the very blood of life. I remember everything. It's all stored in my heart. The forty-three years we were together have to live somewhere. What happened during those forty-three years?

153

My mother used to ask for morphine when she had liver pain, back in the seventies, but we never knew what was causing it. The family is a clamor of never-explained illnesses.

Did she drink? No, not at all. But I don't know. I don't know anything. I orient myself by love. By the loss of love.

The pain abated after she turned fifty, and she stopped asking for morphine.

We could legalize drugs once and for all. But the government insists that its citizens experience the agony of solitude, insists that they live and die alone.

My father died alone.

My mother died alone.

It is nature's greatest revenge, showing up in hospital rooms and destroying all human pacts—it destroys the pact of love and the pact of family and the pact of medicine and the pact of human dignity—and it calls up the laughter of the other dead, the dead long gone, who mock the newly arrived corpse.

My parents never had a camera. My father never took a photo. And my mother hated having her picture taken. She thought she always looked awful in photos. She hated photography. I don't like being in photos either. My mother and I don't want to leave any evidence we ever existed. Sometimes I would try to take a photo of her—either she wouldn't let me or she'd rip them up if I managed it.

The handful of photos I inherited are untidy, bent, some torn. She didn't dare destroy them completely—she just hid them in deteriorating neglect, hoping they would vanish on their own. But I found this one.

I imagine she couldn't bring herself to rip this one up. Somebody must have snapped it and given it to her as a memento. The photo of the boy allows us to date it. It was taken outside an old movie theater in Barbastro that no longer exists. It was called Cine Argensola. The building was demolished more than ten years ago

because the concrete had started to disintegrate. But that's not how we can date the photograph. We can date it through the poster behind the figure of the diabolical child. It's a poster for a Spanish movie called *Los Palomos*, from 1964, starring Gracita Morales and José Luis López Vázquez, both of them dead now, of course.

The hand that's not holding the palm frond looks like a copper prosthesis. My mother hated mementos; that hatred was instinctive for her, and also somewhat cultivated. She despised mementos—for her, they provoked disgust and shame.

Wickedly, she knew that nothing should be remembered. That would mean having power over death.

What did the diabolical doll in the photo come into this world to do? He came to make a go of it in a country called Spain.

I eat a cookie while studying the photo of the diabolical doll. I think about hunger, fits of hunger. My mother always said I was a nightmare to feed when I was a kid. Yes, it seems that was true. My aunt Maria Callas said so too. I refused to eat. They had to fight to get me to eat. I nearly starved to death. If only I'd kept at it, fully embraced malnutrition—I wouldn't be harvesting corpses right now, listening to the music of the dead. I knew what I was doing; I didn't want anything to enter my body, didn't want anything external to intrude, to contaminate my organs, my blood, my unblemished flesh. I didn't want my stomach, liver, kidneys to be touched by life. I wanted to return to where I'd been; I wanted to return to my mother.

I had to be taken to the hospital when I was just three years old because I wasn't eating. Now, ironically, I eat out of anxiety. I spend my days tallying what I eat, counting calories. In eating, a person is seeking the regeneration of life; food keeps the machines of life in order, but machines age, and fuel is wasted on bodies that are no longer useful. Hungry old people have bodies that no longer function, that only waste food the way cars burn oil—high-consumption, low-production cars.

That's what old people are, high consumption coupled with low production—that's aging.

The relationship between the two sisters, Maria Callas and Wagner, was special, quite unspoken and quite deep. Maria Callas was goodness personified, but that goodness didn't appeal to Wagner. Maria was eight years older than Wagner. They grew up together and knew each other well.

I don't know which of the two died first. Oh yes, it was Maria Callas, right, and Wagner didn't go to her funeral, just as I didn't.

Neither of us went to Maria's funeral.

I'm so much like my mother, I'm exactly the same.

154

There's a sentence I expect to hear on the lips of my parents' ghosts when I go to them. They'll tell me, "We barely remember you."

It's the same sentence that hovers in Valdi's and Brah's thoughts when they look at me—"We barely remember you."

A couple of years before her death, my mother was bloated; a couple of years before his death, my father was gaunt: a balloon and a walking stick.

I just got out of bed on Ranillas. Today I don't have a thing to do the whole damn day. People who are alone neglect their hygiene. I didn't inherit good hygienic habits from my parents; how the hell were we supposed to bathe in that tiny bathtub? And another disaster gradually befell us too: over time, less and less water came out of the faucets, till there was barely a trickle. The pipes were clogged by mineral deposits. They needed replacing. Since my mother was renting (she rented her whole life), that job and its cost were the landlady's responsibility. The landlady flatly refused; she wanted my mother to leave because she was a long-time tenant and her rent was very low.

She'd been there since 1960.

The landlady wanted to make more money. She was the daughter of the original owner, who'd died young of a heart attack. My mother saw practically the whole family die over the years. First was the man who'd erected the building and rented out the apartments, whom she'd gotten along with and liked. Then she saw his widow die, who'd inherited the business. It's a shame she didn't see the daughter die. The daughter saw my mother die instead.

Either you see people die or they see you die.

My mother was retaining fluids and barely eating. She didn't understand why she was getting fatter when she didn't eat.

The diabolical child didn't eat. The man the diabolical child became eats and eats to avoid hearing the noise of the world, the noise of living things. Living things make noise as they decay.

My father always ate fast, really fast; his was an atavistic desire to eat, passed down through the millennia, in memory of a time when hunger reigned across the planet, in memory of the Spanish Civil War, in memory of a principle of universal precariousness, a moral and existential principle. He ate fast, and the diabolical child refused to eat because he didn't want to become another man who eats too fast, another man with an unhealthy relationship with food, the kind of man who derives from other organisms a satiety that fails to satiate.

155

My father's death was also the disappearance of a body language, a set of particular movements, an eye color, that I will never see again. A kind of expressivity in the hands, arms, eyes, lips, legs. And if I forget him, I forget those gestures. Death is more absolute and effective with people of whom we have no videos.

It's a kind of energy that disappears. If there were videos of my father, I could remember his gestures, but there aren't any, because he never wanted there to be, because he knew this moment would arrive, the moment to end all moments, the final day of his life, the moment when we realize that there is no evidence that a particular human being ever walked the earth.

It is the immensity of goodbye, the way it swells and expands. I will never see him again, I repeat as a mantra. And the immensity of goodbye is evident there. Faith, then, is natural; it's impossible to accept the idea that you're never going to see him again, for the simple reason that he's right there. If I reach out my hand, I touch his light.

He doesn't move.

He's there, and he's looking at me.

156

I used to run into my father in the elevator. He was neatly dressed, always in his suit. He seemed very clean despite not having a shower. I'm talking about 1978, 1979, somewhere in there. I never knew he was in the elevator. The elevator door would open and there he'd be. He'd smile at how startled I was when I opened the door, as if he'd been rehearsing his sudden apparition, as if he were Hamlet's father.

My father looked great in the elevator. Those old elevators that were all wood and glass. He looked like a duke in a doored casket. I saw the elevators in that building change. It was the first building with an elevator in Barbastro, and in the sixties it was known as the "elevator building." There was even a super, named Manuela—she didn't last long. She and my mother didn't get along at all. She had a small room, which disappeared when the elevator was remodeled. In that room was Manuela, who was pretty unfriendly. My mother used to say she was a witch. I was scared of her. One day she vanished into thin air, and the room where she used to lurk was swallowed by the machinery for the new elevator. But I can see her before me right this moment: she was an elderly lady with glasses and a bun, small, hunched, complaining about the trash, appearing as if by magic, bickering with my mother, but at the same time it makes me happy to remember her, because a superintendent always brings joy to a building—supers symbolize hope for a building, for the concrete, the pillars, the walls, the stairs, the façade, the landings, the lightbulbs, the plaques with the residents' names. The building was all rental apartments, so there were always people passing through, people who were in Barbastro a few years for work and who then left for other cities. My parents made friends or acquaintances with their neighbors, but those neighbors would eventually disappear. Everybody left. They'd find a better job or get a promotion and move, transferring to larger cities. Only Wagner and Johann Sebastian remained, out of their whole section of the building, like survivors, composing music for nobody. As for Manuela, the superintendent, I have no idea where she came from or where she went, whether she had family or if maybe she was a ghost.

157

The two of them are young and they get ready to call me in the darkness. I am not there. I never have been. Yet I was foretold by everything millions of years ago. All of us have been foretold. I can travel back in time and see Johann Sebastian caressing Wagner and kissing her and I am there, waiting to be summoned.

My origin is in his pleasure; in his melancholy after love is the source of my insatiable spirit.

I see the room—it's the fall of 1961, mid-November. The cold hasn't descended yet, it's nice out, and they've opened the door onto the bedroom balcony to let the moonlight in. They are so young, so enormously young, that they believe they're immortal. There they are, naked, with the balcony door flung open.

It's gotten a little chilly, says Johann Sebastian. And he gazes at Wagner's nakedness and I am already there in her belly. Wagner lights an L&M. The bedside lamp gives off a dim glow. An immense happiness suffuses the room. The walls, the curtains, the sheets are singing; the night is singing. By the start of the new year they'll have learned that Wagner is pregnant. But they have no inkling of the baby that's on its way. Even I don't know what kind of baby is on its way. Johann Sebastian, that November night, having invoked me inside of Wagner, steps out onto the tiny balcony of the apartment that will be my apartment and looks at the night. The air is full of incantations. He looks at the buildings across the street—they've just moved into this new building, with an elevator that still smells of varnish; the street is unpaved, everything new: the wooden blinds, the tile floors, the walls, the bedroom doors, which close perfectly, though fifty years from now not a single one will close, they'll all be broken, crooked in their frames. I never saw that new apartment; I only saw its deterioration. But on the night I was conceived, the building was brand-new, recently built, pristine-smelling.

The dead cannot be awakened, because they are resting.

But that night in November 1961 existed and it continues to exist. That night of love, that modern apartment, the freshly painted walls, the newly purchased furniture, the couple's young hands, the kisses, the future that is only a thrilling fantasy, the power of bodies—all of that is still in me.

Glorious November night in 1961, tranquil, pleasant, sweet. You are still alive. Night that is still alive. You do not leave. You dance a dance of love with me.